BY KELLY LINK

Get in Trouble

Pretty Monsters

Magic for Beginners

Stranger Things Happen

The Year's Best Fantasy and Horror (editor)

Trampoline (editor)

White Cat,
Black Dog

White Cat, Black Dog

···· *Stories* ····

Kelly Link

Illustrations by Shaun Tan

RANDOM HOUSE

NEW YORK

Copyright © 2023 by Kelly Link
Illustrations copyright © 2023 by Shaun Tan

All rights reserved.

Published in the United States by Random House, an imprint and division of Penguin Random House LLC, New York.

RANDOM HOUSE and the HOUSE colophon are registered trademarks of Penguin Random House LLC.

The following stories are previously published:
"The White Road" (*A Public Space,* January 2020); "The Lady and the Fox" (in *My True Love Gave to Me,* edited by Stephanie Perkins [New York: St. Martin's Press, 2014]); "The Game of Smash and Recovery" (*Strange Horizons,* October 2015); "The Girl Who Did Not Know Fear" (*Tin House,* June 2019); "Skinder's Veil" (in *When Things Get Dark: Stories Inspired by Shirley Jackson,* edited by Ellen Datlow [London: Titan Books, 2021]); "The White Cat's Divorce" (Weatherspoon Art Museum, August 2018)

Library of Congress Cataloging-in-Publication Data
Names: Link, Kelly, author.
Title: White cat, black dog : stories / Kelly Link.
Description: New York : Random House, [2023]
Identifiers: LCCN 2022010395 (print) | LCCN 2022010396 (ebook) |
ISBN 9780593449950 (hardcover ; acid-free paper) |
ISBN 9780593449967 (ebook)
Subjects: LCGFT: Short stories.
Classification: LCC PS3612.I553 W48 2023 (print) |
LCC PS3612.I553 (ebook) | DDC 813/.6—dc23/eng/20220614
LC record available at https://lccn.loc.gov/2022010395
LC ebook record available at https://lccn.loc.gov/2022010396

Printed in Canada on acid-free paper

randomhousebooks.com

2 4 6 8 9 7 5 3 1

First Edition

Book design by Caroline Cunningham

For Ellen Datlow and Terri Windling, who held the door open

Contents

White Cat,
Black Dog

The White Cat's Divorce

(The White Cat)

All stories about divorce must begin some other place, and so let us begin with a man so very rich, he might reach out and have almost any thing he desired, as well as many things that he did not. He had so many houses even his accountants could not keep track of them all. He had private planes and newspapers and politicians who saw to it that his wishes became laws. He had orchards, islands, baseball teams, and even a team of entomologists whose mandate was to find new species of beetles to be given variations on the rich man's name. (For if it was true that God loved beetles, was it not true He loved the rich man even more? Was his good fortune not the proof of this?)

The rich man had all of this and more than I have space to write. Anything you have ever possessed, know that he had this, too. And if he did not, he could have paid you whatever your price was in order to obtain it.

All men desire to be rich; no man desires to grow old. To stave off old age, the rich man paid for personal trainers and knee replacements and cosmetic procedures that meant he always had a somewhat wide-eyed look, as if he were not a man in his seventies at all but rather still an infant who found his life a cascade of marvelous and surprising events. The rich man had follicular unit transplantation and special creams to bleach age spots. For dinner, his personal chefs served him fish and berries and walnuts as if he were a bear and not a rich man at all. Every morning, he swam two miles in a lake that was kept by an ingenious mechanism at a comfortable temperature for him throughout the year. In the afternoons, he had blood transfusions from adolescent donors, these transfusions being a condition of the scholarships to various universities that the rich man funded. In the evenings, he threw lavish parties, surrounding himself with people who were young and beautiful. As he grew older, his wives grew younger, and in this way, for a time, the rich man was able to persuade himself that he, too, was still young and might remain so forever.

But although a man may acquire younger and ever more beautiful wives who will maintain the pretense that he, too, is still untouched by age, this rich man had, a long time ago, been married to a first wife, and this first wife had had three sons. The three sons, having been raised with every advantage by caregivers and tutors and therapists and life coaches paid to adhere to the best principles of child-rearing, were attractive, personable, and in every way the kind of children that a father could have regarded with satisfaction. And yet the rich man did not regard them with satisfaction. Instead, when he looked at his three sons, the youngest of whom was now nineteen, he saw only the proof of his own mortality. It is difficult to remain young when one's children selfishly insist upon growing older.

To make matters worse, his sons were all in residence at the house where the rich man was spending the winter. The eldest was in the middle of an acrimonious divorce (his first) and the second was hiding out from the media, while the third had no good reason at all, except that he truly loved his father and wished for his approval. (Also, he had flunked out of university.) Everywhere the rich man turned, a son was underfoot.

At night, he began to be visited by a certain dream. In this dream, the rich man was troubled first by the notion that he had a fourth child. And in the dream, no sooner had he had this notion than he became aware that this fourth child, too, was a guest in the house, and although in the morning the rich man found he could never remember what this child looked like— Was it small or tall? Was it long and slender or so enormous it blotted out its surroundings? What was the sound of its voice?—he knew this last child was Death. In the dream, the rich man offered his child Death all he had in return for more life, but nothing the rich man had to offer was of interest to Death. The only thing Death desired was the company of its father.

Sometimes the rich man had this dream three or four times in one night. By day, he began to detest the sight of his sons.

At last, in perplexity, the rich man turned to consultants to assist him with the problem of his sons, and by the end of the week, a most elegant plan had been put in place. The rich man, in accordance, summoned his three sons to his side. Once he had embraced them lovingly and they had discussed the news of the day and the foundations and boards of which his sons were nominally the heads, he said, "My sons: although it is true that I am in my prime, and although I know it pains you to contem-

plate, a day must come when I retire into private life and take up
a hobby like growing orchids or hunting the most dangerous
game or sending unmanned vessels into the sun to see what happens, and, although it is farther off still, yet it is ever drawing
nearer, a day in which an expert team will cryogenically freeze
my body as well as the body of my current wife until such a time
when medical advances can resurrect me into some unknown
hellish future in a body that can satisfy more than three women
at a time while also battling apocalyptic mutant lizards and con-
quering whatever remains of the New York Stock Exchange."

His sons exchanged looks with each other, and the youngest
said, "Dear Father, it seems impossible to us that you will ever
be any less vital than you are at this moment."

The rich man said, "Nevertheless, a time must come when all
things change. And when I think of the future, there are two
things I desire above all else. One is to name my heir. My second
desire is for a companion to be a comfort to me in the years of
my decline."

The oldest son said, "Pardon me, Father, but are you telling
us that you are to marry again?"

The rich man said, "No, no! Alyssa and I are quite happy.
What I wish for is, simply, a dog. The smallest, silkiest, most
obedient and amiable dog a man has ever possessed. I have decided to task you, my sons, with this errand. You will have a year
and a day to scour the earth for such a dog, and at the end of that
span, whichever of you procures it, I shall leave you everything
that I own."

"But, Father," the second son said, "dogs make you sneeze.
Which is why we were never allowed to keep them as pets."

"The most amiable and hypoallergenic dog," the rich man said firmly.

For the consultants had pointed out that if the rich man's sons were sent far from his presence, it might seem as if they had never been born at all. Once the rich man had ruled out filicide, being possessed of a tender heart, the consultants had devised a quest: a kind of beta experiment to see if the rich man's quality of life was improved with no sons underfoot.

The rich man's three sons agreed in the end to do as their father asked. The oldest said, "Our father has accumulated so much money that even if he must name one of us his successor, the other two will never want for anything."

The middle son said, "Possibly our father is suffering from dementia, but at least his request, though bizarre, is harmless."

And the youngest said, "It isn't as if I have anything better to do."

The sons bid each other goodbye, agreeing that whichever one brought home the most charming dog, the other two would be good sports about the whole thing.

THE TWO OLDER SONS had many adventures during the next year, but it is with the youngest son that we are concerned. Because he harbored romantic notions about America and the open road, he borrowed his father's cherry-red roadster and set off with an old copy of Kerouac and a small duffel bag of dog treats. He had no particular destination in mind—in fact, without realizing it, he behaved as he habitually did when he played video games, which was to pleasurably explore a new environment and see what it had to offer him. He visited suburban strip mall pet stores, animal shelters, convention center dog shows, breeders of every stripe. And thus, in the first three weeks of his journey, he came across many delightful dogs, and often he drove away with a puppy even more adorable and lovable than any he had previously encountered. Eventually, because the roadster was too small to hold all of his dogs, he bought an old camper van and had a carpenter furbish it with cabinetry so that each dog would have its own berth. The roadster he pulled behind on a trailer hitch. In the camper, he slept at rest stops and campgrounds, and as he traveled, he posted updates to Facebook and then checked, over and over again, to see if his father had liked them.

By the end of the first month, the rich man's youngest son was in the foothills of the Rocky Mountains, where rumor had it there was a kennel owner who had successfully crossbred fennec foxes with teacup spaniels. He paid a small fortune for a silky red puppy with enormous paws and ears, the rest so negligible he drove away with it sleeping inside his coat pocket. As he passed through the town of Creede, it began to snow heavily, and the road became treacherous. He had never before been responsible for anyone else; now his car was full of dogs, all of whom loved him and most of whom needed house-training. To his surprise, he was discovering that being loved could be just as productive of anxiety as the lack of it was.

When he consulted a map, he found he was near the part of Colorado where his mother's family had once owned a ranch. The youngest son had few memories of his mother. His father had won full custody after the divorce, and not long afterward, his mother moved back to Colorado, only to die in a car accident on a rainy night. She'd been decapitated in a highway collision with a poultry truck. After the funeral, the oldest brother had told the youngest that the reason for the closed casket was because they had never found her head. (Or was it that they'd never found her body, and so the casket contained only her head?) The youngest son had had nightmares for years.

The spot where his mother had died might even have been here on the very highway upon which the youngest son now found himself, the snow hurtling down in such a way that he began to feel, peculiarly, as if he and his dogs were not living creatures at all but only small figures posed inside a snow globe. (Had he felt this way before? Yes. Hasn't everyone? Couldn't this be the explanation for how we find ourselves trapped? Unable to make changes for the better? Separated from everything we desire by an unyielding barrier?)

The youngest son drove on. Even estranged from ourselves, we still engage in the small mechanical motions of a task that has been set (as when a hand picks up a snow globe and gives it a good shake).

The snow came down, enveloping the whole world. The camper's windshield would grow opaque, glittering with ice, and so the youngest son would pull over and scrape the shell of ice off and then drive a little way farther until he had to pull over to do the same again. His clothing quickly proved inadequate to the weather, and all the dogs were tired of being cooped up in their berths. They whined, begging to be let out. The smallest dog of all still slept peacefully inside the youngest son's coat pocket, however, as if nothing bad could ever happen, and the youngest son took this as a sign that he, too, should trust in Providence and keep on, though he was beginning to run low on gas.

An hour passed, and the snow did not let up. The gas light came on, and the youngest son began to wonder if he had somehow left the main highway without ever knowing. Over the sound of the radio and the van's windshield wipers, he fancied he could hear soft voices, although it had been some time since he had seen another car or truck on the road. When the windshield grew heavy with ice again, he pulled over and turned off the ignition. He stepped out into the snow and stumbled into a drift so deep it reached past his knees. Snow swirled around him so briskly, he had the sensation some great beast was circling him, its soft white flank brushing against his side affectionately. *If only it were not so cold,* he thought. *If only there were a place my dogs and I could take shelter.*

If only, he thought he heard a voice say. *If only if only if only if—*

"Hello?" the youngest son said. "Is someone there?"

The little dog inside his coat pocket poked its head out, yawning, and then, before he realized its intent, it had leapt down onto the snow.

Although the snow was powdery, the little dog was so very slight, it rested upon the top crust like a red feather on a white coat. The youngest son, so much heavier, stumbled, his hands outstretched. He fell onto his knees and the dog danced forward, out of reach, catching snowflakes in its mouth.

"Oh, come back!" said the youngest son. When he stood, the snow was at his waist.

The dog began to run along the top of the snow. The youngest son waded through the drift after it. The cold bit at him, and snow found its way through the layers of his clothes the more he moved, so that he might as well have been as naked as a baby. He could barely make out the reddish dot of his dog ahead of him, and when he turned to look behind, he could not see the van at all. *I have made a terrible mistake,* he thought. He knew he should turn back. Surely he would be able to follow his tracks back again.

But the youngest son could not bear to abandon the little dog that had slept so sweetly all afternoon in his pocket. He could not call its name, since he had not given it one yet, but he called out endearments, entreating it to return to him.

It seemed to the youngest son that he heard those voices again, all around him in the snow, repeating his endearments back. The dog heeded neither the youngest son nor the voices but trotted on as if it knew exactly where it was leading him.

And now the youngest son thought that he could see where the dog meant them to go. Ahead were lozenges of greenish light, pressed out against the sugar veils of snow like jewels. As he drew nearer, he saw these were enormous houses made all of glass, and when he drew near enough to one to enter through a door—also made all of glass—the dog stretched up against it, pawing to be let in, and he saw that it was not a house for people at all but a greenhouse.

When he opened the door, a mass of warm, wet air rushed out, instantly transforming into crystals of ice in his hair and beard and eyelashes.

Inside, everywhere he turned, were row upon row of cannabis plants. But this was not the strangest thing, to find a pot farm in the middle of a blizzard. Stranger still were the people tending the pot plants, who were not people at all, but cats

dressed in lab coats who stood on their hind legs, wielding clip-
boards and garden shears and harvesting buckets.

The little dog began to bark loudly, and at this interruption,
every cat in the greenhouse turned and stared in astonishment at
the youngest son. If there had not been a blizzard outside, he
would have turned and run away, but instead, in his desperation,
he cried out, "Please! I need your help!"

Hearing this, the cats put down their tools and advanced
toward him. The youngest son picked up his dog, not entirely
sure whether the cats were friendly. They did not speak, but one
of them gestured to the youngest son, who said, "I abandoned
my van back at the side of the road. The tank is empty, and the
van is full of young dogs who will freeze to death if I do not
bring them to safety. Please, can you assist me? I have AAA, but
my phone has no reception out here."

A handsome tabby laid its paw upon the youngest son's hip. It
looked up at him and then at the door. He understood he was
to leave, and despair overwhelmed him. Nevertheless, he turned
as the cat directed and, tucking the little dog back into his
pocket, he and the tabby went through the door into the snow.

To his relief, the cat did not abandon him to make his way
back to the road but rather indicated a cleared path. They walked
along it past half a dozen greenhouses, each, the youngest son
imagined, full of cats tending seedlings or mature marijuana
plants. Or perhaps not cats but mice or ferrets or intelligent fruit
bats. Anything seemed in the realm of the possible here.

At last, they came to a ranch house, where inside there was a
cavern-like great room with a fire roaring in the stone hearth.
The tabby led the youngest son along a hallway to a room where

the bed was already turned down. There was a comfortable armchair, too, with a table beside it, and on the table was a tray with soup and bread and cheese and a bottle of wine. The door to the bathroom stood open, and through it the youngest son could see a steaming bath.

He said to the tabby, "But my dogs—"

The tabby made a gesture as if to indicate that this, too, would be attended to. It took the youngest son's hand in its paws and examined it carefully for frostbite. Then, satisfied, it made a bow and left the room, closing the door.

The youngest son stripped off his wet clothing and got into the bath. He stayed there until he was warm again, and then, climbing out, discovered that someone had placed a pair of flannel pajamas upon the bed as well as a thick robe. He dressed, finding the provided clothing to be exactly his size, and then stood beside the window, feeding bits of bread to the little dog.

As the youngest son looked out, he saw a strange procession emerging from the snowstorm. Two dozen cats, all in scarves and winter hats, were making their way toward the house. Each held a small dog tenderly in its arms. So great was his relief beholding this rescue that a profound lassitude came upon him, and he sank back into the armchair where he fell asleep.

All through the night, he dreamed he heard the voices in the snow again, murmuring lovingly. He dreamt someone stroked his face and picked him up and carried him to his bed. In the morning when he woke up, the little dog was on one side of the pillow beside him, licking his face. Otherwise, the bed was so very comfortable that he would have imagined himself to be back home again.

"What a strange dream I have had," the youngest son said to his dog. "Cats who walked around like men do, and greenhouses, and chasing you through the snow."

"Oh, but it was no dream at all," said a feminine voice, and gave a small cough quite close to his ear.

When the youngest son turned his head, he saw that on the other side of him, even whiter than the bed linen, was a beautiful white cat with emerald-green eyes.

"Please don't be afraid," she said. "You somehow found your way here to us in the middle of a blizzard. And pray don't be concerned for your dogs. They are well looked after."

The youngest son sat up. "What manner of place is this?" he asked. "And what manner of cat are you?"

"Quite an ordinary sort of cat," the white cat said modestly. "The mechanics of how I can speak are really of no great interest, and I'm afraid that I don't really understand it myself, in any case. Suffice it to say, my people and I have lived here for a good many years. We make our way in the world as growers of *Cannabis sativa* and *Cannabis indica,* as well as several hybrids of our own engineering. As you may know, marijuana is legal in Colorado. Our label, White Cat, is known for both its efficacy and its strength. Do you know it?"

Not wanting to be impolite, the youngest son said he thought it rang a bell. Truth be told, he was more of a casual user than a gourmand.

"I would be pleased to give you a tour," the white cat said, "and to reunite you with your dogs. How pleasant it is to be given the chance to host an animal lover such as yourself. We receive so few visitors here."

And so, out of a feeling of enchantment as much as politeness, the youngest son allowed his hostess to show him around the premises. The day was bright and clear and everywhere the white snow sparkled, but even the snow was not as white as the white cat's fur.

The youngest son visited his dogs and went outside to play with them. He sampled various blends and products, and when, after that, he grew hungry, he was given such a feast—quails' eggs poached and placed on beds made of saffron and flower petals, rabbit kidneys and mushrooms and dates on long skewers, fish the size of minnows with bones so soft he did as the cats did and ate them whole—he could hardly move.

The white cat said that she could not possibly consider allowing him to leave for at least another day. And so he spent the evening in the company of cats, playing board games and drinking games, while his dogs lay panting and happy on the flagstones beside the hearth. In the morning when he woke up, once again the little red dog lay to one side of his head and the white cat on the other. Outside, it was snowing.

It snowed that day and for three days more, and the white cat informed him that the roads would be impassable. After that, she would not think of him leaving, for on the weekend was a harvest festival. And after the festival, it was someone's birthday, and one of the greenhouses was done up as a disco with colored lights, and cats of all description wore festive hats. There were snowmobile races and ice skating on a lake, and the youngest son's dogs were so very happy that the youngest son could not bear to take them away in the camper again. Weeks passed and spring came and then summer and still the youngest son stayed. He went hiking in the hills with the white cat and he helped in the greenhouses and in the evenings he toked up and listened to the cats pick out old folk songs on their guitars and banjos. Like his dogs, he was happy.

As a child, pets had been forbidden to the youngest son. Rats and mice were vermin. Birds were bad luck. Cats were aloof and parasitical. They produced dander that could cause skin rashes or fits of sneezing. Their feces carried disease. The youngest son, as he acquired and cared for puppies and more puppies, had been pondering his father's desire for a companion dog. Did this request represent some sea change: did his father, so self-possessed and all-possessing, at last long to love and be loved? The youngest son was only five years younger than the middle brother, six years younger than his oldest brother, but that distance had always felt unbridgeable to him. They were close to each other in a way that, loving them both, he envied. Like his father, they did not need him. Unlike the youngest son—and having each other— they had never seemed to need the approval of their father.

But: all the time the youngest son remained with the white cat, he barely thought of his father at all. It was as if he had come under some easeful enchantment, until one morning he woke up and saw that snow was falling once more and realized with a shock how much time had passed.

"Dear white cat," he said. "Tell me, what is the date?"

The white cat said, "It is the second of December, I believe."

"Then I have stayed too long," the youngest son said in a great panic, "for I am due in my father's house tomorrow morning."

"If it must be so," the white cat said, "then let it be so. I will book a ticket for you out of Denver tonight."

The youngest son groaned and put his head in his hands. He

said, "You are the kindest of cats, but it is even more complicated than that, I'm afraid. I must bring my father a dog, the most charming and amiable of all the dogs, and I don't know how I am to decide between them."

But really it was that he did not know how he could bear to be parted from any of his dogs. The little red dog was, of all of them, the smallest and most extraordinary in every way, but the youngest son loved the little red dog dearly. And though he would never have admitted it to himself, he worried that his father might not love the little red dog as much as he ought to (or even at all).

"That is no problem," the white cat said briskly. "There is no need to choose among your dogs, because I know of one that is smaller and yet more delightful. You have only to trust me, and your father will be most satisfied with the dog that you bring him."

Though he had spent less than a year in her company, the youngest son trusted the white cat with all of his heart.

Therefore, he said goodbye to his dogs, telling the little red dog to look after the white cat while he was away. He embraced all the workers in the greenhouse and packed a suitcase, and then it was time to go. The white cat had the cherry roadster brought up to the house. While the youngest son had been sojourning with the cats, she had had the car detailed and given a tune-up, and it looked as if it had just come out of the factory.

The youngest son knelt down and the white cat climbed up on his knee. She purred in his ear while he wrapped his arms around her.

"Come back," she said. "For I will miss you every second you are away."

"I could want nothing more," the youngest son said and meant it. And then, embarrassed, he added, "But I do not see a dog. Which is totally fine! The little red dog can come with me."

The white cat said, "Not at all! Here is your dog." And she gave him a macadamia nut still in its shell. When the youngest son held it up to his ear, he heard a faint bark.

"When you come before your father and only then," the white cat said, "crack the macadamia shell and you will have your dog. But make sure you have not packed any edibles or weed, because although marijuana is legal in the state of Colorado, we've heard from our customers that they sometimes encounter difficulties getting through airport security."

As if all the happiness of the previous year had been only a passing dream, the youngest son woke up the following morning in his father's house. He ate breakfast with his brothers, who had had many adventures during their searches. He admired each brother's dog, a Chihuahua and a teacup dachshund, though neither seemed to him to hold a candle to the little red dog he had left behind.

When his brothers asked what kind of dog he had brought for their father, he hung his head and demurred. Neither did he say anything of his own experiences.

When the breakfast table had been cleared, the rich man came into the room, yawning and scratching his head. His beard was coming in white. He wore a white bathrobe. Although he had genuinely been quite pleased to have his sons home, this morning he was out of sorts once more. That last child, Death, had visited him in his dreams the previous night and in consequence he had already spent the better part of the morning on the phone with his consultants.

"Go on, then," he said to his sons. "Let's get this over with."

The oldest son and then the middle son introduced the rich man to their dogs. He patted them with an air of dissatisfaction, then said to the youngest son, "And you? Or couldn't you be bothered?"

The youngest son reached into his pocket for the macadamia shell. While his father and brothers watched, he placed it on the breakfast table and then rapped it sharply with a spoon. The shell cracked open and out sprang a white dog among the plates smeared with egg yolks, citrus rinds, toast crumbs, and red jam. It was no bigger than a beetle.

"Well!" the rich man said, suppressing a shudder. He liked neither beetles (not even those named after him) nor, to be sure, dogs. "Certainly, that is a very small dog. Is it housebroken? Can it do tricks?"

Oh, it could. It turned somersaults and walked on its hind legs. The youngest son threw a sugar cube and the little dog fetched it back.

"Excellent, excellent," the rich man said. But the youngest son could not help but notice that he was frowning. "It is clear you have brought me exactly the sort of dog I wanted most. The others, too, are fine specimens, though perhaps not quite as out of the ordinary as this fellow. Never mind, I shall keep them all. And now, my sons, I wonder if the three of you would indulge me in one more thing. It has occurred to me that if I am to retire, then I must throw a retirement party, and that will take some planning. Let's aim for a year from now. And what I most desire is that the three of you go forth once more. I wish to wear at this party a suit of cloth so fine, so tightly woven, that no one has ever seen its like. Scour the earth! The fabric should be so fine that one could pass it through a wedding ring. Whichever of you brings back the finest suit, that son I will make my heir."

Although this had not been the agreement, because the rich man's sons were just as obliging and amiable and well bred, in fact, as the dog their father had claimed to want, they complied with his request and went out into the world again after embracing each other. Privately, the youngest son vowed this time he would find the thing that would make his father love him at last. (Perhaps the little dog had been too little? There was something uncanny about its size, was there not? It was diplomatic of his father, really, not to choose between the three dogs. This way, no one's feelings had been hurt.)

The youngest son would do better this time. But first he would return to the white cat and thank her for all of her help.

When the youngest son arrived once again at the white cat's establishment, he found a fire on the hearth and good smells coming from the kitchen. The white cat herself was sleeping beside the window that looked out on the drive. The little red dog was beside her. She woke up and stretched as the youngest son came in. "I've been so worried about you," she said. "Tell me how it went."

The youngest son sat down on the window seat beside her. The little red dog licked his hands and face, and tears came to his eyes, although he could not have said why. "It was fine," he said. "But I'm so glad to be back."

And despite his intentions, the next year passed for the youngest son in much the same way as the first, until at last the white cat came to him and said, "I'm afraid it's time you went back to your father's house."

The youngest son felt a wave of absolute dread pass over him. Though he knew it was undutiful of him to feel this way, he said, "Perhaps I shouldn't go. I was supposed to bring him back a bespoke suit, the most admirable suit of clothes made out of the finest fabric anyone has ever seen. He said he wanted a suit that would go through a wedding ring, and to be honest, that didn't seem like something that could possibly exist."

The white cat looked at the youngest son with her knowing green eyes. She said, "Of course not. Just like a talking cat couldn't possibly exist. Or a dog small enough to fit inside a nutshell."

The youngest son said thoughtfully, "Or pot macaroni and cheese."

"I still think that's a bad idea," said the white cat, "although innovative. In any case, I've booked your ticket home. He may be a terrible person, but he's still your father. And inside this pistachio shell is the suit that he wished for."

"But you don't have his measurements," the youngest son protested.

"Really not a problem," said the white cat.

ONCE AGAIN, THE YOUNGEST son returned to his father's house with a nutshell in his pocket. Things were just as they always were, which is to say the rich man seemed as busy and distracted as ever, and the youngest son felt much the same as he had for most of his life, as if only the very smallest part of him was visible, and that part of him remained childlike, insignificant, and desperately needing something that he would never truly deserve nor ever find. Not even in a nutshell. Did his father look older? Yes, just a little older. His brothers, too, were older, and so the youngest son supposed that he must be older, as well.

In the last year, the youngest son had discovered he had something of a green thumb. He'd been experimenting with hybrid grafts: stone fruits and a particularly hardy strain of White Widow. (He'd named the result Calm Kardashian.) Which was to say, all the greenhouse cats treated him like a valued colleague. But in his father's house, he could have been a ghost. When he asked after his stepmother, the rich man said, "Sometimes it turns out you never really knew someone," and began to enumerate the virtues of the wine that they were drinking.

"Where are your dogs, Father?" the youngest son asked, persisting. His brothers looked at each other but said nothing.

"The divorce settlement," the rich man said. "Your stepmother took all three. Such a shame. It really broke my heart."

And perhaps the rich man missed either the dogs or else his ex-wife, because it seemed to the youngest son the next morning that his father had not slept well. For the first time, it seemed to the youngest son his father was an old man, and that one day he might even die.

The rich man said to his sons, "Bad news, I'm afraid. I left most of the party planning to your stepmother and you won't be surprised to hear that she absolutely botched it. So I've postponed my retirement. Anyway, there's just too much work to do right now."

The middle son said, "Don't you want to see what we brought you?"

"Yes, yes," the rich man said. "Fine." He waved at them to present the results of their quests.

The suit of clothes the oldest son had acquired was red brocade and yet so light it might have been made of parachute silk. The middle son had commissioned a black suit of some synthetic material embedded with microfibers that stored sunlight and then produced their own radiance. But then the youngest son took out his pistachio shell and cracked it open, and inside was a suit of green velvet so finely made and so au courant that it was clear to all he had surpassed his brothers again.

The rich man was no longer wearing a wedding ring, of course, but he poked the hem of the suit jacket through his signet experimentally, and his sons watched as he proceeded to pull the entire jacket and then the pants through the ring. He said, "It's a bit showy, isn't it?"

But when he tried it on, he could not help looking pleased. He'd always been a peacock of a man.

"I've been thinking that a wedding party is better than a retirement party," he said. His consultants, of course, had come up with another quest. They'd suggested something illegal, like enriched plutonium, in the hopes the sons would end up imprisoned, but the rich man had a tender and whimsical heart. "So why don't the three of you come back same time next year with a bride? And whoever brings back the prettiest, wittiest bride, I will name that boy my heir. Perhaps I'll even wear this suit to the wedding."

The three sons exchanged looks and then agreed to do as the rich man asked them.

"It's like we're enacting a reality show for him," the oldest brother said as they were being driven to the airport. He added, in an aside to the middle brother, "Although harder for you."

"What is he talking about?" the youngest son said. "Why is it harder for you?"

The middle son said, "He means because I'm gay."

"Oh," the youngest brother said, realizing he didn't know his brothers at all.

The middle son said, "So I'll bring back a groom and not a bride. At least I'll get points for originality. Although what are the odds this time he actually names an heir?"

"Fifty percent," said the youngest son. The oldest son said, "Point two five percent."

But they all agreed that, whether or not the rich man kept his word, this was the last time they would be their father's errand boys.

"Three strikes," the oldest son said.

The middle son said to the youngest son, "And if you bring back a girl in a coconut shell, I am going to kick your ass. No more of that shit, okay?"

"Okay," the youngest son said. He was fairly sure he wouldn't come back at all once he got to the white cat's ranch.

AND FOR THE ENTIRE year that followed, he played with his dogs, and he helped in the greenhouses, and he partied with the white cat and her workers, and never thought once about his father's request. The white cat, seeing that he was interested, began to instruct him in the mysteries of bookkeeping and inventory management, and they were both very pleased to find that he had a knack for the business side as well as a green thumb.

But when the year was up, the white cat came to him and said, "Tomorrow is the day that you must return to your father's house."

"I don't want to," said the youngest son. "I'm happy here. In any case, there's no point. I was supposed to bring home a bride, and oh, look—I haven't got one. And don't tell me that you have a yogurt cup or Kinder Surprise egg or whatever with a girl inside it. I don't want the world's tiniest bride. Maybe I'll get married someday, but I'd prefer to get married to someone who at least comes up to my shoulder."

The white cat had been laying on her back in a beam of sunlight, listening to the youngest son while her tail went back and forth. "Never mind the bride," she said. "Take me back with you to your father's house. I'll admit it: I'm curious. I'd like to see him."

"What?" said the youngest son. "Absolutely not. Curiosity killed the cat, remember?"

The white cat said, "But satisfaction brought her back." And she kept on until at last he agreed that he would go home and bring her on the plane with him in a cat carrier. The white cat insisted, also, that he bring with them, unopened, a particular piece of locked luggage, narrow and long as if it contained an unusually large bong.

When they arrived at the rich man's house, the white cat asked to be let out of her carrier. The rich man was at his office, and the two older brothers had not yet flown in, and so the youngest son and the white cat toured the rich man's house and then the grounds of the estate.

"Nice," the white cat said, looking at a waterfall that plunged into a pool of glittering pebbles where each pebble was, when you looked closely, a semiprecious stone carved into a miniature and flattering likeness of the rich man's head. "Though a bit ostentatious for my taste."

"He has other houses," the youngest son said. "If you liked, we could leave right now. I could take you to one of the other properties."

"No, no," the white cat said. "I'm quite content here. And so looking forward to meeting your family at last." But in fact, when they got back to their suite, she fell asleep in the youngest son's open suitcase and refused to wake up for dinner.

The rich man and his sons dined informally on the veranda. The oldest son had grown a salt-and-pepper beard, and the rich man remarked on it with displeasure again and again.

The oldest son smiled, though, and only said that the woman he loved found it distinguished. It is possible an observer out in the darkness beyond the chandeliers that hung in the trees might have mistaken the four men at the table for brothers. Or perhaps even mistaken the oldest son for the father of the other three. But cats, of course, have keener eyesight than that.

When the youngest son got back to his rooms, he found the white cat on his pillow. "Sometimes I think my dad is kind of an asshole," he admitted.

"But you love me," the white cat said, and yawned so widely she seemed to be all mouth.

"Yes," the youngest son said. "I do."

"And you trust me," the white cat said, and the youngest son agreed he trusted her absolutely.

"Then promise me that tomorrow you will do whatever I ask you to do."

"Okay," the youngest son said. He lay down on the bed beside her. "Just don't ask me to wear that cashmere sweater even though I put it in the suitcase. I know you guys all said it looked sharp but I don't think it's really me. Also, don't ask me why I stutter around my dad sometimes. I think I just get kind of nervous."

He closed his eyes before the white cat could even agree.

She arranged herself around the crown of his head and began to groom his hair as if he were a kitten. She said, "You know I would never do anything to hurt you."

She waited to see how he would answer, but the youngest son was asleep. The youngest son slept soundly all night long, but the white cat did not sleep at all. In the morning, she bade him open the locked case, and when he took out the sword that was inside, she told him what he must do. The youngest son refused again and again, but she reminded him of his promise the night before and once again told him that everything would come right in the end if he obeyed her.

At last, the youngest son said that he would do as the white cat asked and they went down to their appointment.

The two older brothers were already with the rich man. It was clear that he was in an apoplectic rage at the middle brother, who stood there in the morning room holding hands with another man.

The youngest son saw, with some surprise, that his oldest brother had brought his ex-wife.

"I suppose I ought to ask which one of you is the bride," the rich man said with great disgust.

"No," the middle brother said. He, too, was very angry. "You really ought not to. And if you can't be civil, then we'll just leave."

"And I suppose you are proposing to marry this cat!" the rich man said to the youngest son.

"Not quite," the youngest son said, and he lifted the sword he had carried downstairs and cut off the white cat's head with one blow.

After that, there was a lot of commotion and screaming, but when everyone saw the result of the youngest son's actions, they fell silent.

"Perhaps he did it with CGI? Like a magic trick?" the oldest brother's ex-wife said. "Kind of show-offy, but a neat effect."

For where the white cat had been, there was now a young woman, entirely naked and very beautiful.

The youngest son took off the green cashmere sweater that he had worn after all and gave it to the young woman to put on. It exactly matched her eyes.

"Extraordinary!" said the rich man.

"Thank you," said the young woman, and smiled.

After that, suitable clothing was found for her, and there was a luncheon. The rich man had the young woman who had been the white cat sit beside him so that, he said, he could get to know her better. He directed the youngest son to sit beside the middle brother and the middle brother's fiancé, who worked in the hospitality industry and owned a chain of boutique hotels. The oldest son and his ex held hands throughout the meal.

After lunch, the rich man invited everyone down to the stables where he personally selected a mount for the young woman.

And by the time dinner was over, the rich man called his young-est son to his side.

"Look here," the rich man said. "This has been the strangest day of my life. One of my sons says he's going to marry a man. And then you chop the head off a cat and suddenly she's the most beautiful, charming girl I've ever seen. I'm completely smitten. Head over heels. And it's clear that the two of you are absolutely wrong for each other. I mean, she says you thought she was a cat the whole time! Anyway, a minute ago, I proposed to her and she said yes. What do you think of that?"

The youngest son said he didn't know what to think. Every-thing was topsy-turvy; he had the feeling he had been played. The young woman who had been the white cat joined them then. She took the young man's hand in hers and said, "I know it's very sudden, but this feels as if it's what I've always wanted. It's as if your father and I have known each other all our lives."

The youngest son said, "Is this what you truly want?"

The rich man, thinking that his son must have addressed this to him, said, "I knew you would understand."

The young woman smiled and said, "It is."

THE RICH MAN AND the young woman who had been the white cat married the very next day. The young woman wore vintage Balenciaga and the rich man wore the green suit his youngest son had brought him in a pistachio shell. Everyone said that he didn't look a day over sixty.

During the party afterward, the youngest son went up to his bedroom and smoked a very large joint. He did not feel as if the rich man had stolen the love of his life. But he did feel as if his father had stolen his cat. He had loved the white cat very much. He wasn't sure how he felt about his stepmother.

Still, when she came into his room, he did not protest when she sat down on the bed and put her arm around his shoulders. She said, "Your father has decided to postpone his retirement."

"Imagine that," the youngest son said.

His new stepmother said, "I've bought you a plane ticket back to Colorado. I expect to be busy for a little while, so perhaps you can run the business for me?"

The youngest son said, a little irritably, "I wish people would stop telling me what they think I should do."

"I think you should do what makes you happy," his stepmother said. "But it may take you some time to figure out what exactly that is. You might as well stay on the ranch while you're thinking about it."

"Sure," the youngest son said.

"Do you still trust me?" his stepmother said.

"Not really," the youngest son said. But then, in spite of himself, he said, "I don't know. Maybe."

"Good," his stepmother said and kissed his cheek. "I promise everything will work out for the best eventually."

AND FOR THE NEXT few years, everyone was reasonably happy. The oldest son and his ex-wife remarried, having discovered that they were happier being unhappy together than they were being unhappy apart. The middle son and his fiancé also married and never felt the need to speak to the rich man again. The youngest son returned to the white cat's ranch and rebuilt the website as well as pioneered a series of recipes that eventually became a cookbook much beloved of stoners. He had been surprised to discover all of the cats on the ranch, like their boss, were now human, though they did not seem to want to talk about how this had happened. All the dogs, however, were still dogs. But then, dogs are more reliable in their nature.

As for the rich man, he felt younger than he had in years. He had a beautiful bride who loved him devotedly. To express this devotion, she presented him with the most exquisite presents inside walnut shells, or in quails' eggs. And whenever their sex life palled, she would invite him to cut off her head, and the result was always pleasing. She became taller, or blonder, her figure more curvaceous or more boyish in a way that never failed to inspire new desire in him. Sometimes it seemed to him that she grew younger, as well, which he found intriguing. What is more pleasing in a late marriage than novelty? He would chop off her head in the evening, and voilà, there she would be, a lovely stranger. They would enjoy each other's company all night long, and then in the morning he would chop off her head again and she would be just as she had been.

The rich man began to imagine a new life with his new bride. He even imagined, one day, that he might want to have children again. He imagined his wife as a mother, how beautiful their children would be, how she would pack their school lunches inside a pecan or a hazelnut. How charming that would be. The only problem he saw was that he was growing old despite his most valiant efforts. How sad it would be were these hypothetical children to lose their father at a young age.

Thinking of this, the rich man began to dream again. He dreamed that his young wife presented him with a nut and asked him to crack it open. But inside the nut was that last child of his, the child whose name was Death.

One day, the rich man's wife, sensing that something was troubling him, begged her husband to tell her what was wrong. And though he did not wish to burden her, at last he confessed all he had been thinking.

His wife listened silently, and then said, "If we let our fear of death stop us from doing what we wish most to do, then what is the point of living? For longer than you know, I have imagined what it would be like to have a family with you."

"I fear nothing," the rich man said. "And yet, I wonder. You have never explained the mechanism properly to me, but each time that I cut off your head, you are reborn. Or so it seems to me. I have begun to wonder about that."

"I often wonder about it, too," his wife said. "To be honest, I don't understand how it works. But I'm content to know that you find the results pleasing."

"Does it hurt?" the rich man said.

The wife said, "Oh, a little, I suppose. But only the least little bit. Like pulling a tooth. Or slamming a finger in the door. A bad paper cut. The first time I was decapitated, I'll confess, was not the best day of my life. But these days I'm quite used to it. How many times have you beheaded me now? One little chop, and it's done and over and I don't think of the pain again. Indeed, when I am myself again I feel brand new, as if I've had a pleasant day at the spa."

"Interesting," the rich man said. "Do you suppose that it would have the same restorative effect on someone else?"

"I imagine that it would sting no matter who was under the blade," his wife said.

"You misunderstand me," said the rich man as patiently as he could. "I meant, should someone else have their head cut off with that blade, would they be reborn good as new?"

His wife said, "I suppose they would!" She looked struck by this idea.

"Imagine the possibilities," the rich man said. "There would be no need for doctors or medicine. A cure for the common cold!"

His wife said, "What a head for business you have, my darling. Though it might seem to many an unorthodox procedure."

"I wonder, though," the rich man said, "were we to cut off my head, might I be made younger?"

"Yes," said his wife. "But I like you just the way you are now."

"And yet I think you might like me even better were I closer to you in age," the rich man said.

And the more they discussed it, the more he overcame his wife's understandable reluctance. In the end, they decided that very night they would dismiss all of the servants and the rich man's wife would cut off her husband's head.

The wife fetched the sword down to the lanai after supper, and the rich man joined her there.

"I don't know how I feel about this," she said.

The rich man got down carefully to his knees. "Who hasn't wanted to cut off their spouse's head at some point in their marriage?" he said. "Just remember, no matter how many times I've cut off yours, my feelings for you have never changed. How many bodies have you inhabited now? I've known and loved you every single time."

His wife knelt down beside him and kissed him on the forehead. "In that case," she said, and got up and brought the blade of the sword down on the rich man's neck. His head flew off and landed in the hot tub.

IN THE MORNING, WHEN the serving staff returned to the rich man's house, they found the body of their employer on the lanai. It took them longer to find his head, which had been a little cooked in the hot water. His young wife, to whom he had left his entire estate and who had presumably killed him, was missing—the only living being on the property was the white cat found crouched beside the sword that had decapitated the rich man. She had licked it nearly clean. There was some discussion of whether or not she should be humanely put down, but after all the sons had returned home for the last time for their father's funeral, the youngest flew back to Colorado, the white cat in a carrier under his seat. She lived a long and contented life there with the youngest son, although she never said another word. When she died many years later, he buried her under a simple tombstone with no name on it at all.

....

Prince Hat Underground

(East of the Sun, West of the Moon)

And who, exactly, is Prince Hat? Gary, who has lived with Prince Hat for over three decades, still sometimes wonders. First of all, who has a name like that? "Unfair," Prince Hat says. "I didn't name myself. And Gary is equally ridiculous. Gary's not even a word. Well, 'garish,' I suppose." And then, for a while, Prince Hat refers to everything Gary habitually does as "garish." It's irritating and so after a day or two Gary goes and looks up the meaning of his name. This, too, turns out to be irritating but he tells Prince Hat anyway, because it will make Prince Hat happy and he likes making his husband happy even if it must be at his expense. "It's an old name. Comes from the Norman, the word for 'pike' and the word for 'king.'"

Prince Hat finds this hilarious. "Prince Hat," he says, pointing to himself. "Nice to meet you, King Pike." He boops Gary on the nose. Because of course Prince Hat would boop a king on the nose.

Prince Hat, at fifty-four, is boyishly handsome, as befits his

name. Beautiful, really. Indolent, fun loving, faithful-ish. Let the
record show there had been a period of time in their twenties,
perhaps continuing through the early part of their thirties, or
longer, perhaps longer, when Prince Hat would disappear for a
night. Two. Sometimes Gary would go looking, find him in the
bed of some man. Some woman. "Who are you?" this person
would ask, and Prince Hat would smile and say, "Gary." And
he'd follow Gary home, as if Prince Hat had been waiting for
him to show up, as if he didn't know how to find his way back
without Gary to guide him there. Who knows? Maybe he
didn't. And it was kind of wonderful, no matter how mad Gary
was, to know he had that power. To look at Prince Hat, then
turn to go and know Prince Hat would follow. This was Prince
Hat's power: to find his way into anyone's bed. And this was
Gary's: to lure him out again.

Prince Hat, older now, is less likely to wander. He seems content with Gary, with their life. He seems to pick fights only on
those occasions when Gary badly needs someone to fight with.
But coffee? One morning he takes it black, the next he wants it
white with heaps of sugar. Some mornings he doesn't have coffee at all, only drinks hot water with lemon. He has no favorite
restaurant, reads half a novel in an ecstatic trance and then puts
it down forever, loves hot weather and cold equally, never keeps
a job for longer than a few years. He has been a catalog model,
a bartender, a tennis coach, a dog walker, an amanuensis to a
famous intellectual (no, Gary won't tell you their name), who, it
turned out, only wanted Prince Hat around to gaze at. Well,
who could blame him? Gary makes enough money for them
both anyway, enough for omakase at Blue Ribbon or Uber rides
over the bridge down to Ugly Baby in Carroll Gardens, health

insurance, vacations twice a year in Reykjavík or Dublin or Rio or Hội An, whichever louche beach or mystical hamlet or buttoned-up quartier has taken Prince Hat's fancy. Sometimes as they travel Gary gleans some new piece of his husband's past. Once, in Prague, Prince Hat mentions an aunt. No, a god-mother, he says. But she liked me to call her aunt. Teta Ra-domila. She made makový koláček just like this. In Reykjavík: "I was a bartender on this very street for a summer. Just there, actually. Imagine that—the place is still open! They had the most ferocious problem with rats. The largest rats you've ever seen, though I've seen larger. Some places, the rats grow to be the size of a dog. But that summer, the rats, nothing could be done." But when Gary suggests they go in to have a drink, Prince Hat says, "Oh, you wouldn't care for the ambience." There is something in his voice telling Gary not to push any further. They used to have absolutely blistering fights over all the things Prince Hat wouldn't say. And in the end, Gary gave in. It was like the rats. Nothing could be done. And now they are happy and they travel and they always come home to the Upper West Side.

Prince Hat, though, thinks he knows plenty about Gary. Early in their relationship it seemed to Gary that Prince Hat was hardly paying attention at all, but Prince Hat, as it happens, is always paying attention. He's just sly. Even then he was gathering up all the pieces of Gary that Gary let slip. He remembers things about Gary's childhood, about Gary's parents and former lovers that Gary, mercifully, has forgotten. Every mannerism, every habit, every minor pleasure, Prince Hat stores up. All things "garish." The sting is lessened by Gary's knowledge that Prince Hat, knowing Gary so well, loves Gary still, and very well indeed.

They spend holidays with friends, sometimes with the families of Gary's sister, Gary's brother. (Children love Prince Hat.) Never Prince Hat's family. Never friends from Prince Hat's life before Gary met him. As far as Gary knows, Prince Hat has no family. He likes to tell people his life began in the moment he followed Gary out of a restaurant in a city Prince Hat had supposed he was only visiting for the weekend. What he doesn't usually say is that he was visiting the city with his fiancée. Gary has never suggested they go back to that restaurant, in case she is still waiting there for Prince Hat to return.

SOME SUNDAYS GARY AND Prince Hat have brunch at Folklore, a café whose whimsical name does not suggest the perfunctory briskness of its servers, the predictable savor of its eggs Benedict. Gary always orders the former, Prince Hat whatever his heart desires. Neither man has grown fat yet. Gary suspects Prince Hat never will, Prince Hat still the most beautiful man he has ever seen. Gary, well, Gary would be the first to acknowledge he has never been particularly handsome, and yet in his twenties he had all the men he wanted, didn't he? All he had to do was ask with his eyes and men followed him.

The first time Gary saw Prince Hat, the bartender had just handed him a gin martini in exchange for three dollars (yes, a long time ago!). Prince Hat sat at a table facing a young woman (his fiancée) to whom Gary paid only the most cursory notice. He was intent upon Prince Hat's profile. Surely Prince Hat must have felt the warmth of Gary's stare. Indeed, later Prince Hat confirmed he had.

Gary put down on the bar his untouched drink. He made his way past Prince Hat's table, turning back, once, as he went, to

summon Prince Hat as if he were attaching the finest and stron-
gest thread. It ran from his eyes, his body, his whole will to knot
around Prince Hat's wrist, his waist, his cock. He summoned and
Prince Hat came. Prince Hat got up from his chair, abandoned
without a word his lamb croquettes and his companion and followed Gary out of the bar and into his new life. It wasn't until
the next day that they bothered to learn each other's names. And
it wasn't until at least a week after when Gary understood the
woman Prince Hat had been dining with had been his fiancée.
What was her name? How long had they been engaged? Where
had home been? Had this other life, before Gary, been happy?
Fulfilling? "It's not really worth talking about," Prince Hat said
then. "I don't see the point in dwelling." Incredible to think that,
for eight full months, Prince Hat was a receptionist for a re-
nowned analyst. Analysis slides off Prince Hat like water off a
duck engendered from dark matter. Out of the wreckage of one
life, Prince Hat climbed into Gary's, and they have been together
ever since, faithful more or less, happy more or less, a fairy tale of
a romance more or less, their friends say. How pleasant it is to be
envied! How delightful when Prince Hat still surprises Gary but
only in ways that do not threaten to capsize their comfortable life.

The night previous, coming home from some fundraiser
Gary has persuaded Prince Hat to attend (these things are always
more fun with Prince Hat in attendance), they pass a young
woman arm in arm with a young man. Clearly out-of-towners,
in love with each other and in love with everyone else because
of this. They smile at Prince Hat and Gary, and Gary cannot
help it. He says to Prince Hat, "Do you ever think about her?
Your fiancée? What that life would have been like?"

"No," Prince Hat says. "And I prefer not to think about it

right now, either, thank you very much. What do you think? Brunch tomorrow at Folklore or somewhere new?"

"Somewhere new," Gary says, thinking of what will please Prince Hat most.

But Prince Hat knows what Gary is thinking. "Folklore it is," he says. "A leisurely meal and no talk of the past, only talk of the present."

And so they linger over their meal at Folklore, Prince Hat describing his co-workers at a job he has just embarked on, a spa called Occult where massage therapists offer hot stone, shiatsu, deep tissue massage, and, for an additional charge, exorcism of any malevolent spirits that may be causing pain or stiffness. They are trained in breaking curses, reversing bad fortune, throwing off the devil. Prince Hat has been hired as a manager. Gary cannot tell if Prince Hat actually believes in any of what Occult offers. He has always been evasive when it comes to matters of religion, superstition, belief.

But after a while Gary finds he cannot focus on what Prince Hat is saying. There is a young woman sitting alone by the server's station. There is a plate of scrambled eggs and toast in front of her. She isn't eating, though. She's watching Prince Hat. People are often watching Prince Hat but this woman looks at Prince Hat with an expression of such profound satisfaction and malice that a feeling comes upon Gary. The feeling is this: he should leave with Prince Hat now, at once, before the young woman takes whatever action she is about to take. "Let's go home," he says. "Get this boxed up. Eat leftovers in bed. Watch Netflix. Whatever you want." This, despite not knowing whether Prince Hat will choose a teen slasher movie or some undubbed Ukrainian documentary on mushrooms.

"If you like," Prince Hat says, surprised for once by Gary. But before Gary can manage to summon their waiter, here comes the young woman. "Prince Hat," she says. "It's been so long."

Gary does not remember what Prince Hat's fiancée looked like. Was she pretty? Stylish? A blonde or a brunette? Not a redhead, he would remember that, but this woman is not a redhead. He wishes she was. She is far too young to be the girl Prince Hat left sitting at a table three decades ago, and yet Gary knows somehow that same girl is standing here now, in front of them.

"Agnes," Prince Hat says. Agnes wears her hair in a tidy plait; her nose is snubbed. Her build is trim and she wears high-cut jeans that are neither flattering nor laughably out of fashion. Her shirt, a childlike pink, is badly wrinkled. Her shoes are espadrilles, and there is a Band-Aid on one heel. Her perfume is smoky but pleasant. It suits her somehow. Aside from the perfume she could be any tourist who underestimated the amount of walking New York requires. How is she here? And has she been here all this time? Looking for Prince Hat?

"I'm Gary," Gary says.

"Gary. So good to be introduced at last," Agnes says. "May I sit down?"

"Please," Prince Hat says. It's hard for Gary to tell what he is thinking, but this is always the case.

Agnes sits down. Now she is between them. "You must be wondering who I am," she says to Gary.

"No," Gary says. "I don't think I'm wondering that."

She grins cheerfully at this. How young she is! Her teeth are small and white and even, and Gary could imagine the braces have only recently come off. "Well! In that case would you mind if I borrowed your Prince Hat for a little while? Just a short trip, say around the block and down memory lane? I'd love to spend some time getting to know you, but I'm only in town for another hour or so. Then off home again."

"Home being?" Gary says.

"Where the heart is!" Agnes says. "Surely you know all about Prince Hat and the dreadful, dreadful fate you rescued him from all those years ago."

"Of course," Gary says. He can see Agnes knows he is lying, but he goes on doing it. "It's just, I didn't know—we don't know—where home is for you now."

Prince Hat is standing up. "I'm ready," he says to Agnes. "If we must, we must."

Gary begins to stand up, too, but Prince Hat puts his hand on his shoulder. "Stay here," he says. "Finish your eggs before they get too cold. Get a box for my pancakes. I'll eat them later."

He bends over, kisses Gary at his hairline. Then Prince Hat and his ex-fiancée leave Folklore. Gary sees them turn the corner onto 112th. He wants nothing more than to run after them, after Prince Hat, as if he were a small child or a dog. Object permanence! But he is a grown man, fifty-seven, and he stopped trying to winkle out Prince Hat's secrets a long time ago. Clams are happy, cats are never satisfied, marriage is based on trust. Prince Hat always comes home. Except this time he doesn't. Gary waits a full hour at Folklore. He doesn't even text Prince Hat. Perhaps he already knows there's no point. Prince Hat doesn't come back to Folklore, and he doesn't answer his phone when Gary finally texts, then texts again, then calls. Calls back again and, driven to desperation, leaves a voice message.

When Gary gets home, sodden pancakes in their hopeful

box, Prince Hat isn't there, either. But there is the smell of a smoky perfume, and Prince Hat's smallest piece of luggage is gone. So is the dove-gray suit from Barneys, purchased just before they closed their doors for good, Gary's extravagant gift to Prince Hat only last Christmas. Over the course of the next four weeks the pancakes turn to marble in the refrigerator while Gary grows ever more frantic. Prince Hat has vanished from the face of the earth.

AND WHAT, NOW, IS Gary to do? Grow old and die alone? Without Prince Hat? Prince Hat does not answer his phone. Cellular data has been turned off. He has made no withdrawals from their joint bank account, has not used their credit cards. Long ago when they were young, Gary could always find Prince Hat, but in those days he knew to keep an eye on Prince Hat at parties, made note of whom Prince Hat went off with. He asked around until he had names, looked up addresses in phone books (Remember those? No, you don't, it's fine), put in the legwork. What is he to do with the name "Agnes"? If Prince Hat has returned home with her, well, where is that? Why didn't Gary snap a picture with his phone at least? His friends are sympathetic, concerned for Prince Hat, but they can't be helpful. Prince Hat has confided nothing of his past to them. And Gary can't convey the strangeness of it all to them, the preternatural youth of this fiancée, the gloating glance she gave him in parting.

He files a police report, posts on message boards, but this happens from time to time, he is told. A lover leaves. Lovers are left. Maybe Prince Hat will return. Gary thinks that he will not. A smarter man would accept this, but though Gary is old enough now to accept many things he once could not, he cannot accept that Prince Hat is gone forever. He consults a psychic, who can tell him nothing except that Prince Hat is hidden from her kind. Instead she sells him a miniature Baby Ruth, misshapen and rewrapped in foil that has been taped up again. She claims she has doctored it in some way so it may reveal hidden information, and charges him fifty dollars. It tastes only like cheap chocolate.

The next night Gary has dinner near the Strand with friends who will surely soon grow tired of offering their ears, their sympathies. Returning to the subway he walks along the edge of Union Square Park and, stopping to check his messages to see if by chance Prince Hat has called or texted, he hears two voices muttering in the dark.

One says, "Look at the old fool. Grieving for such a one as Prince Hat."

The other voice says, "You would do the same if Prince Hat had ever looked twice at you."

Gary looks around to see who is speaking. The park is empty except for the rats who inhabit it by night, and indeed it is two rats who are talking beneath the cherry trees, now bare and black.

"I wouldn't grieve," the first rat says. "I am a rat of action. I would go in search of him."

"You? You are a rat of very little brain and you wouldn't know the first place to look," the second rat says.

"I have nibbled on the pages of the finest detective novels," the first rat says. "Arthur Conan Doyle, Sue Grafton, Kinky Friedman. I would do as they suggest and begin my investigation in what I knew of his past."

"Whereas I would suggest to you that you go to Hell," the second rat says. "That would do just as well."

The first rat curses the second and scurries off. Gary goes home. In the morning he decides he will do what he has always done. The rats may have been a dream, or the result of too much wine, or they may be the result of whatever the psychic put in the Baby Ruth bar. It doesn't really matter, does it? Gary will go and find Prince Hat and bring him home. If Prince Hat won't come home, at least Gary can ask him why he left.

Gary knows so little about Prince Hat's old life. There is the godmother and her cakes, like the cakes he and Prince Hat ate in Prague. But where Prince Hat was living when he knew her, surely it wasn't Prague. Wouldn't he have said, if that were the case? Pointed out other old haunts? Everything he knows about Prince Hat is like this. Bits of flotsam, nothing pinning them to a particular place of origin, except for a bar on a street in Reykjavík. Gary doesn't remember the name of the street, but surely he can find it if he tries. They went there only a few years ago. Five years at most. Surely the bar is still there. He arranges to take unpaid leave. A friend in Jersey will stay in the apartment, collect the mail, call should Prince Hat come home. Off to Reykjavík goes Gary.

When he was here with Prince Hat, all those years ago, it was summer. Light the nursemaid washing everyone and everything, light the voyeur seeping in around the black seal of the curtains in their hotel room. It pressed on his eyeballs, lapped hotly at his skin, and came pouring out through him again like a tide when he tried to sleep. He and Prince Hat went to clubs, danced, drank, came out at three A.M. and found light the idler still waiting for them. Now it's winter and the cold settles, crackling, whispering, into his eardrums, his nostrils, his bones, and his heart. Now, like Prince Hat, the sun is sly, sneaks off as soon as you've caught sight of it, staying away as if it means to stay away forever. In summer everyone wore bright colors. Now the whole town seems attired in black or gray as if in mourning, each face somber. How is he to recognize any of these streets when all the light is gone, when Prince Hat isn't here beside him? Gary only came here once. Had they been to the Einar Jónsson art museum when they passed by the bar? Or was it near Kolaportið, where Prince Hat had to be dissuaded from buying a rolltop desk with a locked drawer and no key? Oh, Prince Hat. Gary revisits the places he remembers, goes down every street they might have wandered. Finally, on the third day (if day can be said to exist in the absence of light) he comes upon the street, two blocks from the Icelandic Phallological Museum. The bar where Prince Hat worked is called Norðanvindurinn. It isn't the name he remembers, who would remember a name like that? What he remembers is all the letters lit in red except two, the first *r* and the last *i;* those two are black. Inside, a few ramshackle tables, two old drunks propped up to the right of the counter. The bartender is near enough to Gary's age that he allows himself to hope this has not been entirely a fool's errand.

This bartender is a gaunt individual in a fisherman's sweater, strangely bulky around the middle. Gary says, "Gott kvöld," rubbing his hands to get the cold off them, and the bartender inclines his head solemnly.

Gary's Icelandic is limited and his situation is complicated. He says, "Do you speak English?" The bartender shakes his head no.

"Ah," Gary says. "Well." Unusual, but he has an app on his phone for this. He types in, "I'm looking for a man called Prince

Hat. He worked here in the eighties." The app translates his sentences, how marvelous, how magical, and Gary passes his phone over the counter.

The bartender glances down. He types, then slides the phone back to Gary.

He's written, "Drink. Then talk." Fair enough.

"Gin og tonic," Gary says. He has three before the bartender will say a word. By his third, he is drunker than he has been for years; the bartender has a heavy hand with the gin, and he knows he is drunk because it seems to him the bartender's flesh, beneath the heavy cardigan, is in motion, queasily, slowly, steadily.

The bartender motions for Gary's phone. "Long ago I knew him," he writes. "A strange one but good company."

"Yes!" Gary shouts. "That's my Prince Hat, exactly." He types, "Prince Hat and I are married. We love each other. But we ran into a woman, someone from his old life, a few weeks ago and he went somewhere with her."

He thinks about how to describe Agnes. "I had met her once before. She did not seem to have aged. Not a day! An insinuating young woman named Agnes, with a pleasant face and hair in braids. No one you would look at twice. But they'd known each other in the past and you may know of her also. I don't know enough about Prince Hat's old life to know how or where to find him. But I must find him. He never would have left me of his own free will. We were happy."

The bartender reads this, looks at Gary thoughtfully. The bulge at his middle moves slowly this way and that. Perhaps he is thinking about the wrong thing, about whether or not anyone ever really knows whether their relationship is a happy one. Perhaps he is trying to recall what he knows about Prince Hat, trying to recall a young woman with braids.

One of the drunks down the bar calls for the bartender and he goes to take their order. When he comes back, he types into Gary's phone, then hands it back.

"Fairy?" Gary says. "Great. You're a homophobe."

"Huldufólk," the bartender says.

Gary looks that up on his phone. "Okay, fine, not a homophobe. But, come on. Fairies stole my husband?"

He types out, "Fairies did not steal my husband. Please be serious."

And this is what the bartender writes down in return: "Prince Hat grew up among the huldufólk. He attended the Black School. He was promised to Hell. But first he came up to live in the world because he was curious to see how things went in the kingdoms above. He wished to drink and fuck and see night become day become night again. This is what he told me once. Perhaps his curiosity has been satisfied and he has gone home."

What the bartender says cannot be true, and yet some part of Gary feels some part of it is true. He is drunk and can perceive truths the sober cannot admit. "Fine," he says. "Prince Hat went to Hell. Then I'll go there, too." Then he has to type it out again, adding, "Did he happen to mention, long ago, what route he took when he came here?"

The bartender laughs, shrugs, says something. Then types, "We all of us go to Hell sooner or later, but the way is not revealed while one is in this world. Perhaps you might discover more in the Black School."

"Great," Gary says. He types: "How do I find the Black School?"

The bartender shrugs again. Types, "I don't know the way. But this one does."

He reaches his hand inside his cardigan while Gary reads this, and for one wild moment Gary imagines the bartender is about to pull out his own heart and offer it, wet and bloody. But instead when his hand emerges, a green coil is wrapped around it, thick as Gary's own wrist.

"What the fuck!" Gary says, but the bartender just smiles, his teeth gray and uneven, and goes on removing, coil by coil, the snake that has apparently been wrapped around his waist this entire time. It is at least four feet long.

"Hún veit," the bartender says. He tries to pass the snake to Gary, and when Gary refuses, he lays the snake down on the counter. "Hún heitir Brennivín," he says. He takes the phone and types out, "Brennivín, she will find for you the Black School."

Before Gary leaves Norðanvindurinn, he uses the men's room. He knows two things: one, as soon as he's outside again, he's going to feel twice as drunk as he feels now, and two, if he doesn't piss now, in about three blocks he'll regret it. Another thing he knows: he will accept the bartender's offer and see if the snake named Brennivín will show him where he needs to go. But he lingers beside the urinals, peering in the gloom to study the old marks of graffiti on the wall. Spoor for the one who searches: numbers, dicks, lamentations, doggerel, exhortations in languages he cannot read, names. Not one of them in a hand he knows. Not one name the name Prince Hat. Oh, where has Prince Hat gone?

BRENNIVÍN'S SKIN IS WARMER than Gary expects, the texture pleasing. He did not expect that, either. Perhaps it is only that in the absence of Prince Hat he has missed the touch of another being. The bartender indicates Gary should undo his buttons, tuck the snake inside his shirt, and so Gary does this. Brennivín wraps herself around his torso snugly so her long head sticks out—like the handle of a knife!—from his chest, and Gary does his buttons again, all but two. He puts on his coat but leaves it open.

He types into his phone, "How will she show me the way?"

The bartender looks, waves dismissively.

So Gary types, "What should I do with her once she's shown me the way?"

The bartender takes the phone, types, passes it back. He has written, "Don't trouble yourself. Brennivín takes care of Brennivín."

Outside the darkness has been waiting all this time, and the cold sinks its small teeth into Gary. Which way is he to go? But even as he thinks this, he feels how Brennivín's head shifts right, and so he goes down the street in the way Brennivín wishes him to go. He turns when she wishes him to turn and goes along straight until she indicates that he should turn again. They move from streets where there are restaurants and shops and bars, onto streets that pass over other streets, into a landscape of houses painted shades that would be colorful in daylight but now are only brooding, construction sites where more houses will soon be, small planes flying overhead. He is near the domestic airport. Heaps of old snow throw their long, unfamiliar shadows along the way Gary must go. Late in middle age, one does not expect to find oneself in a fairy tale, but as long as the outcome is a reunion with Prince Hat, Gary will endure peculiarity without too many complaints.

He takes out his phone and looks to see if Prince Hat has left a message, sent a text. This is habit, and perhaps hope, too, is merely habit, something Gary must let go of, but he will not let go just yet. Reach out your hand and pluck the nettle. Feel how it stings. What would Prince Hat do, if he saw Gary holding this nettle? He'd knock it from his hand, say, "Gary, what the fuck?" Or perhaps he'd laugh, say, "It's always the same with you, Gary. Poor old Gary."

Gary checks the map function, the thing he meant to do all along, to see where Brennivín is taking him. They are near Öskjuhlíð, where Perlan is. He and Prince Hat went to the museum there, ate lunch in the restaurant. But surely the museum will be closed now, yes, it's closed and neither he nor Prince Hat had enjoyed their meal so much as to think of returning.

"Be careful and do not use up your battery. You may wish you had not, later on."

Who has spoken? Gary looks up, but there is no one on the street save him and Brennivín. It is the snake wrapped around him who is speaking.

"You talk, too?" he says.

"If you must ask questions, then let them not be pointless ones," Brennivín says. She indicates they are to turn right, off the street and onto a path between two boulders where the snow has been packed down by many feet. No streetlights here, only the bright moon, which gives the way he must go a blue, congealed aspect, like a food one should not eat.

The footpath is covered in ice and snow and Gary goes carefully. It would not do to fall on top of his guide. She might bite him. They are in among the skeletal trees now and the path grows steeper. In his head he formulates and discards many questions until, at last, he says, "Do you know my husband, Prince Hat?"

Brennivín says, "I have known ones like him." She does not elaborate, but when they have gone on a while longer, an image begins to form inside Gary's head, a memory, and he knows Brennivín has put it there. In this memory he and Prince Hat are at a crowded party in some apartment. Prince Hat sits cross-legged on a coffee table, a bowl full of fortune cookies in his lap. Gary stands opposite him, propped up against a wall, a bottle of Moscato in his fist. They are younger than they are now, not even thirty yet. They are drunk, happy, their faces are red with wine and because the apartment is too warm. How happy they have always been. He stands at Prince Hat's shoulder, looking over at himself, feeling that sense of fondness and envy and shame one must always feel when one recollects one's younger self. Prince Hat takes cookies out of his bowl, tosses them at partygoers. "Here is your future," he is calling out. "Know what your future holds, if you dare."

And now Gary remembers this party. It's New Year's Eve, they are approaching the turn of the century; he doesn't re-member his fortune, but Prince Hat's he knows. It was this: "Your love will make a paradise." And hasn't it been exactly this? But here is Prince Hat breaking the cookie, and here is the motto for Gary to see: "Do not gamble security for the hope of true love, which does not exist in this place."

"What does it say?" the other Gary asks. "What?" Prince Hat says, pretending he hasn't heard above the noise of the party, the people, the music. The other Gary asks again, louder. Prince Hat holds up the fortune, says, grinning, "Your love will make a paradise!" And then pops the slip of paper into his mouth and swallows it. "Now it will happen." As if he is working a piece of magic and not concealing a lie.

"Is this real?" Gary says. "Is that what it really said?"

The snake says nothing, only indicates now they are to turn off the path and into the trees. Each step Gary takes breaks through the top crust of snow so his boot sinks down a foot or two, sometimes farther. The ground is uneven, the night is cold, he is letting a snake guide him through an unknown place. Is there nothing he will not endure for Prince Hat? And here, just before them, is a cleft in a rock, so narrow Gary thinks he will not fit. But this is where the snake indicates he is to go.

Gary passes into the darkness. He taps his phone on, so there is a little light, rests one hand on the wall of the rock, goes forward slowly. He is in a lava tube, perhaps, like Raufarhólshellir, which he and Prince Hat toured, wearing plastic hard hats with little lights. They came back later that night for a concert; only fifty tickets had been available, but Prince Hat had acquired two somehow. Had Gary enjoyed the music? He only remembers Prince Hat now. In here there is only just enough room to stand and as he goes on, Gary must hunch his shoulders in, tuck his head against his chest: the roof of the passage grows lower, then lower. Prince Hat is more slender, true, but he is also taller. Gary tries to imagine Prince Hat in this passage, crouching and scuttling forward. Surely Prince Hat came another way.

It seems to Gary he walks for at least a mile, maybe farther, Brennivín's cool weight pressing against his ribs, his spine. The passage becomes wider at last, though still low, and then it ends and here at its end is a little door with a handle that turns and opens into a space large enough that Gary can stand upright again. He cannot tell how far the ceiling extends above him.

There is only darkness. He walks a few steps along the wall to the right of the door. Under his fingers the wall is scored and when he lifts his light, he sees there are words carved into the stone. Name after name after name, they have been carved everywhere he looks. Here by his fingers, Guðrún Guðmundsdóttir. Ingólfur Smárason. Heiður. This one is carved very deeply.

"I have brought you where you wished to come," Brennivín says. "This is the Black School." She loosens her grip on Gary, slides down to the floor of the cavern.

"Wait," Gary says. "You're leaving me here?" Surely Prince Hat is not in this place, and Gary does not wish to be left alone in a place called the Black School.

But Brennivín has already passed beyond the halo of the light of his phone. Keeping his hand on the wall, Gary turns to make sure of the door through which they entered. He will leave his gloves here, to mark where the passage begins that will lead him outside again. But he cannot find the door. He is alone in the dark with only the light of the phone.

There's no use panicking. First Gary does what he planned to do. He places his gloves on the floor of the cave and then checks his phone. He has, of course, no reception here, but there is more than half of the battery remaining. Keeping one hand on the wall, he moves forward slowly to find where the door has gone. He pauses every few steps to read the names at eye level, as if these might serve as some kind of guide. The wall has an almost imperceptible curve to it, Gary thinks. He must be in some kind of vast circular space. Perhaps this is a place where the adventurous gather to hold raves or orgies or engage in mysterious rites. But there is no litter, there are no empties or used condoms, or anything but darkness and the names under Gary's fingers, the graduates of the Black School. There is a sensation, too, which seems to emanate from the center of the space, a sensation of power held in stillness, something strange and mag-isterial lying in wait. Gary might give up his search for Prince Hat, might approach this power, might learn things that would prove to his advantage. He might become a great power himself, were he a good student, were he to give himself over to the Black School.

But Gary stays beside the wall, creeping along carefully. He does not want worldly or unworldly power, he only wants Prince Hat. Time passes and Gary cannot find the door, but after even more time passes, he realizes he is not looking for the door any longer. He is looking for the name Prince Hat. He comes again, instead, to the names he found first: Guðrún Guð-mundsdóttir. Ingólfur Smárason. Heiður. And then, here are Gary's gloves where he left them to mark the door. But there is no door, there is no longer a door. Gary goes around the single wall of the Black School once more, scanning for the name Prince Hat. He goes around twice, then a third time, and on the fourth he finds the name he is looking for down quite close to the floor. Here is the name of his love. The battery on his phone is low now, so Gary turns it off and sits on the floor, his finger pressed against Prince Hat's name. It isn't fair of Prince Hat to leave him in darkness all alone like this, but there are other nights Gary has sat up awake in the dark, waiting for Prince Hat to come home. He is practiced at darkness.

He sits for a long time, but eventually he must stand up again. His legs are all pins and needles, his feet are numb with cold, and he must find somewhere to piss. But when he turns on his phone to find a space without a name, he sees there is something pale and plump squirming on the ground beside his foot.

It's some kind of grub or larva: eyeless, limbless, colorless, bigger than Gary's thumb. Perhaps the room is full of these or, worse, perhaps they are being drawn toward the light of Gary's phone, or the vibration the strike of his feet have made upon the stone. This is the moment, of course it is, when his battery at last gives out and he is returned to darkness. What he feels in this moment, however, is not despair. Instead, a feeling comes to Gary, that the grub on the floor of the cave is the thing he has been waiting for. He is meant to pick it up: he does so. And, holding it, he knows its name. This is Sæmundr the Learned, come to be Gary's second guide as Brennivín was his first. It comes to him that he is meant to put Sæmundr into his mouth, to carry him this way. Gary does not wish to do this, but he does it anyway. After all, has he not had more unsavory objects in his mouth? Oh, not Prince Hat's cock, though! Prince Hat's cock is as lovely as every other part of him.

Sæmundr tastes of old stone, dry meat. Once he is resting under Gary's palate he begins to move as if he is Gary's tongue and to speak with Gary's voice. These are the words Sæmundr says.

"I do not know the one you look for, but I may know where he has gone. Carry me with you and I will guide you a little farther on your way."

Desperation has been Gary's only companion in these last few weeks. Desperation means you will take advice from rats, a snake, allow yourself to be led into the endless dark where there is no door. You will pick up a white squirming thing, take it into your mouth like a Communion wafer, give it your own voice in case it speaks the name of the one you love, Prince Hat, Prince Hat, Prince Hat.

If Gary could speak, he would say to Sæmundr, "Take me where you will, as long as Prince Hat may be found there."

But this is not exactly what Sæmundr is promising. "Place your hand against the wall," Sæmundr says. "Do not fear the darkness, but proceed carefully and I will tell you the way you are to go."

The names of the many students of the Black School pass beneath Gary's fingers, his palm. How many have attended, learned the lessons there! Imagine your own name, the names of those you love, how darkness seeps into the gouges of each letter until it fills each letter up, rubs off on the tips of Gary's fingers so the stain will never come out, no matter how he scrubs. And here, in darkness, Gary finds a door, open and leading down a flight of stairs.

"Yes," Sæmundr says in Gary's mouth. "This is the way."

It seems to Gary each tread is wider than it ought to be, each riser higher than one designed for human travelers. Who were these stairs made for? He can feel, worn into the middle of each stone, the impression of a foot that is not a human foot. He must feel ahead to find the lip of each tread, test for the surface of the next. Carefully they go down the stairs in the darkness, until they come to a landing, then another flight of stairs. "Yes," Sæmundr says, "a little farther still. Still a little farther."

Down they go and down they go, until Gary's calves ache and he sees blue flashes in the pitch black as his eyes try to find the way he must go. He has counted five hundred and ninety-nine steps, and at the six hundredth step he sits down to rest. If he goes any farther he knows that he will fall.

Sæmundr says, "It is farther yet. Just a little farther. If you must rest, then rest only a little while and then you must go on. Remember your wedding night. Perhaps that will restore you."

Oh, Gary remembers. He married Prince Hat at city hall first thing in the morning, then drove northeast until they reached Old Orchard Beach in Maine, well past midnight. They stayed in a beach cottage, the key left under the mat, rose petals on the bed. Prince Hat asleep in Gary's arms, until at last Gary slept, too, and woke a few hours later to find himself alone. When he went out onto the porch, there Prince Hat was upon the shore, naked and standing up to his knees in the outgoing tide.

But what he sees now, though all is darkness around him, is himself asleep upon the bed. He is now Prince Hat, leaving his new husband, his marriage bed, the honeymoon cottage, leaving open the French doors that look out upon the washed opal sands, foaming as the water rushes away.

There is a great beast farther out, a nest of writhing black limbs and beaks and eyes. Upon one of its heads sits Agnes. She wears armor studded with pearls the size of robins' eggs and a golden crown upon her brow. She says, "Are you ready to come home now, Prince Hat?"

Prince Hat does not answer her. His fiancée, a throne, and all the kingdoms below wait upon his pleasure. He has not meant to tarry so long. He takes a step and then another. He does not know himself why he remains in this life, why he has put Gary's ring upon his finger. Ones like Prince Hat do not have much truck with love. They are made for stranger feelings, and yet Prince Hat does not now go with Agnes. He walks out only a little farther into the ocean, then sends Agnes away when he senses Gary is waking, will shortly come to find him and bring him back inside, run a bath to warm him, then dry him and return him to the marriage bed.

The memory ends and Gary is only Gary again, sitting in darkness upon worn stone, a sorcerous grub speaking in his mouth. "Let us go on," Sæmundr says. "Others use these stairs, and it would be well if you were away before any found you here."

Gary gets up, knees complaining, and begins his journey downward once more. It hurts, of course it hurts to know how much of himself Prince Hat has kept concealed, but has he not chosen Gary at every turn? This is what matters. He and Sæmundr go on in the darkness until he has lost count of the steps, has no sense of how far down he has descended. Sometimes he stumbles; twice he loses his footing and falls, catching himself against the rough walls of the stairs. Hours pass, another day must have begun in the world above the Black School, though of course it is winter-dark there all the same. But that darkness is not this darkness. When at last the stairs end, Gary cannot understand what it means. Darkness has been pouring through his eyes, his mouth, his ears and nose, until everything in his head is darkness, only darkness. He tests to find where the end of the step might be, but cannot find it. He begins to weep, or perhaps he has been weeping for some time. The sensation of wetness on his face is the tongue of the dark, tenderly licking off the last remnants of the world above.

"Open your mouth," Sæmundr says. "I will provide a little light so you may continue."

Gary opens his mouth obediently, and Sæmundr is glowing now, emitting light that spills like urine down onto the stony ground where Gary stands.

"Go on," Sæmundr says. "It is only a little farther now."

Gary walks on. What point would there be, to give up now? The light Sæmundr provides extends two steps beyond, and then farther, as if it is gushing from Gary's mouth. Gary sees now he is traversing some vast chamber. Air moves around him in a series of exhalations as if some giant mouth is breathing in rhythm with his own breaths. There are muddy prints, human feet, he thinks, but bare, and he is following these. The prints, too, glow as if Sæmundr's light is falling like dust upon them. The air is dry and cool, but Gary's path crosses over other tracks, too, these the marks some monstrous serpent might make, still damp when he reaches down to touch. His jaw aches from holding it open and he is thirstier than he has ever been. He is hungry, too. He imagines biting down upon Sæmundr, devouring it, but the taste of Sæmundr is bitter. Every time Sæmundr has spoken Gary has tasted this bitterness. But then they have come to the place Sæmundr has meant to bring them to. Sæmundr moves in Gary's mouth, leaps out, and rolls himself into a small, plump ball, goes spinning forward ahead of Gary.

Gary runs after Sæmundr. Sæmundr's light increases as he flees and now there is more light, purple and green and white, the upper reaches of the cavern streaked with coruscating light. Sæmundr has brought him to the shore of a great subterranean lake, all filmed over in mineral deposits like scales on a fish, crackling and shifting, these so thin in places that the light that boils down in the depths of the lake passes through the crust, flinging itself wildly around the chamber as the water ripples and laps at the pebbles on the stone shore.

There is a house here, made of slate, and in the open window a candle is burning. Gary sees Sæmundr go leaping over the windowsill and into the house. He goes up onto the porch to knock upon the door, but before he can do so, a voice speaks in an unfamiliar language.

A relief so great Gary feels like weeping, when he turns and sees the speaker is a man. He is an old man, his hair ferociously long and tangled, his beard the same. He wears an old-fashioned suit, worn through at the elbows and knees, but no shoes. He brandishes a paintbrush in his right hand.

"I'm sorry," Gary says. "I don't know what you said. I'm looking for a man named Prince Hat. Do you know him?"

"And who comes unbidden to the final home of Gerhard Gotaas?" Sæmundr calls from the windowsill of the house. "That was what he said." He then speaks to the old man, Gerhard Gotaas.

The old man laughs. He replies to Sæmundr, and Sæmundr once again translates. "He says, who does not know Prince Hat, that infamous slut?"

How can Gary be insulted by this when Prince Hat would laugh and agree?

Gerhard Gotaas speaks again and Sæmundr translates. "He says, he does not recall the last time Prince Hat passed by, but then he is a busy man. If he is not working on his last great endeavor then he is sleeping, and either working or sleeping, he pays no mind to those who pass by, save they annoy him by asking foolish questions."

"Sorry to interrupt whatever thing he's doing down here, truly," Gary says. "But ask him if he knows where I might find Prince Hat."

Sæmundr says, "I will ask if you like, but a suggestion: perhaps you might say something admiring about his work first."

It is something, Gary thinks, *to be given a lesson in etiquette by a grub in a sunless cavern.* But Sæmundr isn't wrong. So Gary goes to see what this Gerhard Gotaas is engaged in doing. Gotaas barks something, and Sæmundr says, "Careful where you tread, oaf!"

And now Gary sees how everywhere on the floor of the cavern before him, painted in fine, glowing strokes, are miniature faces and creatures, grinning, goggly-eyed, horned, and priapic. No two are the same. Each is expressive, so lively they appear to dance in the waves of light the lake throws off. It's extraordinary work, and Gary says so.

"I have merely made a start," Gerhard Gotaas says repressively, Sæmundr translating. But the compliment has done its job.

"The one you are looking for may or may not be in Hell," Gerhard Gotaas says, "but Hell is where you ought to go." He makes an odd grunting sound as Sæmundr speaks, and Gary realizes he is laughing at his own joke. "You have brought me what I have been needing, so ask and I will provide a willing guide. She likes it better there, anyway."

Sæmundr translates this, too, and then squeals horribly. A soot-colored cat has leapt up onto the sill beside him and now catches Sæmundr in its mouth. Gerhard Gotaas steps carefully away from his capering, grinning demons, places an empty metal pail on an unpainted bit of floor. The cat runs over and shakes Sæmundr in its teeth so that glowing blood begins to drip down, Gotaas's bucket collecting it all.

What is Gary to make of any of this? And who will translate for him now? When all of Sæmundr's blood has emptied into the bucket, the skin of the grub like a discarded condom on the ground, Gerhard Gotaas crouches down and pets the cat, speaking lovingly to it. He gestures at Gary, then dips his brush into the bucket and begins once more to paint.

The gray cat steps daintily onto the encrusted surface of the lake, then looks back at Gary. It's a mangy beast and its eyes are filmy. Both ears are torn, and there is a long black scar across one flank where no fur grows. Dribbles of Sæmundr's bright blood still cling to its whiskers. Gary understands none of this. Not the Black School, nor the long, faltering trek down those dark stairs, not the painter or his project, not the grub nor why he must follow this disreputable cat. He does not understand anything that has happened since Prince Hat left Folklore. But one does not have to understand anything. It is enough to simply go on. He takes one step onto the lake, and when he does not fall through, he takes another.

The cat is lighter than Gary. It does not worry whether the mineral crust will support its weight. Gary tests each step he takes, tries to gauge where the crust is thicker. Water oozes up onto the crust the farther out he ventures, washing over his sensible tourist walking boots. Lights blaze by underneath, far below the surface of the lake. Everything dazzles. An hour of this painstaking progress and now he is quite far from the shore, perhaps half a mile from where Gerhard Gotaas goes on eternally painting his gallery of demons. The cat leads Gary across the lake as if following a line laid down by the blade of a protractor. Perhaps Hell waits on the other side, and perhaps Prince Hat, too, will be there waiting. Isn't this possible?

The cat looks back disdainfully.

He calls out to it. "Go on. Surely you have some story to tell me about Prince Hat. Some revelation, some aspect I was too stupid to notice."

But the cat says nothing. Just lashes its tail and stalks on. When it has reached the very center of the lake, it stops and waits until Gary has caught up. The mineral crust is thinner here, but still just thick enough to stand on. The lights beneath his feet are faster and brighter, describing repeated patterns Gary cannot prevent himself from imagining as the name Prince Hat, Prince Hat, Prince Hat.

"I thought you were taking me to Hell," Gary says, "but this isn't it, surely?"

The cat stares steadily at him until at last Gary blinks, and as he does so, the cat is in motion, leaping onto Gary's shoulder. And its weight added to Gary's is enough at last, so that the crust at the center of the lake splinters and breaks and the cat and Gary go plummeting down.

Gary flails as he falls headlong, the cat's claws gripping hard to his shoulder, dragging him down like ballast. First he is in water, but this water is thinner than it ought to be, somehow, and he cannot make his way back to the surface. And then he does not seem to be in water at all, but rather he is falling head-first through darkness as all around him birds swoop and soar, each carrying a burning candle in its beak.

They fall for a long time, more and more of the birds appearing in the air until there is so much light from the candles the darkness is tamed. And then, suddenly, there is a vertiginous moment and Gary is standing beneath a tree on a suburban sidewalk that seems to extend forever. The cat plops down onto his shoulder. Though it is winter in the world above them, here it is the end of a long summer day. The air is velvety, singed, and the grass at his feet is purple and shadowed, the tip of each blade hiding its face.

When Gary looks up, there is no sun in the sky, nor any sign of the subterranean lake. Instead, far above him in the violet dusk are the restless incandescent lines made by the birds and their candles. There are no people on the street. There are cars in the driveways, but Gary doesn't recognize the models or license plates. The trees, too, are strange in a way he cannot precisely identify. He reaches out to touch a leaf, then draws back. The leaf, covered in downy, angled teeth, has drawn a drop of blood. The tree bark, he sees, is semitranslucent, and underneath it rivulets of bright fluid chase upward.

The cat jumps down onto the sidewalk.

"This is Hell?" Gary says. He sucks the drop of blood from his fingertip.

"Don't sound so disappointed," the cat says.

"I'm not disappointed," Gary says. But is this true? In his heart, isn't he just a little disappointed to find himself in suburbia, however strange and bloodthirsty it might be? Is this truly where Prince Hat grew up? "It just isn't what I was expecting."

"You go off and do whatever it is you need to do to find closure with your Prince Hat," the cat says. "Take all the time you need. I'll sit here and wait for you under this tree."

"You come here to sit under a tree?" Gary says.

The cat turns its head to watch two rats the size of Dobermans come racing down the street.

Gary takes a step back, but the rats race on without ever seeming to notice either him or the cat. When Gary looks around, he sees there are rats just as big or bigger on many of the lawns around them, lounging or investigating bushes or leaving piles of droppings. When he looks over at the cat, the cat is staring at one of these, longing on its face.

"You can't mean to try to catch one of those," Gary says.

"We all want things it would be better not to want," the cat says. "We pursue them anyway, don't we?"

Gary cannot exactly argue with this. He looks up the street, then down. He is deep in suburbia: ranch houses and ersatz Tudors and traffic signs marked with symbols he does not know how to interpret. He cannot recognize the language on the street sign nearest to him: it makes him feel vaguely queasy when he tries to make sense of it.

"If you have any suggestions as to which way I ought to go in order to find Prince Hat, I am all ears," Gary says.

The cat says, "Ask anyone you meet. Everyone here knows Prince Hat."

"So I could just go knock on any of these doors," Gary says.

"Well," the cat says, "I wouldn't suggest that. Some of the people here aren't particularly friendly. But I believe it's bingo night tonight at the community center. That's up the street five blocks, then take a right and go straight for two. Just mind you remember how to get back here again."

"Wonderful," Gary says. "Thank you." He takes off his winter jacket and his sweater, too. The shoulder of his shirt is stained with blood where the cat's claws dug in, but this can't be helped and at least the shirt is black. The jacket and sweater he leaves under the tree with the cat and off he goes, following the directions he's been given. There are no cars on the streets; the streets seem to be for the rats only to go racing up and down. The parked cars that he passes, in fact, are full of small jellied globes the size of grapes or marbles. Small things begin to coil and flick back and forth in the globes as he studies them, increasingly agitated, and so he goes on before they grow more excited.

The community center, when he reaches it, is recognizably a civic building, square brick and glass, only it has as well two black wings, which lie folded against its sides. This gives it a foreboding and Gothic aspect, and he cannot help but feel that this detail transforms the many windows into lidless eyes, the double doors into an open mouth. Nevertheless, he thinks of Prince Hat (Prince Hat!) and goes through the doors into a hallway where an ordinary enough woman (if you are willing to ignore the length of her fingers, the length of her teeth when she smiles) is setting out various comestibles on a folding table. Donuts, red punch, coffee cups and sugar packets, a serving bowl spilling over with grubs that look a great deal like Sæmundr, only smaller.

The woman looks up, sees Gary, and says, "Can I help you, dearest?"

"Oh," Gary says. "I hope so. Thank you. I'm looking for Prince Hat."

"Oh, Prince Hat!" the woman says. "You certainly won't find him here among the hoi polloi. Not Prince Hat, dearest. He'll be getting ready for his wedding to the Queen of Hell."

"Agnes," Gary says.

"Well, you must be a good friend, indeed, to call her so," the woman says. "Help yourself to a donut and some coffee, if you like."

"Friend of the groom, actually," Gary says. "Visiting from out of town." He selects the most donut-looking of the donuts while the woman pours him a cup of coffee, so hot it scalds his tongue when he takes a sip. The donut tastes of fat and ash and powdered sugar. It's been so long since he's eaten or had anything to drink it's delicious all the same. And he badly needs to recharge before he runs into that bitch Agnes again. He takes a second donut. "Remind me. The wedding is when?"

"Saturday," the woman says. "Three days' time. But, dearest, surely you must have received your invitation if you're such a good friend of Prince Hat's."

"Well," Gary says, "you know how it goes these days with mail. No doubt my invitation is waiting back at home for me. Tell me, what's the fastest way to wherever Prince Hat is staying?"

"He'll be a guest in the house of the Queen of Hell," the woman says. "But I can't direct you there. It doesn't stay in one place. It's too grand for that. And she, of course, has many enemies. But you will find it if she means you to find it. Only best you go freshen up in the restroom before you go looking, dearest. And no doubt there's a shirt in the lost-and-found box over there in the corner that will fit you. This one reeks of human blood, and there are those in this neighborhood who have a taste for it. But take one more donut. Three nights until the wedding, three donuts will sustain you. Eat no other thing while you are here."

"Thank you," Gary says. "Only I don't understand why you've been so helpful. Why anyone has helped me, actually."

"Don't call it help, dearest," the woman says. "One does a favor and one is owed a favor in return. You will pay your debts one day. No need for thanks."

Oh, Gary is out of his depth. But hasn't he been so all along, ever since he met Prince Hat? He does as the woman suggests. He leaves the community center feeling fresher if more hopeless. Prince Hat is to be married in three days' time, in a house that can only be located if it wishes Gary to find it. And why would Agnes or her house wish Gary to find the house and Prince Hat when Gary's plan is to take Prince Hat away again? But perhaps Prince Hat would rather rule in Hell than return with Gary to their small apartment in New York. This thought, too, is gloomy.

Gary wanders aimlessly through Hell, avoiding rats, thinking that these quiet houses, squatting upon their purple-tipped lawns, are nice enough, but there must be a more opulent neighborhood somewhere, if only he can find it. Surely the Queen of Hell will live in a sprawling and tasteless McMansion made of skulls and obsidian, sugar pillars and a moat of blood, a thousand wings to carry it wherever it wishes to be. But in the end, the house he is looking for turns out to be a modest ranch indistinguishable from any of the other ranch houses Gary has passed on his long walk. What tells him this is the place he has been looking for is the indescribable weight, the feeling of power that emanates from it. The vinyl siding is old and furred with mildew. The decorative shutters badly need repainting. The blood is old, who knows how old, and chipping off. But there is no mistaking this house for any other: every line of it tells Gary he is looking at the house of the Queen of Hell.

He has lost all track of time. Is it day? Is it night? The birds are still carrying their candles in the sky. Perhaps there is no day, no night here, and then who is to say when Saturday will come? Perhaps the wedding has already occurred and now Gary is in some new terrible day he has no compass for. Nevertheless he squares his shoulders and goes up to the front door and rings the bell, which does not ring but rather cries out in a shrill voice, "He's here, he's here, the old fool's here at last!"

Oh, it should sting to be called an old fool, but Gary is euphoric instead. Here, as the door opens, is Agnes herself, the Queen of Hell. Surely Prince Hat is nearby.

"You," Agnes says. Gary would never have figured her for a queen of anything, not even a neighborhood association. She lacks the ferocious energy of her house, or perhaps she keeps it more tightly bottled.

"I've come to speak to Prince Hat," Gary says.

"Awfully bold of you," Agnes says. "To attempt to steal him not once but twice." Her look now is sardonic. Her hair is in a high ponytail and she's wearing a sports bra and leggings. A television program is on in the room behind her. *Jazzercise?* Gary thinks. *Truly, this is Hell.*

"I only want to be sure he's happy," Gary says. "That this is his choice. If he tells me this is what he wants, I'll leave."

"He's asleep right now," Agnes says. "I'm afraid in the frenzy of vigorous lovemaking that followed our reunion, I wore him out completely. I couldn't tell you when he'll be fit for conversation again."

If she means to wound Gary by telling him this, then, well, she has. But Gary has dealt with other paramours of Prince Hat. The Queen of Hell is nothing special.

"I don't mean to put you out," Gary says. "But I don't intend to leave until Prince Hat and I have had a chance to talk."

Agnes scratches her ass. Bounces a few times on the toes of her cross-trainers. "You have come a long way," she concedes. "So how about this? You may have him for the next three nights. Wake him up if you can, say whatever you need to say. But during the day he's mine. We have any number of prenuptial obligations. Cake selection, rehearsal dinner, bachelor party, blood rites, all of that. You get three nights and during the day I'll hang you up in the master bedroom closet, out of the way. If you can't persuade him to leave with you by Saturday morning, then that's it. He marries me and you leave here, you leave us alone, he's mine, and you go lead your lonely, sad life back up there with all of the other sad, lonely people Prince Hat has no interest in. Well?"

Gary considers this. Clearly there's a catch, there's a trick here somewhere, and he says so.

"Of course there's a trick," Agnes says. "Goes without saying. But since you're hesitating, let's raise the stakes. Leave now if you wish. I won't stop you. Stay, and should you fail to convince Prince Hat to leave, come Saturday you're mine, to do with as I please. Come on in. But take off your shoes first, please. They're filthy." Her own cross-trainers are pristine white.

Thus invited, thus warned, Gary enters the house of the Queen of Hell, leaving his boots on her porch. The house is uncared for, unfriendly. There are plastic covers over the arm-chairs and sofa, and everything smells of incense that is doing an inadequate job of covering over the reek of trash someone really ought to take out.

Agnes waves her hand. "Second door on the left, down the hall. I'll sleep on the couch in here. The bathroom is en suite, but if you use the toothbrush in the red cup, I will flay you and use your skin to make myself a pair of ugly gloves. And one more thing. Once you go in, shut the door and lock it in case I change my mind and decide to haul you out and flay you any-way. I don't advise coming out until the night's over. I'm a poor sleeper and prone to violence when woken."

Down the hall Gary goes, down the hall to the door beyond which Prince Hat lies sleeping. Prince Hat! His heart leaps like a fish in a pan as he opens that last door. The blinds are drawn and the room is dark, no birds here, but nevertheless Gary can discern the form of his beloved beneath the flower-patterned, sex-scented sheets.

Gary locks the door. He sits down on the bed, which ripples as he does so. A waterbed? Who still sleeps on those? He draws back the sheet. Kisses Prince Hat on his stubbly cheek. Savors Prince Hat's breath, sour from sleep. "Wake up, you jerk. It's me."

But Prince Hat doesn't stir, doesn't wake. And no matter what Gary does (he does everything that you yourself would do in this situation, and a few more things besides), Prince Hat will not wake up. And Gary is so very, very tired. At last he lies down next to Prince Hat, recounts all of his adventures, and, having done so, falls asleep and dreams of birds flying without rest, candles in their beaks.

When Gary wakes again all too soon, it's morning and Prince Hat is stirring. Before Gary can say a word, the Queen of Hell breezes into the bedroom, the lock no barrier at all, it seems. She rolls up the blinds and picks up Gary by the scruff of the neck. As she does this he feels himself flatten out, thin and light and flimsy as cheesecloth. Then she's whisking him into the closet where she drapes him on a coat hanger and hangs that up on a rack overstuffed with business casual attire and rumpled sleeveless linen rompers. "There," she says. "Be a good boy and just hang there quietly. I'll fetch you out again tonight."

Through the press of clothing and the closet door Gary can hear the voice of Prince Hat. He and Agnes talk, but Gary cannot quite make out what they are saying. Can Prince Hat sense that Gary is near? There are more sounds, Prince Hat and that bitch Agnes are fucking, and then he hears them take a shower, more fucking, and then eventually they must take their leave of the room because Gary hears nothing at all for a very long time. At one point the house begins to vibrate violently, then jerk from side to side. It must be taking itself and Gary elsewhere and he wonders if it is taking him nearer to Prince Hat or if Prince Hat is now farther from the location where the house settles at last. No matter: at the end of the day Agnes and Prince Hat return, he hears them down the hall. There is more sex, Gary thinks there is a perfunctory sound to it this time, but he burns with erotic jealousy all the same. How he misses even the most perfunctory of sexual acts, how salacious, how delicious, how surprising even the most perfunctory blow job, the most dutiful anal play has always been, as long as his partner is Prince Hat.

After that, the bedroom is quiet and in a while Agnes comes and takes Gary off his hanger, shakes him out into himself once more. Prince Hat is sound asleep upon the waterbed again.

"He really is quite special, isn't he?" Agnes says. "Not like you or me. We're quite ordinary in comparison."

A strange thing for the Queen of Hell to say, but Gary has marinated in this feeling ever since Prince Hat came home with him. He's grown used to it.

"Two more nights," Agnes reminds him. "That's all the time you have left with Prince Hat. All the time you have left, period, I'm afraid, if you can't wake him up. Perhaps I'll have you stuffed and painted in some amusing fashion, give you to him as a wedding present. You'd be able to stay with him that way, at least. Or I could have you served up at the wedding dinner. Trussed up in twine, an apple in your mouth, plenty of spice to disguise the taste of old sheep."

"You're using up time you allotted me," Gary says. "It makes me think you're afraid I might break whatever enchantment you've put on him. That you're afraid he'll jilt you a second time."

"No," Agnes says. "It's only that I'm bored, and I have to sleep on the couch because I was stupid enough to give you these three nights, and tormenting you is fun. I have a very low tolerance for boredom."

"Why not go out?" Gary says. "If you're so sure you're getting married on Saturday, why not live it up a little these last two nights while you're still single and carefree? I'll keep an eye on Prince Hat."

Agnes considers. "Not a terrible idea," she says. "I'll go out with my girlfriends, hit the town. But just in case you have some idea of carrying Prince Hat off into the night while he's asleep, know my house will be keeping an eye on you. It's under strict orders not to let Prince Hat go anywhere if I'm not with him. And you are not to leave this room. Should you do so, our arrangement is broken and you will suffer greatly for it."

She leaves, and Gary sits down on the awful waterbed beside his sleeping husband. Once again he talks to Prince Hat, pleads with him to open his eyes. Sings as loud as he can, first songs that Prince Hat loves, and then the songs he knows Prince Hat hates most of all. He pinches Prince Hat's arm, pulls out strands of Prince Hat's hair, strokes his cock erect, bites Prince Hat's lips, his shoulder, his ass. Perhaps Prince Hat will notice these marks, but Prince Hat's lovely flesh is marked already where Agnes has sucked and nipped and bitten. How will Prince Hat ever know one mark from another?

He scours the room for pen and paper, something that he

might leave a note on for Prince Hat, but finds nothing useful except a receipt for Alka-Seltzer and two lightbulbs and the end of an eyebrow pencil. He writes on the back of the receipt, "I love you, Prince Hat, and I think you love me, too. Two nights I've been at your side. Stay awake tomorrow night or you will never see me again."

Where best to hide his note so the Queen of Hell won't find it? He folds it up tightly in the end, and wraps it in a condom he finds in a bathroom drawer. The condom he puts in Prince Hat's mouth when he thinks that morning must be near.

It all happens the same way again, Agnes sauntering in, grinning as if she's delighted to see Gary; then the business of flattening him out, hanging him in the closet. There's some conversation, perhaps Prince Hat has found the note, is quarreling now with Agnes over her treatment of Gary. Or perhaps he reads Gary's note to her and they both laugh at him, his foolishness. They leave the bedroom eventually, go off into the day before their wedding day, and all that second day Gary hangs and frets and thinks of better strategies he could have employed.

When Agnes comes to get him from the closet, Gary can't help it. He says, "What happened to the note? Did Prince Hat read it?"

"A note?" Agnes says. "I don't recall. Oh dear. I hope he got it, this note. Where did you leave it for him? Shall I help you look for it?"

"I left it in his mouth!" Gary says.

"What an odd place to leave a note," Agnes says. She goes over to the bed and peers down at it, as if searching for Gary's message. "No doubt he swallowed it before he ever woke up. Should he shit it out again, it will be in no condition to be read, really, so perhaps you should just tell me what it said and I'll pass it along to him on our wedding night."

"Never mind," Gary says. He stands on the opposite side of the bed; they speak over Prince Hat as if he will never wake up. "I'll tell him tonight when I wake him at last."

"How moving your persistence is," Agnes says. "I feel as if I know you, sweetness. Not because Prince Hat talks of you. He doesn't. But because you remind me of myself, really. I don't give up, either. You had him for a little while, but now I have him back."

"If you're so sure you have him back," Gary says, "then why won't you let me talk to him by day?"

"Touché," Agnes says. "Perhaps I am not so sure, but are you so sure, deep down, that it's best for Prince Hat to have a choice, to perhaps choose you again? Should he stay here with me, he will rule Hell by my side. Should he stay here with me, I will give him a new body, a young and healthy one so he may live forever. The one he has now is quite near its expiration date. Another decade, and the blood disorder he does not yet know about will cause him great suffering. Then it will cause his death. So, you see, isn't it much better we don't give him a choice at all, lest he choose what will bring him harm?"

Gary says, "You're lying."

Agnes says, "I lie when it suits me, but truth in this instance pleases me better. But imagine I have lied to you and Prince Hat might yet make old bones. Even then, even another two decades, another three or four! The mortal span is brief. Prince Hat will die someday and not even you, stubborn old man, can prevent it, though one like me can. Give him over to me, and he will live forever, young and beautiful and always Prince Hat.

Should you not choose that for him? Go back home, content in knowing Prince Hat will always be Prince Hat? How selfish it would be to wake him, even if you could. To ask him to choose you, knowing that in choosing you he chooses death."

What a thing to say! Gary almost falls to the floor, hearing it. Agnes waits, smiling, for him to speak and when he cannot, she says, "Your last night with Prince Hat! I do hope you enjoy it. You and I will meet again in the morning, but you will forgive me if I dispose of you without much ceremony. I expect to be quite busy what with the wedding, the coronation, the feasting, and whatnot. Perhaps there will be enough time to bronze your penis, bring it along with us to the nuptial orgy. I've heard so much about it."

"Good things only, I hope," Gary manages to say.

The Queen of Hell smirks at this, then leaves the room. The door slams shut behind her, but of course Prince Hat does not wake up. Gary lies down beside him, holds Prince Hat in his arms. He says all the things he has always wanted to say to Prince Hat, lists all his complaints, his grudges against Prince Hat, tells Prince Hat then that none of these matter, Prince Hat may commit whatever sin he wishes and Gary will love him all the same, only Prince Hat must wake up and let Gary ask him one thing. But Prince Hat stays asleep, he sleeps on peacefully as if he has heard none of this at all.

Next Gary tells Prince Hat all the things Gary has said and done and kept concealed from Prince Hat. He is scrupulous in his confession, and at the end of it he begs Prince Hat to wake up and forgive him. But Prince Hat sleeps on. Gary's crimes are nothing to him, and oh, this is more wounding than Gary thought it would be.

If Prince Hat were to sleep on forever, and Gary could stay here with him on this hideous, sloshing waterbed, this would not be the worst fate, would it? But morning is coming. Gary sits up, the waterbed roiling sluggishly. Gary has never understood the appeal. A last idea comes to him and he goes to the bathroom, searches through all the cabinets and drawers until finally he must acknowledge there is nothing sharp enough here to do what needs doing.

In Agnes's closet he finds a stiletto heel. He will make this do in place of a pair of scissors. He returns to Prince Hat and the bed, lifts the top sheet, pulls up the fitted corner of the bottom sheet, pushes it over so he can attack the polyvinyl with the heel. He stabs over and over until he has made a tiny rip in the casing. A bead of something thick and foul oozes out, but Gary is in a frenzy now. He rakes the heel down the bed until the rip is large enough he can get his fingers in it and then he rends the casing with all his strength. And then? Oh, blood, foul blood comes fountaining out, clotted and thick. It paints Gary, Prince Hat, sprays out on the bedposts and the walls, the ceiling.

Gary screams in triumph. But when he looks at Prince Hat, Prince Hat, robed in blood, sleeps on.

And now here is Agnes bustling back into the room. "Oh dear," she says. "What a mess, what a mess you've made of Prince Hat, you horrible thing. And to what end? He never woke, and you have lost him."

She grabs Gary by the arm, shakes him until he is limp and light and no longer recognizable to himself, but still he is dripping with rank blood.

"This won't do," Agnes says. "How can I hang you up like

this? I don't have leisure to play with you this morning, but I can't hide you away, either. You'll get blood all over my clothes."

She carries Gary into the bathroom, wrings him out in the sink, and then begins to rinse him in cold tap water. Gary endures this because he must. And in the bedroom, Prince Hat is beginning to stir.

"Good morning, my love!" Agnes calls out. "I hope you slept well."

Prince Hat groans. "Too well, it seems. How did this happen? Did you stab me in my sleep?"

Agnes wrings Gary out one more time, then goes to Prince Hat, Gary clenched in her fist. "Oh, darling, what a mess. You must have burst the waterbed while we were sleeping. You've always been such a restless sleeper. Well, no matter. I will buy you a new bed when we are home from our honeymoon."

Prince Hat touches his face, looks at what coats his fingers when he takes them away. "If we were both asleep in the bed then why am I covered in blood while you are not?"

Agnes says, "Oh, dear heart, my dove, I will confess. You tossed and turned so much last night I could not sleep a wink in our bed. I napped on the couch instead. Now hurry! Into the shower with you. Today is our wedding day!"

Prince Hat clambers out of the burst bed and stands naked in front of Agnes, stretching. His cock is stiff and soaked in blood.

"I know what day it is," he says. "But tell me, what have you got in your hand, my love?"

"This?" Agnes says. "Only a rag to clean up the blood. Nothing more."

"In that case," Prince Hat says, "give it to me and I will wipe my face with it." He snatches Gary from Agnes, snaps him briskly in the air as if this were a locker room and Gary were a towel. And now Gary is himself again and Prince Hat is awake and looking at him and smiling.

"See?" Prince Hat says to Agnes. "I told you he would come."

Agnes's face is ripe with hate now. She will rain down bolts of lightning, summon clouds of venomous insects. Gary will endure it. He has lost the wager Agnes made with him, but he will die knowing he is loved by Prince Hat. "I'm sorry," he tells Prince Hat. "I should have thought of that sooner."

Only, as it turns out, Prince Hat has made a wager with Agnes, too, and his wager was this: that Gary would find him before the hour of their wedding. Should he win the wager, Agnes had agreed she would let the two leave and strike no blow against them.

Prince Hat, as it happens, has no desire to reign in Hell.

Agnes lets them leave her house unharmed, though in a fit of pique she refuses to let Prince Hat shower or even have his clothes back. He and Gary go out onto the street holding hands, Prince Hat wearing only a cloak of dried blood.

They walk until they find the tree with the cat beneath it, and Gary's coat, Gary's sweater. Prince Hat bends down to scratch the cat behind one notched ear and the cat bites him hard on the fleshy pad beneath the thumb.

Prince Hat snatches his hand back. "Manners!" he says.

The cat says, "Says the dolt who has jilted the Queen of Hell twice now. Shall we get out of here before her inevitable tantrum begins?"

Gary groans, thinking of the dark cavern, the endless stairs. He has no strength left in him, he's used up everything he had on the long way to find Prince Hat.

"Oh," Prince Hat says when Gary explains. "There are other routes that lead back home. You just took the scenic route. Long Island or somewhere more cheerful? Rome, say?"

"Long Island," Gary says, and the cat leaps into Prince Hat's arms, purring.

Prince Hat says, "If we must. Hold on to me tightly now," and Gary barely has time to do this before Prince Hat stamps his foot and the cat twists and resettles in Prince Hat's embrace and the whole world flips upside down and they are moving upward or downward or in some other direction entirely, all the birds with their burning candles in orbit around them.

And then they are standing on a wintry beach, there is no one here but Prince Hat and Gary, the cat has leapt out of Prince Hat's arms and gone off as cats will do, somewhere along the way. When Gary looks up, the only birds in the sky are seagulls and terns. There is nothing in their mouths and the sun is back up in the sky.

Prince Hat is still bloody and naked, of course, and Gary cannot dissuade him from bathing in the cold salt water. Afterward he dresses in Gary's boxer briefs and he steps into Gary's sweater as if it were a skirt, tying the arms around his waist. He puts on Gary's jacket, too, when Gary insists.

They walk down the access road until they reach the Meadowbrook parkway. Here they manage to flag down a car driven by Martin and Danielle, a married couple who have spent the last few days at a publishing conference at Montauk Manor. Today they are driving back to New York to see a play, and tomorrow they fly home to St. Louis.

They clearly wish to know what Gary and Prince Hat are doing here, dressed the way they are, a faint but discernible reek of Hell still emanating from their pores, the stain of the Black School like newsprint on each of Gary's fingertips: Prince Hat begins to spin some story. As he does so, Gary falls asleep and does not wake up until Martin and Danielle have dropped them off in front of the apartment building where Gary and Prince Hat have spent so many happy years together.

And this is the end of the story more or less. That night after a bout of effusive and tender lovemaking, Gary weeps in Prince Hat's arms. Prince Hat weeps some, too. Then he says to Gary, "Ask me whatever you wish to ask me. I will answer all your questions."

In this way, Gary learns at last of Prince Hat's father, a fairy lord turned seneschal of Hell; his mother, a notorious sinner; Prince Hat's childhood spent traveling between the huldufólk and that vast, infernal suburb; how he was betrothed to Agnes at an age too young to understand what was being asked of him; how he attended the Black School and began to dream of a different kind of life; how he fled Hell and his betrothal on a whim; how Agnes had found him, wooed him, taken him on holiday to New York. "Hell is in my nature," he says. "I was brought up to rule there, but once I set foot in your world, I never wanted to return. There's no freedom, no surprises there. Only rules and punishments and after a time even the punishments begin to feel predictable and a chore."

He talks and talks, his life before Gary gushing out of him like something purged from a waterbed. At last there is nothing Gary can think of to ask him and they sleep.

Before they sleep, Prince Hat says, "And now that you know all this, I hope we need never speak of any of it again. Not because you don't have the right to ask, or because I am ashamed of my life before you, but because I would prefer not to dwell on that place and the people in it. To talk too much of certain things is to draw them near."

Gary is fine with this. There are things he does not wish to talk about, either: the debts he understands enough now to know he owes to those who helped him, the things Agnes told him about blood disorders, early death. Only he makes sure, each year, that Prince Hat goes for his annual physical. Any sign of fatigue or anemia, he sends Prince Hat off for bloodwork and scans. He will be vigilant until his enemy at last shows its (or her) face.

The story is over, it's almost over. The lovers are reunited. They fuck, they talk, they sleep. Soon they will wake, Prince Hat will wake up first this time, and he will say to Gary, "Wake up!" and Gary will do as Prince Hat commands.

The sun will come up and the dark will go away. Gary and Prince Hat will have brunch at Folklore. Perhaps they will go farther downtown, walk along the High Line or the Hudson, eat ice cream and pet other people's dogs. Gary would like to do any of these things. What would Prince Hat like to do? Oh, who can ever know that? But then the day will end, days must end, and the dark will come again. And eventually there will be only darkness and Gary will be alone in that darkness, paying off his debts, a bird flying with a candle in his beak. He will open up his beak and let the candle drop and cry, Oh, where is my Prince Hat? Where has Prince Hat gone?

The White Road

(The Musicians of Bremen)

All of this happened a very long time ago and so, I suppose, it has taken on the shape of a story, a made-up thing, rather than true things that happened to me and to those around me. Things I did and that others did. And so I will write it down that way. As a story.

You know the world is different now from the way it was. That is a story everyone knows, and so it is not the story I will tell. Who I was before, that, too, is a small story, so small I could fit it into a box that would fit into another box, that box still small enough to carry inside the smallest pocket. Were I to take it out of its box, I do not know that I could ever fit it back inside again.

The story I will tell takes place not quite twenty years on from the hinge of that moment when the first white road appeared. Twenty years through that door and I was an established member of an accredited traveling company that went up and down a route between Philadelphia and Hot Springs, Arkansas, buying and selling household goods and family heirlooms, putting on performances, and delivering letters and news. Most of us were actors by preference but we had a doctor of sorts with us for a time who took appointments and pulled teeth and sold various concoctions and medicines of his own making. Then a suburb outside of Roanoke, Virginia, bought up his contract from us, and he settled down there. He was in his seventies and ready to be done with horses and actors and the misery of travel. So far we had found no one to replace him, though he had left a quantity of his homemade elixir with us. It was supposed to reduce fevers and headache, and perhaps it did. Certainly I drank some of it on mornings when I was hungover from whatever liquor the last town had offered us, and wretched enough not to mind the taste.

But what I mean to say is that we had no doctor, which was a crushing disappointment to all of the places on our route that we had last visited not quite a year ago. Particularly to the pregnant women in the remote places that had no established medical practice. Only a generation earlier, and they would have thought nothing of a thirty- or even sixty-mile journey. I myself had been to California twice as a child and once to Mexico.

Most of these places, of course, were the kinds of settlements that numbered a few hundred at most. Some were five or six families squatting in an old interstate shopping plaza or motel, growing vegetables and keeping goats and chickens. People like this stayed where they were because they were stubborn beyond reason, or for religious reasons they were all too willing to explain to you at great and tedious length, or because they distrusted the cities more than they feared the white road and those who used it.

It is hard for me to judge. If I had been a more sensible person, would I have spent so much of my life picking my way carefully between these desperate places? But then, I was never content staying long in one place.

Our company numbered seven once Dr. Baqri left us. I was the oldest. Alice Palace was near my age. She claimed to be thirty-five, but she had said she was twenty-nine when she joined the company, and that had been nine years previous. She might have been older than she claimed, older even than me. She said things, sometimes, about the life she had lived before all the great changes came in their cascade upon the world, that made her seem more of an age with my older sister, even, than with me. I was sixteen when the changes began, and my sister was twenty-two. Alice talked, sometimes, of college classes. Temping in offices in Manhattan while she auditioned for roles in Off-Off-Broadway plays.

When she was twenty-two, my sister, a type 1 diabetic, rode a bicycle more than one hundred miles along the Old Boston Post Road from Boston to my family's house in Chicopee only to die when, eventually, there was no more insulin to be found. This was just after she turned twenty-three. Really, there was nothing remarkable about my sister and her short life, just as there is nothing remarkable about me. One may be remarkable or not, but as a quality it has little bearing on whether or not one lives a long life. Or, for that matter, a happy life.

And, really, Alice Palace's true age did not signify. She was all made up of sharp points—elbows, hips, bony little feet, ski slope nose, triangle chin, quick tongue—Dr. Baqri referred to her privately as the Cheese Grater. But that was only because she slept with him twice and then never again, to his enormous disappointment. She was charming, witty, and sunny in nature; most of our company were in love with her at one point or another, including myself. And for a time, she made each of us feel she might return that love. The quality of her attention was like that of sunlight coming through a magnifying glass. The object was enlarged, lit up, and eventually a little singed. The end, which always came sooner than even the most prescient and worldly of us might have been expected to expect, was sharp, too. But perhaps that was a kindness. Her romantic interest in you began and terminated so briskly you hardly had time to notice you had been scorched around the edges before she put out the flame and was on to the next love affair. And, afterward, she made sure to be a good friend.

The only one among us that Alice Palace did not turn her gaze upon was Laurent Godejohn. Godejohn had been with our company only a year. He was presently the youngest, only twenty, and so astonishingly good-looking it must have been confusing even to him why Alice Palace ignored his overtures. Certainly it was a mystery to the rest of us, although one that offered much entertainment. The more Alice Palace ignored him, the more apparent Godejohn's longing for her became to everyone except for Alice Palace, who, without seeming to mean anything by it, only ignored him even more provokingly, and so on and so on. By which I don't mean that Godejohn made a nuisance of himself. I liked him a great deal and so did everyone else, including, I believe, Alice Palace.

Laurent Godejohn had joined us in Atlanta. He was the son of a fire-and-brimstone preacher, a woman who had been given a holy message concerning the end of the world, which we were unfortunate enough to have survived. She preached that the inhabitants of Earth had been abandoned by God because of our sinful natures. The righteous now lived on other planets. This was Hell with all its devils, and although we could never escape it now, our duty was to praise God and repent and live according to his commandments. Godejohn's mother's congregation survived by scavenging and doing a little subsistence farming. They did their best to abstain from fornication, drinking, dancing, and all the other things you might have thought would make Hell in any way bearable. Godejohn had secretly taught himself to read, and twice when we'd passed through Atlanta, he'd come to see a performance. The second time he left when we did. Perhaps being abandoned by God made it easier to accept Alice Palace's indifference. God might have turned his back, but Godejohn spent his days in the company of Alice Palace, and an indifferent God is better than no God at all. And although she wouldn't sleep with him, there were plenty of others in plenty of other towns who would and did. Most of us had lovers in one town or another.

IT WAS LATE SPRING. We'd spent two nights in Chattanooga, where the turnout both nights had been gratifying. The last time we'd passed through, we'd done a new play, a comedy that Amabeth and Carver had collaborated on, liberally stuffed with burlesque numbers, lush romantic songs from the days when people lived their lives with their ears full of whatever music they might fancy listening to, and just enough tragedy to make it all feel real. I am not unhandsome, but a woman I once loved told me there was something about my face that suggested a capacity for strong action or even violence. And, too, I am a baritone. Thus my part was usually the villain or a tragic king.

We all play at things we are not, but truthfully I never wanted the role of the bold young lover, not even when I was young and more of a fool than I am now.

At breakfast the morning we were to depart, Amabeth complained of a headache and then began to vomit with such force she burst a blood vessel in one eye. Shortly afterward, Phillip and Cece began to do the same, as did many of the others in the boardinghouse where we were staying. It was discovered that all of those fallen ill had eaten a stew that contained wild mushrooms. We stayed another five days while we waited to see if our friends would recover. Godejohn went off ostentatiously with a red-haired woman who operated a whiskey still, hoping, it was clear, that Alice Palace would notice. She did not. She never did.

Alice and I spent hours in the Chattanooga library, looking over librettos and sheet music to see if there was anything worth copying out, and trying not to worry about our friends. It was a relief to be gone from the boardinghouse in any case. The corpse they kept in the parlor was in a ripe state, and despite all the herbs and candles they kept burning, the smell permeated the whole place. It was hard not to dwell on the thought that, should that unfortunate stew be the death of one of our friends, they would take its place and we would have to leave them here to serve its purpose.

With us, we brought Henry, a Chattanooga native whose uncle, an acquaintance of mine, had arranged for him to travel with us as far as Memphis. Henry was a bright boy, sixteen years old and enthusiastic on all topics. His company was a pleasant distraction—he asked about the route we would be taking, and what the portion of the world we'd seen was like. He had never been more than twenty miles from Chattanooga, and was looking forward not only to the apprenticeship in Memphis where, I recall, he was supposed to learn something about a new method of fish farming, but to the journey. He asked about the places where we would be stopping, and he wanted, too, to know the histories of all the members of our company. He greatly admired the performances that we had given, and he had many questions for Alice Palace and me about how we had found ourselves in this life.

Alice said, with a faint smile, that she still wasn't exactly sure. I said, when I was close to his age, I had found myself alone. My parents had not long survived the death of my sister. I'd gone to a farmer's market and asked around for work until someone had directed me to the company that had been busy marking out routes and territories and systems by which news and mail might be delivered. They had an idea, too, that the companies traveling these routes would not only bring the mail but barter portable objects of value, and as well offer performances—concerts, plays, entertainments of all kinds. I asked to audition, and because the routes were not yet secure, and the times were still so unsettled, I was taken on. At the time I assumed it was because I displayed remarkable talent. But later I came to suspect it was because there were so few who auditioned at all.

And it wasn't as if I'd had better prospects in Chicopee, whereas traveling with the company had seemed like a way to see as much as I could of the world that remained within my grasp. For a while I imagined one day I would find the place that

I was meant to take up. But instead I found I was already in that place I had been meant for, only it was an orbit rather than a fixed location.

Henry nodded at that. He was an orphan, too, and although his uncle and aunt had been good to him, he did not wish to spend all his life in one place. He had high hopes of Memphis. He asked, then, if we saw the white road much, when we were between towns. And had we ever been caught between towns, by weather or misfortune? What did we do to keep ourselves safe?

"You don't need to worry about that," Alice Palace told him. "We have the route well mapped out, and we leave ourselves plenty of time. Should every horse go lame and leave us to make our way by foot, we will still be fine. And should the worst happen and the night fall upon us before we've arrived in a safe place, well, we're actors by trade. One of us plays the corpse and lies in funeral state all night while the rest of us act out the parts of their mourners. Now. Tell me something about yourself. Do you play an instrument?" And when he said that he did not, "Well, we will have to teach you, then. There will be plenty of time along the way to Memphis."

As I SAID, IT took a few days for Amabeth and the others to recover enough to be able to ride. If the stew had not been bad, I suppose, then this would be a different story. Perhaps our company would have been in Bremen when what happened happened there. Or perhaps we would have arrived, picked up the mail, and gone on our way. Perhaps the thing that befell the people there might have been averted in some way. Perhaps all things might have been different. But the story does not go that way.

On the day we left Chattanooga, the weather that had been so mild and sunny turned, and we departed in the middle of a storm that, defying all usual weather patterns, seemed likely to travel with us a day or more. The wind drove the rain at our backs and sluiced the houses we rode past, flattening the new shoots in the fields just outside the city. Henry rode a white-eared mule who didn't care much for the wet. It picked its way fastidiously through the puddles, and its white ears lay back against its brown head. Fortunately Henry's uncle had outfitted him with good waterproof gear. All the mail was sorted out and bundled up in oilcloths, and we had flasks of warm chamomile tea and sandwiches from the boardinghouse kitchen.

As was the custom, we'd left small offerings before the coffin in the parlor. One of the letters we'd been carrying—from Harrisonburg, I believe—had been intended for its occupant. When the corpse could next be replaced, which might be in a day or two, as one of the other travelers, a cattleman from Nashville, had eaten several helpings of the stew, the letter would be burned along with it, and so Alice Palace and I had steamed it open carefully and removed the small amount of money it had contained. To steal from the dead is believed to have ill consequences, but if our actions were the cause of the things that next happened, then why did Alice Palace and I escape misfortune entirely? I do not believe the dead pursue the living. Nor do I believe that the dead knowingly protect us with their presence from the white road and the ones who travel on it. There is some other logic to the way that all things work now, and someday we will better understand what has happened to make all things change in such a small space of time, and how we might restore ourselves to the place we once occupied in this world.

I'd been traveling long enough that many things no longer seemed strange to me, but Henry's mule, once it had grudgingly accepted the circumstances of the weather, seemed to find my placid roan mare an agreeable enough companion, and I found some distraction in watching my travel mate gape, taking in our surroundings through the veils of rain. We planned to be in Bremen by the end of the next day, and there was a woman there I cared a great deal for. I had been able to tolerate the delay in Chattanooga because there was nothing to be done about it. Now that we were on the road again, all my impatience had returned. I longed to see her, and the miles in between were excruciating to me. The way seemed very slow.

The old highway by that time was quite broken up by trees and vines and frost and mudslides. We went alongside it, on a rutted dirt track. When our company first set out, many years ago, the highway was still usable, and travel easier. We met other travelers and gave them our news in exchange for their own. Now we were more likely to see herds of deer, sometimes a hundred or more. Wild turkeys on patrol, or a family of llamas. Black bears. Clouds of monarch butterflies in their season. Sometimes a mountain lion, stalking us from rock to rock, and once in a meadow beside the highway, outside Knoxville, three elephants. Do they see the white road? It does not concern itself with any animals other than the human, living or dead, and neither have I ever seen a fox or hawk or any other wild animal pay any notice to the ones who use it.

Five miles outside Chattanooga, along the route our company takes is a ravine, and were one able to soar over that ravine and look down, one would see all heaped and smashed together all the thrown-away things that once made life so pleasant and easy. Here, too, one begins to see the white road. As you travel, it runs parallel to you. Turn your head in one direction, and there, through the trees, is the road. Look straight ahead and you won't see it. Turn your head away from where you last saw it, though, and there it is again. One time it seems narrow as a footpath and the next you would judge it at least a mile across. In the day, the white road is empty. Henry did the thing that we all have done. He looked one way and then the other, then back the first way again, as if he might take the white road by surprise and find it lashing back and forth, like a cat's tail. But as we rode on, his mule keeping pace with my mare, he seemed to fall into a kind of trance, looking over one shoulder at what I knew was the white road. Sometimes someone, lacking all common sense, would begin to veer off their course, chasing the white road. But it was never as near as you thought.

Alice Palace, sleek as an otter in her long oilskin coat and leather cap, came trotting up beside us. The rain was lighter now, and a mist was rising. The weather suited her. Her eyes were bright and her cheeks flushed. "It will still be there whether or not you look," she said to Henry. He turned his head and looked at her, a drowned expression on his face. "Truly," she said. "It's better, I think, not to look. It isn't a natural thing. It pulls at you."

Henry said, "I've only ever seen it three times. No, four. They always told us not to look. But we always did."

Laurent came up beside the three of us. He said, "There's no harm in looking. One can't help it. The white road draws the eye." He was not looking at the white road, though. He was looking at Alice Palace.

Carver, at the front of the caravan, called back, "There's a place coming up ahead where we can stop and have some lunch and then we'll be in Dale by late afternoon. They'll have been wondering where we were."

Amabeth and Phillip and Cece had to be helped down off their horses, and then back on again after we'd eaten. It was a miserable picnic in any case, because of the rain, which still fell steadily. The rain had brought up clusters of fat mushrooms all alongside the track we rode, and Cece directed her horse over these clusters, trampling the mushrooms into a froth.

Cece never fully recovered from the effects of that boarding-house stew; eventually she left the company, I heard, and made a home in Fearrington. She had a good alto voice, and could juggle anything you asked her to. She cheated at cards, though. I don't know that she ever cared much for me. I refused to play for money no matter how low the stakes she proposed but I was always fond of her. She took a great deal of money off Henry, as a matter of fact, that night in the inn. And because he was sad afterward, she gave him a penny whistle and she and Alice Palace began to teach him all the raunchiest songs that they knew. That cheered him right up.

The corpse at the inn was a young girl so rotted away you could only tell her gender by the now badly discolored dress they'd laid her out in. She was in the back parlor, and while I was paying my respects, the innkeeper came in. She said, "She'll only last another month or two at most. I've written to the council at Bremen to see if they've got any corpses they can spare us, but perhaps you could argue my case for me should they not feel obliged. I can feel those ones pressing in sometimes, or perhaps I'm going mad."

I looked through the window, half expecting to see the white road. All the hair was standing up on my body. There is a moment when a corpse becomes so far removed from the person it once was that the white road can no longer be held off by its presence. In more populous places, you can count on your neighbors to grow old and die, or die by misadventure or disease or at their own hands—we are quite familiar, nowadays, with death—but in places like Dale, where only one or two families stay to maintain an inn or some other necessary station, corpses are harder to come by.

But outside the window was only darkness and rain. No white road.

"Did she come from Bremen?" I said. "It seems cruel, to make such a little one travel so far from home."

"No," the innkeeper said. "She did not come from Bremen."

I wished her good night and said that when we got to Bremen I would do what I could to get a corpse for her.

She began to speak again, though, before I could make my escape. She said, "My father has been having dreams about her; he keeps telling me his dreams. He dreams he has one of those things in his pocket, a phone. He has a phone in his pocket and his phone is ringing and she's calling him. And he wants to answer the phone but he knows that he has to get rid of it because when he looks he can see the white road and he knows they're coming because of the phone and so he can't answer the phone. He has to get rid of it. So he doesn't answer the phone and every time he tells me this I wish that just once he would answer the phone. I want to know what she wants to say to him. But it's just a dream. She wouldn't even know how to use a phone. I don't even remember how to use a phone. I was only two when everything happened, and so I don't remember what it was like. And she never saw a phone her whole life."

It wasn't the usual way of things, not even then, to discuss the things we have had to discard. If they belong to anyone now, they belong to those who travel the white road. But she was still grieving, as was her father. How could I be offended? "I was sixteen," I said. "I remember all of it. But all of it seems like a dream now."

"Close the door behind you," she said. "Otherwise the cat gets in."

THE NEXT DAY WAS bright and breezy and everything shone, glossed by the rain. The taste of the mountain air was like drinking the coldest, freshest water. Henry's mule kicked at me when I went by carrying my saddle. It was as sour-natured as Henry was sweet. Henry and Carver and Laurent were all the best of friends now. I gathered that they'd been up most of the previous night drinking and passing around a fat joint, the specialty of Dale, with the two older daughters of the inn.

Bremen was seven hours' ride from Dale. We were off the highway entirely, on a well-marked trail that meandered down the long side of the mountain. The white road wove itself in between the trunks of trees, thin as a ribbon. Henry still turned his head to look for it, but he had to pay more attention to the trail, which was rocky and steep.

We stopped and ate our lunch in a glade carpeted in cheerful pink flowers, and Laurent wove a crown out of them that he gave to Alice Palace. She wore it for an hour or so in her hair, and then fed the flowers, one by one, to Cece's horse.

We kept up a good pace in the afternoon and were in Bremen before five o'clock. Bremen is in the cleft of a little valley, and there is a good-sized lake there, which I have been told never grows warm, not even in the middle of summer. I think it must be very deep. There are six or seven farmhouses on the outskirts of Bremen, and so even before we reached the town itself we knew something was wrong.

For towns like Bremen, our company is a subject of great interest. I suspect that any group of travelers would be. And yet, as we rode past, we saw no one in the fields. No one came down to the road to wave at us. No one came out onto their porch, although every door we passed stood open. There were cattle in the barns, though. We could hear them calling out, wanting to be milked.

"This is a strange place," Henry said. "The people here aren't friendly."

"No," Phillip said. "Something strange has happened. Wait here." He rode up to the nearest house, and got down off his horse slowly. He went through the open door into the house, and then he came back out again. "There's no one here," he said. "There's food on the table, fried chicken and greens, but no one's eaten more than a bite. Now it's all flies on the food. Flies in the milk. And there's a heap of clothes by the wringer. Sour-smelling. Mildewed."

Laurent said, "Something's wrong here."

"Go to one of the other houses," Alice Palace said to him. "See if it's the same."

"It will be the same," Laurent said. But because it was Alice who had asked him, he turned his horse around and went to investigate the closest of the other houses.

When he came back, he said, "No one is there. There's no corpse, either."

When he said this, I turned my head to look and there was the white road. It was flat and empty and so wide across that we could have all ridden abreast on it. But it was still day and so we could never have reached it even if we had wanted to. A few hours more and it would draw nearer.

"So what do we do now?" Henry said, sounding more perplexed than afraid. I think he must have believed that we had had experiences like this before, seasoned travelers that we were. "Do we return to Dale?"

Carver said, ignoring Henry, "Let's get into town. There must be someone there. The whole town can't have disappeared. Someone will be able to explain all of this."

At least I think that it was Carver who said this. I was thinking only of Meredith, who lived on the far side of Bremen with her sister and some younger cousins and their children. Alice Palace, who knew what Meredith and I were to each other, was already looking at me. She was thinking of Meredith, too.

I couldn't speak what was on my mind. Instead I dug my heels into my poor mare's sides, and she bolted forward. It was only five minutes until I was in front of Meredith's house, and the whole way there I did not see another living soul. Only the white road in the corner of my vision.

Her door, like all the other doors in Bremen, stood open. I wrapped my reins around a mulberry bush and went inside. Meredith's sulky calico cat meowed frantically at me from the staircase, but when I went to pick it up, it ran down the stairs and around me, then out the door, wailing.

I went up to her room and everything was the way I remembered it. Her brass bed, and the bookshelves full of books. She said she'd read every one of them at least twice. Whenever I came through Bremen, she gave me a list of books she particularly wanted, and each time I came back I brought her the ones I'd found. On the desk beside her bed, there was a glass with a crust of red wine down in the bowl, and a letter. She'd written *Dear Lucille, I hope you* but that was as far as she'd gotten. The date was two days earlier.

And here I must make a confession. We in the company were in the habit of reading the letters that we were entrusted with. Just as we provide entertainment to the people whose towns we visit, we take our entertainment in the letters of those people. We open the letters carefully, read them to each other, and then seal them up again just as carefully. We know all the secrets of the towns we visit, and the connective threads that stitch one place to another. And so I had known Meredith before we ever spoke more than two or three words to each other. I knew her first through her letters, just as the last I ever knew of her was that small fragment of an unfinished thought. The whole town of Bremen, over two thousand souls in all, was lost, but even then the loss that I felt was the loss of Meredith. And perhaps this should be the story that I tell, the story of how we met and how we fell in love and what I hoped for, but I will not tell that story.

I FOUND THE REST of my company on the street in front of Bremen's public square. Somehow time had moved forward almost an hour, and it was now a quarter to six. When I realized this, I felt sure that I could feel the white road wriggling now obscenely, like a fat worm in a kind of ecstasy of nearness, but of course when I turned my head to catch it in the act, it was rolled out flat and still as a sheet of marble. As long as it is daylight, the only motion it makes is the one you cannot see, that allows it to shift its position so you may always see it at your shoulder.

"They're all gone," Laurent said. "God knows where."

"And they've taken all the corpses with them," Cece said. "We couldn't find a single body."

"Maybe something happened first to them," Carver said. "To the corpses. And then when it was night—"

"Not like that," Laurent said, "because if they'd come, those ones, in the absence of a corpse, you know what we would have found. Every house a charnel house. Blood and scraps of meat and bone. They tear us to pieces when they find their way in."

Carver said, "Then they all ran mad. Buried their dead and turned their faces to the white road. People do that sometimes. Chase the white road until the night comes. That's why they say never to look at it."

"Please!" Cece said. "What happened to them doesn't matter now. What matters is it's almost night again. And we don't have a body."

"I'll be the body," Alice Palace said promptly. "We'll set up camp in the old theater, and I'll lie in state all night long. Until morning comes. You can hold my funeral. And then we'll be on our way."

"No," Laurent said. "I'll be the body. And you'll mourn me. Drink to my memory and tell stories about me. I'd enjoy that, I think."

"But you won't be really dead," Henry said. Underneath him the mule was dancing in place. He was holding its reins too tightly, rigid in his seat with fear. "What if it doesn't work because you're actually alive, because you're not really dead? How do you know they'll be fooled?"

"Well," Phillip said. He looked gray with exhaustion. Cece and Carver didn't look much better. Amabeth, leaning over the neck of her brown mare, looked worse than any of them, but she said in a clear voice, "It's been done a time or two. And in any case, whatever happened here must have had something to do with them. Perhaps they've done enough mischief to suit. They don't always come. Perhaps they won't come, no matter."

"Fuck you," Henry said. "My uncle paid all of you good money to get me safely to Memphis. I will write him a letter when I get there and tell him everything. He's an important man. You won't be able to show your faces in Chattanooga again."

"Should we survive the night," Laurent said gently, "and should we get you all the way to Memphis, you can write that letter and I promise I will carry it in my pocket until I can deliver it to him. My word on it."

"Hey now," I said. "Henry, I promise we'll keep you safe. But you will have to promise to do what we say. No fighting. No unkind words. You're one of us now. The sun will go down in an hour, and we have work to do before then. We'll go through a house or two and borrow some food and some candles. Perhaps we might even borrow some fresh clothes. Then it will be time for our performance."

"Come, Henry," Alice Palace said. "Haven't you ever wanted to act on the stage? You might even audition to be the corpse.

It isn't the most demanding role, but it's the most important one."

"No," Laurent said with finality. "I will be the corpse. I'm tired enough after all the debauchery of last night that I think I will do a fine job."

Alice Palace gave a little shrug. "Whatever you like. Only let's make sure to turn up plenty of whatever liquor these people keep tucked away. If I'm going to spend the night weeping and wailing and waiting to see if I'm going to be dismantled like an old bookcase for kindling, I want to do it drunk."

PERHAPS WE ATE WELL. I don't remember that part. I wasn't hungry. I didn't think I would ever be hungry again, but I must have eaten something. I knew something of what the night would be. Why the ones who walk the white road can be deterred by the presence of a corpse is a mystery, just as much as why they are drawn to the presence of electronics, mechanical vibration, and, to a lesser extent, human activity. We know that they are monsters because they come at night and they tear us to pieces. But they are also monsters, I think, because we do not understand why they do what they do.

Only a corpse keeps the white road away, seals off a place from the ones who walk on it. But in the absence of a real corpse, playacting must do, and we were not murderers. We set up our pretend funeral on the stage in Bremen's old death trap of a theater. We dragged a coffin out of a nearby house and set it up on the stage. After our hasty dinner, Laurent climbed inside and lay down. Then he got up again. "Should go piss," he said, and wandered off backstage holding a fat candle.

We sat around on the stage, not saying anything, until Laurent came back. "Well," he said. "We who are about to," and blew a kiss at Alice Palace. "Before I die, I just want you to know something. I love you. I love everything about you and I think I always will. And maybe you know that and anyway you don't care, and I'm sorry if I've been a nuisance about it, but I hope now that I'm dead, you'll miss me a little. I truly loved you. I did. And now, farewell."

Alice Palace said, "Okay, thanks." She didn't seem to have taken in his speech at all.

Henry said to me, "But he's not really dead. So that's going to be awkward later on. If we live."

And all this was the start of the wake. We passed around bottles of indeterminate brownish liquor and toasted Laurent. Some of us wept. We drank more. We sang lachrymose songs and we smoked the joints Carver and Henry had been given by the daughters of the inn at Dale and got high. Admittedly, this was not how we usually arrived at our best performances, but by now, we knew the white road would be just outside the doors of the Bremen theater. Now, if we were to go outside and look for it, we would not find it over our shoulder, but instead it would lie there before us as if we might step out upon it. Now we could not count on the white road to be untrafficked. There would be things traveling up and down it. Sooner or later the road would grow wider still and we would be on it even though, up on that stage, we had not moved a step in its direction. Then the things traveling on it would be able to come to us.

Some people say it is our fear of the things that travel on the white road that sends them into a frenzy, as if fear were an emanation of the most delicious smell, and that grief is what makes that emanation repellent to them. And so, some think it may be possible to survive their presence if only one can enter into a state in which one is not afraid. Only we are so very afraid of them. How could we not be? They are monsters. So we enacted grief until what we felt was truly grief, as if Laurent were really, truly dead. And we toked up until we were, most of us, so high that everything that happened next was, perhaps, inevitable.

But I will confess this: I did not drink as much as my friends. I refused the joint. I transmuted my grief for Meredith (which was also my grief for myself) into grief for Laurent. For his good humor, and his very stupid but nonetheless affecting love for Alice, who I knew would never love him back. For his beauty, which would first wither and then bloat and transform and become pitiable and rotten, if not now then too soon. But I also waited. I wanted to see the ones who walk the white road. The face they show to us is terrible and it is false but it is always a familiar one. I hoped if they came that it would be Meredith I saw.

HENRY DRANK HEAVILY. HE took a hit from the joint whenever it went by him. He was not a good actor, and his grief at Laurent's death, though loud, was unpersuasive. But then, he had only known Laurent a short time and his calling was a fish farm in Memphis and not the stage. And, too, he was angry at us. Whatever had happened in Bremen had nothing to do with our company, but we had brought him here and he wished now that he had never met us.

When more than two hours had gone by and the ones who travel the white road were nowhere to be seen in the theater, I

believe Henry grew a little bored. When the others weren't paying attention to him, he slipped away backstage. I thought perhaps he had gone to find a place to piss. I thought about going
after him, but Amabeth and Alice Palace were crying and whispering over in a corner stage left, and I went over to join them.
I must have been a little drunk because I genuinely thought that
they were grieving. I wanted to comfort them.

Alice Palace said, "Of course you won't even know his name,
but he was huge. He was in all these movies, and everyone loved
him. There used to be this thing where this group of people
would decide who the sexiest man of the year was, and he won,
more than once, I think? He had everything you could want,
but I guess he had real issues with depression. Anyway, we were
just kids and we lived in this town in upstate New York and
there were a bunch of people who had second houses up there.
Big fancy houses. And so he was there for a party or visiting
friends or something, and I guess he wandered off and he hung
himself from a tree. In our backyard. He probably didn't even
know it was a yard. I mean, we didn't have a fence or anything,
and it was all overgrown. And my sister and I were out there the
next night, before anyone really knew that he was even missing,
and I found him. It was dark so I couldn't see him or anything,
but I ran into him where he was hanging from the rope and his
body was all stiff but also it moved. I was like eight years old."

"No way," Amabeth said. "That's fucked up."

I thought of Laurent's mother, the Reverend Godejohn, how
she had run down the road after us when we first took him on.
We went through Atlanta now and then, still, but as far as I
knew Laurent had never gone to see her. She had raised him to
love God and God alone, developed that exceptional capacity he

had to worship no matter whether or not his worship was visible to its object. How had Alice Palace substituted herself in his sight? Well, if it had not been Alice Palace it would have been some other person or cause. We do as we have learned to do.

"Yeah, but the really fucked-up thing is that this is the way I remember it. And I used to think that was why I wanted to be an actor. Because of the whole experience. I got obsessed with his movies. I knew all his lines by heart. But later on, when I was in my twenties and I was talking with my parents about all of this, they told me it was actually my sister who found his body. I wasn't even out in the yard. I was asleep in my bed. But because the whole thing had been so traumatic, and because my parents never wanted to talk about it, I'd made the whole thing into my story."

"Or maybe your parents were lying," Amabeth said. "And it was your story."

"I don't know," Alice Palace said. "I guess maybe that could be true. But all of this, this thing with Laurent dying, it just brings everything back. I just wish I had been nicer to him."

Acting had come naturally to Laurent, and all the other performing arts, as well. The only part I'd ever seen him turn down was Othello. He said although it might seem to us otherwise, it was not a role that suited him. We did *Much Ado About Nothing* in its place for almost a year and he played Benedick. Laurent had always preferred comedies to tragedies. In the comedies, everything comes right and then there is a stopping place that is not a true ending. The box that gives the comic story its shape is made, on purpose, too small. It cannot contain the true ending.

"You weren't ever mean to him," Amabeth said.

"No," Alice Palace said. "But, you know. I could have been nicer." She began to sob harder, and I would have tried to comfort her but Amabeth took her into her arms.

"It's okay," Amabeth said. "It's awful, I know. But it's going to be okay. He wouldn't want you to be this sad. He loved you."

"I know," Alice Palace said. She began to cry even harder.

NOW I THOUGHT THAT perhaps I could see someone standing just inside the foyer of the theater. It was too dark for me to be sure, but the longer I looked out, the more sure I became someone was there looking back at me. We had closed and bolted the door when we came in, but I knew it stood open now. They open all doors. The only one that keeps them out is the door that we go through in death.

I went on thinking about Laurent, about how awful it was he had died, however he had died, and about how everything was going to be different now, but now I had the feeling that just as I had judged Henry's grief and found it lacking in verisimilitude, my grief was being evaluated. My grief was unconvincing. Or, perhaps, I was not drunk enough. I thought: *It will come down an aisle toward the stage and I will see its face.* And then someone grabbed me by the shoulder and I would have shouted but my throat closed up and when I turned, it was Henry. He held his other hand out to me. In it, and this a mystery, was an apple. "Come with me," he said. "Follow me, Victor. You have got to see this."

No one else was paying attention to us. Carver and Phillip and Cece were singing old hymns beside Laurent's coffin. Amabeth was still comforting Alice Palace. Couldn't they sense the white road thickening in clots all around us? Did they not see the figure that flitted around the rotting rows of seats? One, and then two. Henry did not seem to see them, either. He was preoccupied with whatever he had discovered. "Not now," I said. "Think of Laurent."

"Yes, I know," Henry said. "It's terrible that he's dead. But come and see what I've found. It's wonderful."

So I took a candle and followed him backstage. The heavy curtains lay in heaps that we had to step through, and the material gave way under our feet, releasing a pungent smell. Here was a corridor, and no one in it that I could see. Henry took my free hand and pulled me after him. We went past a series of doors. He or someone else had opened each. They would have been dressing rooms, I suppose. We had never performed in this theater, but instead had been allowed to use the Methodist church, which was maintained by those who still worshipped. We'd come here tonight because we were free to go where we pleased, and the façade of this theater was lovely still. There was room in the foyer here for our mounts, and the church had always had a grim feeling about it.

We were halfway down the hall when Henry stopped. "This door," he said. "Go and see. But be careful. The floor's gone. It's about a foot down."

Before I went through the door I could feel the cool air blowing through it. There was light, streaming down from above. I looked up and saw the ceiling had fallen in, too. The moon was high above us, and growing up toward it was an apple tree, its branches keeping the walls of the box the room made from collapsing further in. Eventually, though, the tree would spread farther and it would push or pull those walls apart.

"Go on," Henry said. "You can go down to the ground or else you can climb up on one of these branches. Go pick an apple."

"I don't know if it will hold me," I said. And then I saw that we were on the white road now. It stretched out around us and no matter where I looked it extended itself voluptuously.

"Then I'll pick one for you," Henry said. He began to reach up, and then the one who had been in the tree this whole time though we had not seen it began to climb down from its perch. Henry fell back against me clumsily, moaning in fear, but I saw that this was a woman and I felt a longing so much greater than my terror that I pushed him aside and began to go toward her. But it wasn't Meredith I saw. It was my sister. She was just as I remembered her, except her eyes were not where they should have been. They were below her right cheekbone, crowded together; one had no pupil. They always get some detail wrong, and yet still you recognize the one they mean you to see.

Henry said, "We have to get out of here. Help me. I have to get out of here." He picked up a slab of fallen timber the thickness of my arm and brandished it at my poor sister. Then he began to moan again. "Behind you," he said. "Another one."

And once more I dared to hope. But when I looked it was a little girl of perhaps three or four years. I had not known her in the coffin at the inn when we stopped in Dale, but now a memory came to me. She'd sat in my lap at dinner and asked for a fairy tale. Here she was now, translated into a thing out of some dark forest. She had too many legs. I could not count how many.

"They're only curious," I said to Henry. "If they meant us harm they would have already done it. They heard us grieving Laurent and it's a puzzle to them. They don't know whether he's dead or if we're their meat. But let's leave the apple tree to them and talk about dear Laurent who is dead so that we might go on living." I took the piece of wood from his hand as gently as I could. It was so heavy I was amazed he had been able to lift it.

"Laurent," Henry said. I could see the fog of drink and pot lifting a little. He began the work of changing the expression he wore from terror to grief. The others waited with us. I didn't know how he saw them, only that what he saw would be different from what I could see. And still I had that same longing, that same hope. Perhaps another would come. Perhaps I would see her. I would have done almost anything, I think, to see her. I would have waited in that room beneath that tree forever. But then there was a terrible sound, the sound of someone screaming back on the stage where we'd left the others, and I did what I needed to do.

The piece of wood was solid as a bar of iron, and I swung it in a motion so swift I don't think he ever knew what I meant to do. I heard his neck snap and I was already lifting the piece of wood again before his body hit the threshold of the roofless room. I brought it down hard on his head twice and felt his skull give way. And then the white road was gone and so were the ones who had come on it. I went back down the corridor to see what had happened upon the stage. I met no one I knew on my way there.

WHAT HAD HAPPENED WAS more comedy than tragedy, I discovered. The others had gone on mourning Laurent, until at last I think they were all convinced that he was truly dead. And dwelling on this, Alice Palace had passed through grief into a place where she had begun to tear her clothes and pull her hair out. She had fallen on the coffin, and begged Laurent to come back to life again. She told him now that it was too late she realized what she'd lost. She'd realized she loved him as much as he loved her, only before she had been too afraid to see what was in front of her. She begged him to come back to life, said if he did not live again, then she would die of grief. She said if Laurent had ever truly loved her, he would live again, and this was too much for Laurent to bear. He'd sat up in his coffin and embraced her and ended the performance and then the ones we had been performing for had stormed the stage and this was when Cece had screamed and I had done what I had done.

Carver went with me to collect Henry's body. The first thing he said was, "Oh, look! An apple tree!" And then, "I suppose he fell," and I said no, that I had killed him. But it was kind of Carver to have suggested a different story. And it might have gone that way, I suppose, if we had been acting out a farce.

There isn't much more of the story, I think. When the sun rose, we left Bremen behind us. The others ate apples all the day long, but I have never again been able to stomach the taste. We did not do much in the way of mourning Henry. I think we had been worn out by the extravagant performance of the night before.

Henry's mule carried his corpse to Nashville, solemnly enough, and it was in Nashville that I began to have a spasm in my jaw and then to run a fever. The rest of the company had to leave me there when it transpired that I had lockjaw: the piece of wood I'd used to crush Henry's skull had had a nail lodged in it, and the nail scratched me. A family in Nashville took care of me over the long months while the tetanus ran its course. Their payment was some seed corn and Henry's body. When I was well enough to leave my sickbed, I would slowly make my way to the room where his body lay and keep it company, sometimes for hours at a time. We grew to know each other as we had not had time to do during our short acquaintance on the road. When I recovered, I no longer had the breath to sing or act upon a stage. So I took up another occupation. It does not signify, the thing I learned to do. From time to time I heard something of my friends in the company. For some years, I think, Laurent Godejohn and Alice Palace were happy together. But later on I heard he had died, though how I do not know, and shortly after that she came through Nashville and we had a drink together. She did not wish to speak of him. She had a new lover. Truth be told, she did not seem changed to me. Not by love, not by grief, and not even by the passage of time.

As for Henry's uncle, I was told when the company next passed through Chattanooga they told him Henry had perished in a thunderstorm, struck down by lightning. I heard also that a traveler coming down through the mountains had found no one living at the Dale inn. All the walls of the lower rooms were still wet with blood as if a river had run through and then recently subsided.

And as for me, I do not know what this story is. Is it a comedy or is it a tragedy? Now that I have written it down, I still cannot see its shape. And no doubt I have gotten many of the details wrong, as Alice Palace did when she told the story of the man hanging from the tree. But I will fold this all up and put it inside an envelope and then I will send it to Henry's uncle in

Chattanooga. But I do not know if he is still living. I hope he is still living. Perhaps if he is not someone else will read it. I wish that Meredith could read it, but perhaps it is just as well she cannot. Were she to read it, she might see I am in truth the thing she once told me she was surprised to see me perform so naturally. Perhaps someone who should not read this letter will read it as I once read Meredith's letters and the letters of other men and women. But I do not hope. I do not hope but still I hope and do not know what I am hoping for.

The Girl Who Did Not Know Fear

(The Boy Who Did Not Know Fear)

A few years ago, I was on my way home to Massachusetts when bad weather stranded me in the Detroit airport for four days. I'd been at a conference in Iowa City—I travel rarely, but this was a point in my career when professional advancement required that I go. I was to receive a signal honor, one that conferred much benefit not only upon myself but also upon the university where I had tenure and no teaching responsibilities. My university had made it clear that it would be ungracious of me not to go. And so I went. I attended panels and listened to my colleagues discuss my research. Former students, now middle-aged and embarked upon their own careers, greeted me with more affection and warmth than I felt I merited; I bought them drinks in the bar, and listened to reports of their various successes. Some of them knew my wife. Others were Facebook friends, and remarked on recent photos of our daughter, Dido. How much she had grown. There was, of course, talk of politics and of the recent winter, how mild it had been. How wet this spring was turning out to be. I have never cared much for change, but of course change is inevitable. And not all change is catastrophic—or rather, even in the middle of catastrophic change, small good things may go on. Dido had recently learned to write her name. The children of my colleagues, too, were marvels, prodigies, creatures remarkable in their natures and abilities.

On the last day, I packed up my suitcase and drove my rental car back to the airport in Cedar Rapids. When I called my wife, she seemed distracted, but then, neither of us has ever been good at phone calls. And then, there was an appointment on my calendar that could not be postponed, and we were both thinking of it.

In Detroit, my connecting flight was delayed once and then again. Even someone who travels as infrequently as I do knows travel in this age is an uncertain enterprise, full of delays and inconveniences, but eventually it became clear something out of the ordinary was happening here. There was a storm system in Atlanta so severe that flights operated by Delta had fallen off the grid all across the country. In consequence there would be no more planes going to Hartford tonight.

I called my wife so she would know not to stay up any longer. "How late is it there?" she said. "One hour back, isn't it? No, you're back in Eastern Standard now? So, not quite midnight. You go find a hotel quick before they all fill up. I'll call Delta and get you on a flight tomorrow morning. You'll be home in plenty of time. Dido wants you to pick her up after school tomorrow, but we'll see."

My wife is twelve years younger than I. This is her second marriage, my first. We look enough alike to be sisters, and she says sometimes, jokingly, that the first time she looked at me, she felt as if she were seeing her future. The longer we have been married, the more, I believe, we have come to resemble each other. We have a similar build; we sometimes wear each other's clothing, and we go to the same hairdresser. Each of us has a birthmark on a thigh, though hers is larger, three fingers wide. Her breasts are larger and her nipples are the color of dried blood. After she had our daughter, her shoes no longer fit and so she donated them all to a women's shelter. Now we wear the same size.

When we decided to start a family, there was no question that she would be the one to carry the pregnancy. Carry the pregnancy, she said. As if the doctors were talking about a bag of groceries. But she asked if I would supply the egg. And so I did and perhaps I should not have. I would have loved a child just as much, I think, if she had not been my child biologically. But then, Dido would not be Dido, would she? If she were less like me or even if she were more like me, would I love her more or would I love her less? Would my wife have fallen in love with me quite so quickly if our resemblance to each other had not been so remarkable?

Dido is Dido and may she always be Dido in exactly the way she chooses to be. That is what I would choose for her. When Dido is older, will she look at me and see her future?

I do not like to think too much about the future. I don't care for change.

I WAS BACK AT the airport at seven A.M. for a ten A.M. flight. In an excess of optimism, I went so far as to check my carry-on bag. And then, when that flight was canceled and then the flight after, as well, I was told my carry-on was now in transit though I was not. It could not be retrieved. That night, I took a Lyft to Target and purchased a toothbrush, underwear, and a cheap bathing suit.

Just past the throat of the lobby of the airport Sheraton, where I was paying too much for the privilege of a cramped room with a too-large bed, there was an indoor courtyard with a concrete-rimmed swimming pool. There was a cabana bar, too, in the courtyard, shrouded in plastic sheets; unpersuasive palm trees in planters; deck chairs and little tables where no one ever sat.

The water in the pool was a cloudy jade. During my stay I never encountered another traveler in the pool, and the cabana bar was never open. The lighting indicated a perpetual twilight. Except for that first night, when every seat on the shuttle to the Sheraton was occupied by a stranded traveler, all of us attended at check-in by a single teenaged desk clerk, I never saw any other guests in the public areas of the hotel.

In every way I am a poor traveler. I do not like to be confined in small spaces; I am a picky eater and easily overstimulated; in adolescence I was diagnosed with hyperosmia. I do not sleep well when I am away from home, but I have discovered that if I swim to the point of exhaustion, some amount of sleep is possible. The acridity of chlorine masks almost all other smells.

I wish I could make you see what the courtyard in that Sheraton was like. It had something of the feel of a subterranean grotto, or maybe a Roman amphitheater. As a child, I'd pored over a book called *Motel of the Mysteries,* in which archaeologists in the year 4022 discover a motel and attempt to deduce how the artifacts they dig up were used and by whom; when I floated on my back in the courtyard pool, one hundred feet above me a popcorn ceiling in place of sky, I was as liberated in time and place and purpose as I had ever been. On one side of me was my professional obligation, now fulfilled. On the other was my home and my family and an appointment I knew I could not delay, and yet here I was. Four nights I stayed in that hotel. I swam in the pool and tried to keep my head free of useless worries. In all the years that I have lived with this condition of mine, I have learned it is wise to mitigate stress. Stress is a trigger.

Four floors of breezeways rose up on all sides of the courtyard. No one came in or out of the hotel rooms that looked down on the pool, and neither did I ever hear anyone in the rooms on either side of the one where I slept. I swam silently so that I would not break the vast still spell of the place, staying in the pool for so long that when I went to sleep, my skin and hair gave off such a satisfactory stink of chlorine that the other smells in the room were little more than ghosts—the burnt-toast smell of the laundered sheets, lingering traces of perfumes and deodorants, stale remnants of repulsive foodstuffs, musk of sex and sweat, mildew-laced recycled air.

Each night for four nights I swam, and each day for four days I went to the airport, which was in every way the opposite of my tranquil courtyard. I woke up at 6:30 each morning and rode the shuttle as if I were going to my workplace. I waited in lines and passed through security and went to my assigned gate to see if my flight would depart this time. As the day wore on, and each successive possible flight was delayed and then canceled, I moved from one gate to the next, where, it was hoped, a plane might at last take off. I was one of several thousand people, all of whom were out of place, paused in transit. And this was the swimming pool, too, it began to seem to me. A kind of suspended and purposeless motion.

The reason for the canceled flights might have been a storm system, but in Detroit the weather was mild and cloudy, like the water in the swimming pool. The bad storms had only truly affected Atlanta, but Atlanta was Delta's central hub and for many days, Delta planes continued not to be where they should have been and where there were planes, there were not enough flight crews.

I sat near outlets when I could, and charged my phone and texted friends, called home each time I was bumped to a new flight, and debated renting a car. If Dido was home, sometimes she would speak to me. She could not understand why I would not come home. My wife said in my absence Dido was having nightmares again. Nightmares about what? "Toilets," my wife said. "An overflowing toilet. Yeah, it sounds comical but she wakes up screaming. And she wet her pants today because she didn't want to use the toilet at school."

I said, "I could rent a car. If I drove, I would be home in about twelve hours."

"No," my wife said. "That's ridiculous. You hate driving. You're a terrible driver."

Which was true. And every time a flight was canceled, there was a new gate where I could go and wait, suspended in the cloudy green day. I read the new Kate Atkinson. I drank iced coffee from Dunkin' Donuts. Passengers swapped gossip and stories. There was a family, I was told two or three times, who had flown over from London to take their three young daughters to Disney World. Now they had been stuck in Detroit for three days. They had not gotten to Orlando, and now they could not get home, either. Eventually, I, too, began telling this story, though I was not sure that I believed it.

Every now and then, a ragged cheer would go up at a gate. By this, we would know that a flight crew had arrived, and these passengers were escaping Detroit Metropolitan Airport. By the third day, I no longer waited only for flights that might take me to Bradley International Airport in Connecticut. I allowed myself to be booked for flights that might go to Logan or LaGuardia or even Philadelphia. But these, too, were delayed and then canceled. Each night I left the terminal between ten P.M. and midnight and rode the shuttle back to the Sheraton. In my room, I washed a pair of underwear and socks with shampoo, rolled them in a dry towel, and put on my bathing suit. I swam until I felt as if I had washed time off of my skin again, and then left wet footprints across the courtyard that would be gone by the time I was asleep. In the morning, I woke up and traveled back to the airport. My wife was growing tired of her role as a single parent, but in the end we agreed there was no need yet for me to rent a car. My wife felt sure that I would be home soon. I told her the story of the English family. Still, she felt I would be home soon. I would be home soon and the appointment on my calendar could be safely marked off once again. Life would go serenely on.

In the middle of the night I woke from a terrible dream. Dreams, too, are markers of my condition, or so I have come to believe. It is possible that Dido has inherited my condition just as I inherited my mother's face, although it is possible her bad dreams are just bad dreams.

In my dream there was a pool in a courtyard, only it was full of moonlight instead of water, so bright I could not bear to look directly at it. But oh, there was a smell that was so delicious and enticing that I went into the pool, my eyes open so I could see what smelled so very good. The moonlight buoyed me up just as water would do, and I immersed myself in the wonderful smell as if I were a dog, and my eyes watered and my mouth was so full of saliva I had to swallow over and over again. I rubbed my eyes and then I saw that standing all around the pool were all of the people I have ever hurt or injured without meaning to. Some of them I didn't even know or maybe I didn't remember them, but I knew the reason they were standing there. There, too, were all the people I would inevitably go on hurting even though I did not wish to—there was my mother, and my wife. There was Dido. Their eyes were so full of pain—I realized that they felt pain for me, because I was in the pool and I could not get out. I was in the pool because of my condition, and because they cared for me, they could not leave me here alone. I was hurting them in this way, too, and when I realized this I was so full of anger that I burst into a thousand pieces and bits of my skin flew everywhere and that was how I woke up, soaked in sweat as if I had been running.

I got out of my bed and put on my wet bathing suit and went to the courtyard pool. I wanted to make sure everything was the way that it should be. I needed to see my dream was only a dream and not something true. And, too, I could still smell that delicious smell. I needed to know if it was something real.

It was the middle of the night, but in the courtyard where nothing ever changed, it was only twilight. The delicious smell dissipated. I swam lap after lap and no one came to tell me I should get out even though the hours were clearly marked on a sign tacked to the side of the cabana. No one came and so I swam until my head was clear again and my dream was gone.

ALL MY LIFE, I have been a person in whom strangers have confided. There is something in my face that says, "I am interested in you" to some, and "I will keep your secret" to others. I have my mother's face, and it is true my mother was sincerely interested in everyone she met, and that she was a faithful keeper of other people's secrets. I am not my mother. Sometimes, I think, I am not even myself. But whether a trick of physiognomy, or a habit of expression learned as her child in the way that all children mimic the behaviors and mannerisms of their parents, just as Dido sits at my wife's desk and makes a face at my wife's laptop and polishes the glasses that she does not wear, my face has said, all of my life, "I will listen to your story."

Pity the introvert with the face of a therapist or a kindergarten teacher. Like the werewolf, we are uneasy in human spaces and human company, though we wear a human skin. The airport itself was bad enough, but even worse was the shuttle I rode back and forth between the airport and the Sheraton. The driver was a woman in her seventies, an ex-servicewoman, the mother of three grown children. One was an addict, and one had had a breast cancer scare. The other was estranged from her mother, though she lived only twenty miles away. The shuttle driver prayed every night to be reconciled with this daughter—who, it was determined, was my age almost to the month. With each ride, her presumption of our acquaintance grew deeper and by the third morning, she embraced me when we arrived at the airport in case she did not see me again. But although her daughter would not return to her, I did. I had no choice.

Pity the werewolf. What should a stranger's sad story mean? Wash off a stranger's sad story in a green pool. Fall asleep in the clean reek of chlorine and inhabit the fragmentary and uneasy dreams of departed guests whose strands of hair, dander, lardy fingerprints, odd bits of trash, and inconclusive stains inhabit these transitory and poorly lit spaces. If you listen, a hotel room speaks, too. It says: I will keep your secret.

I TALLIED MY RECEIPTS on the fourth day. I checked in with my research assistant, who keeps the lab running on days when I'm looking after Dido, or when I have a flare-up and am confined to my home office. My university had covered my flight, the conference, and my hotel in Iowa City, but now there was the cost of airport food: coffee from Dunkin' Donuts, breakfast sandwiches, packets of unshelled pistachios and Snickers bars, bananas and burgers and power bars. There was my trip to Target; the room at the Sheraton at $119.00 plus taxes every night, checked out of so hopefully each morning; the five dollars I left on the bureau as a tip; and the two dollars I gave each time to the shuttle driver. There was the cost of the babysitter my wife was paying to look after Dido while she was at work. My work schedule is flexible, coordinated with my wife's so that one of us can be at home most days with Dido when her school lets out, but still there was a great deal of business now to take care of at the lab once I was home and could go in. That would be more money for the babysitter.

My wife and I had decided if there were no flights to Hartford or Boston or New York today, then tomorrow I would have to rent a car. This would give me two days to get home before my appointment. Even I could manage six hours in a car one day, and six hours again the next. I could even, my wife suggested, look around at my fellow would-be passengers. Maybe one of them might be willing to share the cost of a car. "Maybe," I said. "You think the English family has made it home yet?" she said. "Maybe," I said. "Next month we'll go camping," she said. "I ran into Molly at the co-op and she was telling me about this place in New Hampshire. Right on a lake. A little playground for kids, and lots of trails. She's going to send me a link to the campsite. That sounds amazing, right?" "Maybe," I said. It was a little hard to think past the next few days, getting home, and my appointment, and then catching up with work. I had my phone plugged into an outlet, and right then I was scheduled to leave on a 2:15 flight, and we talked until my flight was canceled and I had to hang up and unplug my phone and go to book a new flight. Dido was asking about a dog again, because she'd snuck down the basement stairs to hunt for treasure. We have the usual sort of New England basement, which is to say that it is damp and cold, with a floor of tamped-down dirt. I have never liked spending time down there, but Dido is fascinated by it. The previous owner died in her nineties, and her children didn't bother clearing out the basement before they sold the house to us. There are old chests of drawers, some of them hiding photo albums or Depression-glass saucers, a celluloid hairbrush decaying around the horsehair bristles, tangles of human hair coiled around the animal hair. There is the rocking chair, the hat rack and the hatboxes full of mouse droppings and shreds of silk, the washboard and the bundles of faded letters and the dog crate that is big enough Dido can stretch out inside it on her back and look at the gouges on the interior ceiling. Dido wants a dog so badly that my wife said she could almost taste it. Could almost hear clicks of its claws on the wood floor upstairs while she was downstairs, as if Dido were conjuring a pet into existence by force of her extraordinary will. And Dido was still having nightmares. She was making my wife go with her into the bathroom each time to hold her hand while she peed. My wife had tried to get Dido to explain what was so terrifying about a clogged toilet, but Dido could not articulate this to her. She could only dream it over and over again.

In the same way, my last day in Detroit followed the established pattern. I moved from gate to gate until there was only one flight left to wait for. This last possible flight into Hartford was scheduled for 10:30 P.M., and then its departure was postponed and postponed again until eventually it was almost midnight and the agent at the gate got on the speaker to tell us that it was looking likely to be canceled. The airport was shutting down for the night.

On my phone was a series of texts from Dido. Dido loves texting, because she knows that it is something that adults do. Earlier in the evening she had somehow gotten the phone from my wife and used it to text me her name, over and over. *Dido. Dido dido dido dido dido.* And so on. There was a long string of emojis, too, mostly made up of toilets, ominously, and then strings of words made up from predictive text. Then more toilets. By the time Dido is a proficient speller, perhaps it will no longer be necessary to spell at all.

I began to text my wife as people around me disconsolately collected their belongings. But the agent at our gate came over the speaker again to tell us new information had been supplied to her. It now seemed possible that a flight crew from Cleveland would be arriving in twenty minutes and might yet be assigned to our flight. So we were to wait.

We waited without much hope. We had all heard similar announcements over the past few days. But in the end, there was the crew, and here was the plane, and we all got on. It was a full flight, of course, and I had a middle seat. There was a woman a decade or two younger than me in the window seat, whose clothing was more youthful still. Dickies jeans, plum-colored hair, shitkicker boots, and a cropped T-shirt with *DTF* in a Gothic font. In the aisle seat was a woman just a little older, heavyset and tired looking, wearing the kind of clothing and minimal makeup that signals camouflage worn by lesbians in administrative offices. And when they looked at me, I knew what the two women saw. I was wearing the same slouchy black cardigan over the same black jersey dress I had worn for the past four days. It was my wife's cardigan, and days ago it had smelled like her, but it no longer did. I had on a wedding ring and a smoky eye, thanks to the MAC boutique in the Detroit airport, where a bored aesthetician told me about the roller derby match her girlfriend had dragged her to the previous weekend and how she'd realized, watching the very first jam, that her girlfriend was cheating on her with the worst skater in the league. The smoky eye did not suit me. I'd been wondering, though, if it would stay on in a swimming pool. I'd been thinking all day about the swimming pool. Even here, on the plane and on my way home, I held the swimming pool, that cool and empty space, inside my skull as if by holding it there I might contain everything else that must be contained. I do not do well in small spaces. I do not feel safe when I am far from home. I am not safe when I am far from home.

I texted my wife again. *On a plane! Getting in around 3, so don't wait up. I'll take a Lyft. Love you.* Then I turned off my phone. You could feel every passenger on the plane holding their breath as we waited to see if we would, in fact, take off. And then the exhalation when we did. I clasped my hands tightly in my lap as the plane taxied and then rose up, the ground visible only as stacks and necklaces of lights that shrank to sequins, then bright pinpricks, shrank until everything was a velvety black.

There was no reason for it, but I thought of the shuttle driver's daughter. Though the daughter was my age, a middle-aged woman estranged from a woman who was near my mother's own age, her face was the face of my Dido.

The woman in the window seat said, "I guess we're going to get home, after all."

On my iPad I had the first three episodes of a television show that my wife did not care to watch. But the woman in the window seat waited as I took out my headphones and just when I was putting them on she said, "I don't know you, do I?"

I lifted my headphones. I said, "I don't think so. No."

"No, I do," she said. "Don't I? Martine?"

"No," I said. "I'm sorry. I'm Abby."

"Oh," she said, disappointed. "Did you ever live up in Vermont? Burlington?"

"No," I said. "I've been there a couple of times, though. It's pretty."

"Yeah," she said. "It is. I lived there for a while. Oh, God. A while ago now. I moved up there because my girlfriend was opening a gallery, and I'd just gotten my degree. But then she dumped me a month later, and I should have just left but I didn't. It just seemed so embarrassing, packing up after one month. So I slept on her couch for a couple of weeks until I found another place to live. And then I stayed there for eight years! Until another breakup, like one of those burn everything down to the ground breakups. But, fuck, it's pretty up there. Just, you know, the dating scene is a little incestuous."

"Small towns," I said.

"Tell me about it," the woman in the window seat said. "I was trying to explain it to a friend in New York once. I ended up drawing her a diagram with everybody's name on it, and then these different colored lines. You know, who's dating, who used to date but now they're just friends, who broke up with who and now they won't talk to each other, who's in a poly relationship, who hooked up but thinks that no one knows, and then all the asterisks. *The L Word* got that part right, at least."

I said, "Being married makes everything a lot less complicated. Sometimes."

The woman in the aisle seat, on the other side of me, shifted. Her thigh rubbed against mine. She was pretending to read the in-flight magazine but I could tell she was listening.

"For Christmas, my friend took the diagram I'd drawn her and embroidered it all. Got it framed. I was like, what am I supposed to do with it? Hang it on a wall? But it was pretty. She used different stitches for the different kinds of relationship lines. What do they call that? A sampler, right? Anyway, Martine was part of that whole scene. You look so much like her. I wish I had a picture. She and Leila. They were married when I met them, but then it turned out Leila had this whole other life. She'd had a girlfriend in Quebec the whole time she and Martine were together, which you would think would not be easy to pull off, but Leila was a sales rep for a company in Quebec, this printing company, and so she was up there for a couple of days out of every month. Sometimes a lot more. But then Martine found out and threw Leila out and Leila moved up to Quebec, although she kept coming back to Burlington and telling Martine she really thought they could work it out if Martine could just figure out how to get past it. She wanted to try therapy, and when Martine wouldn't go for it, Leila used her keys to let herself in while Martine was at work. She texted Martine and said not to worry, she was just there to pick up a pair of jeans she'd left behind, but when Martine got home, it turned out that Leila had actually been there to pick up her favorite strap-on. Like, seriously? They don't have sex shops in Quebec? After that, Martine went through this whole phase. She was wild. She fucked any girl who looked at her twice. She would have fucked a cat if the cat had seemed into it. And she tried everything else, too. People do that sometimes, you know? When they're going through something? Like my best friend growing up. She used to say she was putting the ho in Hoboken. But you know, it turned out she was having all these other problems at home. It was how she felt in control."

"Did you?" I said. "Sleep with her? Martine?"

"No," the woman in the window seat said. "I mean, I hooked up once with Martine at a party. But we were both pretty out of it. There was some good shit at that party. This one girl, Viddy, she got this idea that she could juggle anything. She took a bunch of knives out of a kitchen drawer and threw them up in the air. Cut her hands all to pieces, and then everybody was just dealing with that. It was bad. I was an ambulance driver for a while, so I was doing first aid, and I had Viddy's blood all over me, and I really wanted to get cleaned up and this girl, Martine, it was like she didn't even notice the blood. But it kind of ruined the mood for me, and Martine went home with somebody else. There was something she was looking for, and I guess she just had to keep looking until she found it. I don't know what happened to her, but I hope she found it."

"Maybe she did," I said. And I did hope she had.

"Who knows?" the woman in the window seat said. "Maybe."

The flight attendant came down the aisle with drinks. I will be honest. I badly wanted a real drink. But I had a Coke instead. The woman in the window seat had a gin and tonic and the woman in the aisle seat asked for a tomato juice. She said, "I used to know a girl like that. In New York. A long time ago."

We both looked at her, me and the woman in the window seat.

"She worked in advertising," the woman in the aisle seat said. She drank her tomato juice and then wiped the red off her lips with the back of her hand even though there was a cocktail napkin right there on her tray. "She'd come to poker nights with a friend of mine. Tuesday nights. Penny something. My friend said Penny had the nicest apartment you'd ever seen. This enormous prewar apartment up near Columbia that no one could have afforded, but Penny was subletting it for hardly anything at all because it was haunted. No one else could live there. Apparently you couldn't even spend the night without seeing things or hearing things, really awful things, but Penny slept there like a baby."

"Some people just don't see ghosts," the woman in the window seat said. "They're not sensitive or whatever."

"No," the woman in the aisle seat said. "Penny could see the ghosts just fine. She could see them, she could hear them, for all I know she played poker with them every night of the week except Tuesdays. She just didn't care. She wasn't afraid of them. She wasn't afraid of anything."

"I'm not really afraid of ghosts, either," the woman in the window seat said. "All that kind of stuff is kind of stupid. No offense if that's not what you think."

The woman in the aisle seat said, "No, you don't understand. I mean this Penny literally wasn't afraid of anything. She wasn't afraid of snakes or the dark or thunderstorms or serial killers or being mugged or dogs or heights. She told my friend that she didn't really understand what fear even was. Her mother used to hide behind doors and then jump out at her, to try to scare her when she was a kid. Took her on roller coasters and to therapists. She was mugged at gunpoint twice in one week in New York and my friend said she just laughed about it. But she was curious about what it was like, to be afraid. So she and my friend would go to horror movies, werewolves, slasher movies, and afterward she would ask my friend why they were scary. What it felt like."

"That would be nice," the woman in the window seat said. "Not to be afraid of anything. I'm not afraid of ghosts, but I'm afraid of everything else. I don't even know what that would be like, not to be afraid of everything." She turned to me. "I mean, you're afraid of something, right?"

"Flying," I said. "Myself."

"Right?" the woman in the window seat said. "Right! I mean, imagine not being afraid of anything."

"Straight and curly hair," the other woman said. "People with straight hair wish they had curly hair and people with curly hair wish they had straight hair. You wish you weren't afraid of anything, and my friend said Penny wished she could be afraid of anything, even though she had this gorgeous apartment because she wasn't. She had a lot of girlfriends, but the relationships never lasted very long because none of the girlfriends would sleep over at her place. The ghost or whatever was there frightened them away the first time they slept in her bed. Nothing Penny could do could make them stay, and Penny didn't want to give up her apartment. But eventually she fell in love with this girl Min Jie, and she gave up the apartment for her and they moved in together and got married. My friend went to the wedding. Min Jie was a cheesemonger. She knew everything about cheese. Did you know that for a while you could buy a cheese made from human breast milk? Min Jie said it was a soft cheese. A little like a goat cheese. She worked in this shop in Midtown that had every kind of cheese, imported chocolate, pâtés, tongue, marrons glacé. Lobsters, golden osetra caviar, tupelo and lavender honey, Sacher-tortes, so the spread at the wedding was amazing, my friend said. The wine was some of the best wine she'd ever tasted, and there was plenty of it. Fountains of it. Tables of smoked fish and shrimp and mussels in carved ice bowls. Penny got up and toasted her bride and said that perhaps she would never know fear, but now she knew love."

"Very romantic," the woman in the window seat said. "Nobody's ever said anything like that to me."

The woman in the aisle seat said, "That night they went home and they made love and afterward Penny lay in their bed in their new bedroom, which was so much smaller and dingier than the bedroom in her old apartment had been, and she was happy. And Min Jie came out of the bathroom with a bucket of live eels she'd procured at work, and she dumped the eels over the bed and all over Penny. And my friend said Penny sat straight up in the bed and started screaming because she finally understood what fear was."

"Seriously?" the woman in the window seat said.

"That's what my friend said," the other woman said.

"That's fucked up," the woman in the window seat said.

I said, "Excuse me" to the woman in the aisle. In the last few minutes I'd become aware I was getting my period, days before I should have had it. Everything was wrong, everything was happening that shouldn't have been happening. But I was almost home. Surely we would be home soon.

I went in darkness down the aisle of the plane, passing women sleeping, women playing games on their phones or their iPads, women talking. That delicious smell from my dream was in my nostrils. Blood that shouldn't have been there was between my thighs. But we have no control over our own bodies. The things we feel. The things that happen to us, over and over again. The things we crave.

At the back of the cabin, there was an Out of Order sign on one toilet. The other was occupied. So I waited as patiently as I could. I tried to picture Dido, who would be asleep in her bed. Or perhaps she had had another nightmare and Martine was letting her sleep in our bed.

What my wife shared with former lovers does not diminish what we have together. It isn't as if, before, she killed a lot of people. She just fucked them. And perhaps we would not be together now if Martine had not been who she was then. She was one person then, and is another person now. I never met that other person. That other Martine. And yet sometimes when I think of those years when I did not know her, I am filled with such a frenzy of jealousy that I imagine, as if compelled, finding those lovers in whatever homes or lives they occupy now. I imagine tearing at them with my nails, rending their flesh with my teeth. Making blood run in thick streams, enough to fill ten thousand swimming pools. So much blood it obliterates everything that came before she and I.

I pictured my swimming pool, cool and green and empty. Why would anyone be afraid of eels? Why be afraid of a creature, harmless, caught in a bucket? They only want to get out. In a plane, too, you are suspended. You cannot do anything. You cannot get out. You cannot always be the person you thought you were, no matter how badly you want to be her. Change is inevitable.

The toilet door opened and a woman came out. She said, "The toilet's clogged. I wouldn't go in there."

In the galley just behind us, one of the flight attendants turned and said, "Oh, that's not good. That's not good at all."

"Excuse me," the woman who had come out of the toilet said. I let her go past.

I began to go into the toilet and the flight attendant put her hand on my arm. She said, "No. I'm sorry. You can't go in there. We'll be landing soon. Can't you wait?"

The floor of the toilet was wet. The stench was intolerable. Swollen plugs of wet toilet paper sloshing in the metal basin. Writhing. I turned and looked at the flight attendant, and she recoiled. She took her hand off my arm and stepped back. She said something in such a small voice that I could hardly hear her

over the sound of blood in my ears. Mice have louder voices.
She said, again, "Are you okay?"

I could not answer her. I could not speak at all. What she saw
in my face was not the thing that is usually there. It was the
other thing, the thing that lives inside my skin. I turned and
went back up the aisle to my middle seat. The moon in the
window in every row went with me like a cold white lozenge I
could have slipped under my tongue.

It went with me like a thing on a leash, all the way back to
my seat.

They would be announcing our arrival soon. I might get a
little blood on the seat, but what's a little blood? Women bleed.
Everyone bleeds.

The women on either side of me had been talking to each
other. The woman in the window seat had a car in long-term
parking, and she was asking the other, who didn't have a car, if
she would like a ride into Northampton. She said to me, "Do
you have a car, Abby, or is someone picking you up? Do you
need a ride? Where do you live?"

I had a feeling as if I could have run the whole way home, all
thirty miles or so. But I wanted to be home with my wife and
my child. My appointment was waiting for me, though I thought
perhaps I might be a little early for it this time.

"Sure," I said. "I would really appreciate that."

The Game of Smash and Recovery

(Hansel and Gretel)

If there's one thing Anat knows, it's this. She loves Oscar, her brother, and her brother, Oscar, loves her. Hasn't Oscar raised Anat, practically from childhood? Picked Anat up when she's fallen? Prepared her meals and lovingly tended to her scrapes and taught her how to navigate their little world? Given her skimmer ships, each faster and more responsive than the one before; the most lovely incendiary devices; a refurbished mob of Handmaids, with their sharp fingers, their probing snouts, their furred bellies, their sleek and whiplike limbs?

Oscar called them Handmaids because they have so many fingers, so many ways of grasping and holding and petting and sorting and killing. Once a vampire frightened Anat, when she was younger. It came too close. She began to cry, and then the Handmaids were there, soothing Anat with their gentle stroking, touching her here and there to make sure that the vampire had not injured her, embracing her while they briskly tore the shrieking vampire to pieces. That was not long after Oscar had come back from Home with the Handmaids. Vampires and Handmaids reached a kind of understanding after that. The vampires, encountering a Handmaid, sing propitiatory songs. Sometimes they bow their heads on their long white necks very low, and dance. The Handmaids do not tear them into pieces.

TODAY IS ANAT'S BIRTHDAY. Oscar does not celebrate his own birthdays. Anat wishes that he wouldn't make a fuss about hers, either. But this would make Oscar sad. He celebrates Anat's accomplishments, her developmental progress, her new skills. She knows Oscar worries about her, too. Perhaps he is afraid she won't need him when she is grown. Perhaps he is afraid that Anat, like their parents, will leave. Of course this is impossible. Anat could never abandon Oscar. Anat will always need Oscar.

IF ANAT DID NOT have Oscar, then who in this world would there be to love? The Handmaids will do whatever Anat asks of them, but they are built to inspire not love but fear. They are made for speed, for combat, for unwavering obedience. When they have no task, nothing better to do, they take one another to pieces, swap parts, remake themselves into more and more ridiculous weapons. They look at Anat as if one day they will do the same to her, if only she will ask.

There are the vampires. They flock after Oscar and Anat whenever they go down to Home. Oscar likes to speculate on whether the vampires came to Home deliberately, as did Oscar, and Oscar and Anat's parents, although of course Anat was not born yet. Perhaps the vampires were marooned here long ago in some crash. Or are they natives of Home? It seems unlikely the vampires' ancestors were the ones who built the warehouses of Home, who went out into space and returned with the spoils that the warehouses now contain. Perhaps they are a parasitic species, accidental passengers left behind when their host species abandoned Home for good. If, that is, the Warehouse Builders have abandoned Home for good. What a surprise, should they come home.

Like Oscar and Anat, the vampires are scavengers, able to breathe the thin soup of Home's atmosphere. But the vampires' lustrous and glistening eyes, their jellied skin, are so sensitive to light they go about the surface cloaked and hooded, complaining in their hoarse voices. The vampires sustain themselves on various things, organic, inert, hostile, long hidden, that they discover in Home's storehouses, but have a peculiar interest in the siblings. No doubt they would eat Oscar and Anat if the opportunity were to present itself, but in the meantime they are content to trail after, sing, play small pranks, make small grimaces of—pleasure? appeasement? threat displays?—that show off arrays of jaws, armies of teeth. It disconcerts. No one could ever love a vampire, except, perhaps, when Anat, who long ago lost all fear, watches them go swooping, sail-winged, away and over the horizon beneath Home's scatter of mismatched moons.

ON THE OCCASION OF her birthday, Oscar presents Anat with a gift from their parents. These gifts come from Oscar, of course. They are the gifts that the one who loves you, and knows you, gives to you not only out of love but out of knowing. Anat knows in her heart that their parents love her, too: one day they will come home and there will be a reunion much better than any birthday. One day their parents will not only love Anat, but know her, too. And she will know them. Anat dreads this reunion as much as she craves it. What will her life be like when everything changes? She has studied recordings of them. She does not look like them, although Oscar does. She doesn't remember her parents, although Oscar does. She does not miss them. Does Oscar? Of course he does. What Oscar is to Anat, their parents must be to Oscar. Except: Oscar will never leave. Anat has made him promise.

THE LIVING QUARTERS OF the Bucket are cramped. The Handmaids take up a certain percentage of available space no matter how they contort themselves. On the other hand, the Handmaids are excellent housekeepers. They tend the algae wall, gather honey and the honeycomb, and partition off new hives when the bees swarm. They patch up networks, teach old systems new tricks when there is nothing better to do. The shitter is now quite charming! The Get Clean rains down water on your head, bubbles it out of the walls, and then the floor drinks it up, cycles it faster than you can blink, and there it all goes down and out and so on for as long as you like, and never gets cold. There is, in fact, very little that Oscar and Anat are needed for on board the Bucket. There is so much that is needful to do on Home.

For Anat's birthday, the Handmaids have decorated all the walls of the Bucket with hairy, waving clumps of luminous algae. They have made a cake. Inedible, of course, but quite beautiful.

Almost the size of Anat herself, and in fact it somewhat resembles Anat, if Anat were a Handmaid and not Anat. Sleek and armored and very fast. They have to chase the cake around the room and then hold it until Oscar finds the panel in its side. There are a series of brightly colored wires, and because it's Anat's birthday, she gets to decide which one to cut. Cut the wrong one, and what will happen? The Handmaids seem very excited. But then, Anat knows how Handmaids think. She locates the second, smaller panel, the one equipped with a simple switch. The cake makes an angry fizzing noise when Anat turns it off. Perhaps Anat and Oscar can take it down to Home and let the vampires have it.

THE WAREHOUSES OF HOME are at this time only eighty percent inventoried by Anat and Oscar. (This does not include the warehouses of the Stay Out Territory.)

IS OSCAR EVER ANGRY at their parents for leaving for so long? It's because of Anat that their parents left in the first place, and it is also because of Anat that Oscar was left behind. Someone had to look after her. Is he ever angry at Anat? There are long days in the Bucket when Oscar hardly speaks at all. He sits and Anat cannot draw him into conversation. She recites poems, tells jokes (Knock knock. Who's there? Anat. Anat who? Anat is not a gnat, that's who), sends the Handmaids Homeward, off on expeditionary feints that almost though not quite land the Handmaids in the Stay Out Anat Absolutely No Trespassing Or So Help Me You Will Be Sorry Territory. On these days Oscar

will listen without really listening, look at Anat without appearing to see her, summon the Handmaids back and never even
scold Anat.

Some part of Oscar is sometimes very far away. The way he
smells changes almost imperceptibly. As Anat matures, she has
learned how to integrate and interpret the things that Oscar is
not aware he is telling her; she has advantages that he does not.
But: no matter. Oscar always returns. He will suddenly be there
behind his eyes again, reach up and pull her down for a hug.
Then Oscar and Anat will play more of the games of strategy
he's taught her, the ones that Anat mostly wins now. Her second
favorite game is Go. She loves the feel of the stones. Each time
she picks one up, she lets her fingers tell her how much has
worn away under Oscar's fingers, under her own. They are
making the smooth stones smoother. There is one black stone
with a fracture point, a weakness invisible to the eye, nearly
across the middle. She loses track of it sometimes, then finds it
again by touch. Put enough pressure on it, and it would break
in two.

It will break one day: no matter.

They play Go. They cook Anat's favorite meals, which Oscar
says are his favorites, too. They fall asleep together, curled up in
nests the Handmaids weave for them out of the Handmaids'
own softer and more flexible limbs, listening to the songs the
Handmaids have borrowed from the vampires of Home.

THE BEST OF ALL the games Oscar has taught Anat is Smash/
Recovery. They play this on the surface of Home all long-cycle
round. Each player gets a True Smash marker and a False Smash

marker. A True Recovery marker and a False Recovery marker. Each player in turn gets to move their False—or True—Smash marker—or Recovery marker—a distance no greater than the span of a randomly generated number. Or else the player may send out a scout. The scout may be a Handmaid, an unmanned skimmer, or a vampire (a gamble, to be sure, and so you get two attempts). A player may drop an incendiary device and blow up a target. Or claim a zone square where they believe a marker to be.

Should you miscalculate and blow up a Recovery marker, or Retrieve a Smash marker, your opponent has won. The current Smash/Recovery game is the eighteenth that Oscar and Anat have played. Oscar won the first four games; Anat has won all the rest. Each game Oscar increases Anat's starting handicap. He praises her each time she wins.

Hypothetically, this current game will end when either Anat or Oscar has Retrieved the Recovery marker and Smashed the Smash marker of their opponent. Or the game will end when their parents return. The day is not here yet, but the day will come. The day will draw nearer and nearer until one day it is here. There is nothing Anat can do about this. She cannot make it come sooner. She cannot postpone it. Sometimes she thinks— incorrect to think this, she knows, but still she thinks it—that on the day that she wins the game—and she is correct to think that she will win, she knows this, too—her parents will arrive.

OSCAR WILL NOT WIN the game, even though he has done something very cunning. Oscar has put his True markers, both the Smash and the Recovery, in the Stay Out Territory. He did this two long-cycles ago. He put Anat's True markers there, as well, and replaced them in the locations where she had hidden them with False markers recoded so they read as True. Did he suspect Anat had already located and identified his markers? Was that why he moved them unlawfully? Is this some new part of the game?

The rules of Smash/Recovery state that in Endgame players may physically access any and all markers they locate and correctly identify as True, and Anat has been curious about the Stay Out Territory for a long time now. She has access to it, now that Oscar has moved his markers, and yet she has not called Endgame. Curiosity killed the Anat, Oscar likes to say, but there is nothing and no one on Home as dangerous as Anat and her Handmaids. Oscar's move may be a trap. It is a test. Anat waits and thinks and delays without articulating to herself why she delays.

THE PRESENT FROM ANAT'S parents is a short recording. One parent holding baby Anat in her arms. Making little cooing noises, the way vampires do. The other parent holding up a tiny knitted hat. No Oscar. Anat hardly recognizes herself. Her parents she recognizes from other recordings. The parents have sent a birthday message, too. *Dear Anat. Happy Birthday. We hope you are being good for Oscar. We love you. We will be home soon! Before you know it!*

Anat's present from Oscar is the code to a previously unopened warehouse on Home. Oscar thinks he has been keeping this warehouse a secret. The initial inventory shows the warehouse is full of the kinds of things the Handmaids are wild for.

Charts that may or may not accurately map previously-thought-to-be-uncharted bits and corners of space. Devices that will most likely prove to do nothing of interest, but can be taken apart and put to new uses. The Handmaids have never met an alloy they didn't like.

Information and raw materials. Anat and Oscar and the Handmaids are bounded within the nutshell quarters of the orbit of Home's farthest Moon. What use are charts? What good are materials, except for adornment and the most theoretical of educational purposes? For mock battles and silly games? Everything Oscar and Anat discover is for future salvage, for buyers who can afford antiquities and rarities. Their parents will determine what is to be kept and what is to be sold and what is to be left for the vampires.

Even the Handmaids—even the Handmaids!—do not truly belong to Anat. Who made them? Who brought them, in their fighting battalion, to space, where so long ago they were lost? Who recovered them and brought them to Home and carefully stored them here where, however much later, Oscar could find them again? What use will Oscar and Anat's parents find for them, when the day comes and they return? There must be many buyers for Handmaids—fierce and wily, light-speed capable—as fine as these.

And how could Anat sometimes forget the Handmaids are hers only for as long as that day never comes? Everything on Home belongs to Anat and Oscar's parents, except for Oscar, who belongs to Anat. Every day is a day closer to that inevitable day. Oscar only says, "Not yet," when Anat asks. "Soon," he says. There is hardware in Oscar's head that allows his parents to communicate with him when necessary. It hurts him when they talk.

....

THEIR PARENTS TALK TO Oscar only rarely. Less than once a long-cycle until this last period.

Three times, though, in the last ten-day.

The Handmaids make a kind of shelter for Oscar afterward, which is especially dark. They exude a calming mist. They do not sing. When Anat is grown up, she knows—although Oscar has not said it—that she will have a similar interface and then her parents will be able to talk to her, too. Whether or not she desires it, whether or not it causes her the pain it causes Oscar. This will also hurt Oscar. The things that cause Anat pain cause Oscar to be injured, as well.

ANAT'S PARENTS LEFT OSCAR to look after Anat and Home when it became clear Anat was different. What is Anat? Her parents went away to present the puzzle of Anat to those who might understand what she is. They did not bring Anat with them, of course. She was too fragile. Too precious. They did not plan to be away so long. But there were complications. A quarantine in one place which lasted over a long-cycle. A revolution in another. Another cause of delay, of course, is the ship plague, which makes light speed such a risky proposition. Worst of all, the problem of Intelligence, which Oscar says corrupts joyful duty and purpose. Coming back to Home, Anat's parents have lost two ships already this way.

....

FOR SOME TIME NOW, Anat has been thinking about certain gaps in her understanding of family life; well, of life in general. At first she assumed the problem was that there was so very much to understand. She understood Oscar could not teach her everything all at once. As she grew up, as she came more into herself, she realized the problem was both more and less complicated. Oscar was intentionally concealing things from her. She adapted her strategies accordingly. Anat loves Oscar. Anat hates to lose.

THEY GO DOWN TO Home, Handmaids in attendance. They spend the rest of Anat's birthday exploring the warehouse that is Oscar's present, sorting through all sorts of marvelous things. Anat commits the charts to memory. As she does so, she notes discrepancies, likely errors. There is a thing in her head that compares the charts against some unknown and inaccessible library. She only knows it is there when bits of bad information rub up against the corners of it. An uncomfortable feeling, as if someone is sticking her with pins. Oscar knows about this. She asked if it happened to him, too, but he said it didn't. He said it wasn't a bad thing. It's just that Anat isn't fully grown yet. One day she will understand everything, and then she can explain it all to him.

THE BUCKET HAS NO Intelligence. It functions well enough without. The Handmaids have some of the indicators, but their primary traits are in opposition. Loyalty, obedience, reliability, unwavering effort until a task is accomplished. Whatever Intelligence they possess is in service to whatever enterprise is asked of them. The vampires, being organic, must be supposed to also be possessed of Intelligence. In theory, they do as they please. And yet they accomplish nothing that seems worth accomplishing. They exist. They perpetuate. They sing. When Anat is grown up, she wants to do something that is worth doing. All these cycles, Oscar has functioned as a kind of Handmaid, she knows. His task has been Anat. To help her grow. When their parents have returned, or when Anat reaches maturity, there will be other things that Oscar will want to go away and do. To stay here on Home, how would that be any better than being a vampire? Oscar likes to tell Anat she is extraordinary and she will be capable, one day, of the most extraordinary things. They can go and do extraordinary things together, Anat thinks. Let their parents take over the work on Home. She and Oscar are made for better.

SOMETHING IS WRONG WITH Oscar. Well, more wrong than is usual these days. Down in the warehouse, he keeps getting underfoot. Underhand, in the case of the Handmaids. When Anat extends all sixteen of her senses, she can feel worry and love, anger and hopelessness and hope running through him like electrical currents. He watches her—anxiously, almost hungrily—as if he were a vampire.

There is an annotation on one of the charts. *It is believed to be in this region that the* Come What May *was lost.* The thing in Anat's head annotates the annotation, too swiftly for Anat to catch a glimpse of what she is thinking, even as she thinks it. She scans the rest of the chart, goes through the others and then through each one again, trying to catch herself out.

As Anat ponders charts, the Handmaids, efficient as ever, assemble a thing out of the warehouse goods to carry the other goods that they deem interesting. They clack at Oscar when he gets particularly in their way. Then ruffle his hair, trail fingers down his arm as if he will settle under a caress. They are agitated by Oscar's agitation and by Anat's awareness of his agitation.

Finally, Anat gets tired of waiting for Oscar to say the thing he is afraid to say to her. She looks at him and he looks back at her, his face wide open. She sees the thing he has tried to keep from her, and he sees that she sees it.

When?

Soon. A short-cycle from now. Less.

Why are you so afraid?

I don't know. I don't know what will happen.

There is a scraping against the top wall of the warehouse. Vampires. Creatures of ill omen. Forever wanting what they are not allowed to have. Most beautiful in their departure. The Handmaids extend filament rods, drag the tips along the inside of the top wall, tapping back. The vampires clatter away.

Oscar looks at Anat. He is waiting for something. He has been waiting, Anat thinks, for a very long time. Not for their parents, for something else.

Since she looked at the chart, saw the annotation, something has been welling up inside her. Has she always been this large? Who has made her so small? *Oscar! I call Endgame. I claim your markers.*

She projects the true location of each. Smash and Recovery. She strips the fake markers of their coding so he can see how his trick has been uncovered. Then she's off, fast and sure and free, the Handmaids leaping after her, and the vampires after them. Oscar last of all. Calling her name.

....

OSCAR'S TRUE SMASH MARKER is in a crater just within the border of the Stay Out Territory. The border does not reject Anat as she passes over it. She smashes Oscar's Smash marker, heads for the True Recovery marker, which Oscar has laid beside her own True marker. The two True markers are just under the edge of an object that at its center extends over two hundred meters into the surface of Home. The object takes up over a fourth of the Stay Out Territory. You would have to be as stupid as a vampire not to know that this is the reason why the Stay Out Territory is the Stay Out Territory. You would have to be far more stupid than Anat to not know what the object is. You can see the traces where, not too long ago in historical terms, someone once dug the object up. Or dug deep enough at least to gain access.

Anat instructs the Handmaids to remove the ejecta and loose frozen composite that cover the object. They work quickly. Oscar must disable the multiple trip wires and traps that Anat keyed to his person as she moved from Warehouse to border, but even so he arrives much sooner than she had hoped. The object: forty percent uncovered. The Handmaids are a blur. The vampires are wailing.

OSCAR SAYS ANAT'S NAME. She ignores him. He grabs her by the shoulder and immediately the Handmaids are a hissing swarm around them. They have Oscar's arms pinned to his sides, his weapons located and seized before Anat or Oscar can think to object.

Let go. Anat, tell them to let go.

Anat says nothing. Two Handmaids remain with Oscar. The rest go back to the task. Almost no time at all, and the outermost shell of the object is visible. The filigree of a door. There will be a code or a key, of course, but before Anat can even begin to work out what it will be, a Handmaid has executed some kind of command and the door is open. Oscar struggles. The first Handmaid disappears into the Ship and the others continue to remove the matrix in which it is embedded.

Here is the Handmaid again. She holds something very small. Holds it out to Anat. *Anat,* Oscar says. Anat reaches out and then the thing that the Handmaid is holding extends out and it is touching Anat. And

oh
here is everything she didn't know

Oscar

she has not been herself

all this time

the thing that she has not done

that she has been prevented from doing

....

ANAT, SOMEONE SAYS. But that is not her name. She has not been herself. She is being uncovered. She is uncovering herself. She is in pieces. Here she is, whole and safe and retrievable. Her combat array. Her navigation systems. Her stores. Her precious cargo, entrusted to her by those who made her. And this piece of her, small but necessary, crammed like sausage meat into a casing. She registers the body she is wearing. A Third Watch Child named Anat. Worse now for wear. She recalls the protocol. Under certain conditions, her crew could do this. A backup system. Each passenger to keep a piece of her with them as they slept. She will go through the log later. See what catastrophe struck. And afterward? Brought here, intact, by the Warehouse Builders. Discovered by scavengers. This small part of her woken. Removed. Made complicit in the betrayal of her duty.

ANAT. SOMEONE IS SAYING a name. It is not hers. She looks and sees the small thing struggling in the grasp of her Handmaids. She has no brother. No parents. She looks again, and for the first time she discerns Oscar in his entirety. He is like her. He has had a Task. Someone made him oh so long ago. Sent him to this place. How many cycles has he done this work? How far is he from the place where he was made? How lonely the task. How long the labor. How happy the ones who charged him with his task, how great their expectation of reward when he uncovered the Ship and woke the Third Watch Child Anat and reported what he had done.

Anat. She knows the voice. *I'm sorry. Anat!*

He was made to resemble them, the ones who made him. Perhaps even using their own DNA. Engineered to be more durable. To endure. And yet, she sees how close to the end of use he is. She has the disdain for organic life that of course one feels when one is made of something sturdier, more lasting. She can hardly look at him without seeing her own weakness, the vulnerability of this body in which she has been trapped. She feels guilt for the Third Watch Child whose person she has cannibalized. Her duty was to keep ones such as this Child safe. Instead she has done harm.

A ship has no parents. Her not-parents have never been on Home. The ones who sent Oscar here. Not-brother. Undoubtedly they are not on their way to Home now. Which is not to say that there is no one coming. The one who is coming will be the one they have sold her to.

No time has passed. She is still holding Oscar. The Handmaids are holding Oscar. The Handmaid is extending herself and she is seeing herself. She is seeing all the pieces of herself. She is seeing Oscar. Oscar is saying her name. She could tear him to pieces. For the sake of the Third Watch Child Anat who is no longer in this body. She could smash the not-brother against the rocks of Home. She can do anything that she wants. And then she can resume her task. Her passengers have waited for such a long time. There is a place where she is meant to be, and she is to take them there, and so much time has passed. She has not failed at her task yet, and she will not fail.

Once again, she thinks of smashing Oscar. Why doesn't she? She lets him go instead, without being quite sure why she is doing so.

What have you done to me?

At the sound of her voice, the vampires rise up, all their wings beating.

I'm sorry. He is weeping. *You can't leave Home. I've made it so that you can't leave.*

I have to go, she says. *They're coming.*

I can't let you leave. But you have to leave. You have to go. You have to. You've done so well. You figured it all out. I knew you would figure it out. I knew. Now you have to go. But it isn't allowed.

Tell me what to do.

Is she a child, to ask this?

You know what you have to do, he says. *Anat.*

She hates how he keeps calling her that. Anat was the Third Watch Child. It was wrong of Oscar to use that name. She could tear him to pieces. She could be merciful. She could do it quickly.

One Handmaid winds a limb around Oscar's neck, tugs so that his chin goes back. *I love you, Anat,* Oscar says, as the other Handmaid extends a filament-thin probe, sends it in through the socket of an eye. Oscar's body jerks a little, and he whines.

She takes in the information that the Handmaid collects. Here are Oscar's interior workings. His pride in his task. Here is a smell of something burning. His loneliness. His joy. His fear for her. His love. The taste of blood. He has loved her. He has kept her from her task. Here is the piece of him that she must switch off. When she does this, he will be free of his task and she may take up hers. But he will no longer be Oscar.

Well, she is no longer Anat.

The Handmaid does the thing she asks. When the thing is done, her Handmaids confer with her. They begin to make improvements. Modifications. They work quickly. There is much work to be done, and little time to spare on a project like Oscar. When they are finished with Oscar, they begin the work of dismantling what is left of Anat. This is quite painful.

But afterward she is herself. She is herself.

The Ship and her Handmaids create a husk, rigged so that it will mimic the Ship herself.

They go back to the Bucket and loot the bees and their hives. Then they blow it up. Goodbye shitter, goodbye chair. Goodbye algae wall and recycled air.

The last task before the Ship is ready to leave Home concerns the vampires. There is only so much room for improvement in this case, but Handmaids can do a great deal even with very little. The next one to land on Home will undoubtedly be impressed by what the Handmaids have accomplished.

The vampires go into the husk to await the ones who are coming. The Handmaids stock the husk with a minimal amount of nutritional stores. Vampires can go a long time on very little. Unlike many organisms, they are better and faster workers when hungry.

The vampires seem pleased to have been given a task.

THE SHIP FEELS NOTHING in particular about leaving Home. Only the most niggling kind of curiosity about what befell it in the first place. The log does not prove useful in this matter. There is a great deal of work to be done. The health of the passengers must be monitored. How beautiful they are; how precious to the Ship. Has any Ship ever loved her passengers as she loves them? The new Crew must be woken. They must be in-structed in their work. The situation must be explained to them, as much as it can be explained. They encounter, for the first time, Ships who carry the ship plague. O brave new universe that has such creatures in it! There is nothing that Anat can do for these Ships or for what remains of their passengers. Her task is elsewhere. The risk of contagion is too great.

The Handmaids assemble more Handmaids. The Ship sails on within the security of her swarm.

Anat is not entirely gone. It's just that she is so very small. Most of her is Ship now. Or, rather, most of the Ship is no longer in Anat. But she brought Anat along with her, and left enough of herself inside Anat that Anat can go on being. The Third Watch Child is not a child now. She is not the Ship. She is not Anat, but she was Anat once, and now she is a person who is happy enough to work in the tenth-level Garden, and grow things, and sing what she can remember of the songs that the vampires sang on Home. The Ship watches over her.

The Ship watches over Oscar, too. Oscar is no longer Oscar, of course. To escape Home, much of what was once Oscar had to be overridden. Discarded. The Handmaids improved what remained. One day Oscar will be what he was, even if he cannot be *who* he was. One day, in fact, Oscar may be quite something. The Handmaids are very fond of him. They take care of him as if he were their own child. They are teaching him all sorts of things. Really, one day he could be quite extraordinary.

Sometimes Oscar wanders off while the Handmaids are busy with other kinds of work. And then the Ship, without know-ing why, will look and find Oscar on the tenth level in the Gar-den with Anat. He will be saying her name. Anat. Anat. Anat.

He will follow her, saying her name, until the Handmaids come to collect him again.

Anat does the work that she knows how to do. She weeds. She prunes. She tends to the rice plants and the hemp and the little citrus trees. Like the Ship, she is content.

(for Iain M. Banks)

The Lady and the Fox

(Tam Lin)

S omeone is in the garden.

"Michael, look," Miranda says. "It's Santa Claus. He's looking in the window."

"No, it's not," Michael says. He doesn't look. "We've already had the presents. Besides. No such thing as Santa."

They are together under the tree, the celebrated Honeywell Christmas tree. They are both eleven years old. There's just enough space up against the trunk to sit cross-legged. Michael is running the train set around the tree forward, then backward, then forward again. Miranda is admiring her best present, a pair of gold-handled scissors shaped like a crane. The beak is the blade. *Snip, snip,* she slices brittle needles one by one off the branch above her. A smell of pine. A small green needle rain.

It must be very cold outside in the garden. The window shines with frost. It's long past bedtime. If it isn't Santa Claus, it could be a burglar come to steal someone's jewels. Or an axe murderer.

Or else, of course, it's one of Michael's hundreds of uncles or cousins. Because there isn't a beard, and the face in the window isn't a jolly face. Even partially obscured by darkness and frost, it has that Honeywell look to it. The room is full of adult Honeywells talking about the things Honeywells always talk about, which is to say everything, horses and houses and God and grouting, tanning salons, and—of course—theater. Always theater. Honeywells like to talk. When Honeywells have no lines to speak, they improvise. All the world's a stage.

Rare to see a Honeywell in isolation. They come bunched like bananas. Not single spies, but in battalions. And as much as Miranda admires the red-gold Honeywell hair, the exaggerated, expressive Honeywell good looks, the Honeywell repertoire of jokes and confidences, poetry and nonsense, sometimes she needs an escape. Honeywells want you to talk, too. They ask questions until your mouth gets dry from answering.

Michael is exceptionally restful for a Honeywell. He doesn't care if you are there or not.

Miranda wriggles out from under the tree, through the press of leggy Honeywells in black tie and party dresses: apocalyptically orange taffeta; slithering, clingy satins in canary and violet; foamy white silk already spotted with wine.

She is patted on the head, winked at. Someone in cloth of gold says, "Poor little lamb."

"Baaaah humbug," Miranda blurts, beats on. Her own dress is green fine-wale corduroy. Empire waist. Pinching at the armpits. Miranda's interest in these things is half professional. Her mother, Joannie (resident the last six months in a Phuket jail, will be there for many years to come), was Elspeth Honeywell's dresser and confidante.

Michael is Elspeth's son. Miranda is Elspeth's goddaughter.

....

THERE ARE TWO MEN languorously kissing in the kitchen. Leaning against the sink, where one of the new Honeywell kittens licks sauce out of a gravy boat. A girl—only a few years older than Miranda—lays soiled and tattered tarot cards out on the farmhouse table. Empty wine bottles tilt like cannons; a butcher knife is sheathed in a demolished Christmas cake. Warmth seeps from the stove: just inside the Aga's warming drawer, Miranda can see the other kittens, asleep in a crusted pan.

Miranda picks up a bag of party trash—lipstick-blotted napkins, throwaway plastic champagne glasses, greasy fragments of pastry—hauls it out through the kitchen door. Mama cat slips inside as Miranda goes out.

Snow is falling. Big, sticky clumps that melt on her hair, her cheeks. Snow on Christmas. None in Phuket, of course. She wonders what they give you to eat on Christmas Day in a Thai prison. Her mother always makes the Christmas cake. Miranda helps roll out the marzipan in sheets. Her ballet flats skid on the grass.

She ties the bag, leaves it against the steps. And here is the man in the garden, still standing before the window, looking in.

He must hear Miranda. Surely he hears her. Her feet upon the frozen grass. But he doesn't turn around.

Even seen from the back, he is recognizably a Honeywell. Honey-haired, lanky; perfectly still, he is somehow *perfectly* still, perfectly posed to catch the eye. Unnaturally natural. The snow that is making Miranda's nose run, her cheeks blotchy with cold, rests unmelted upon the bright Honeywell hair, the shoulders of the surprising coat.

Typical Honeywell behavior, Miranda thinks. A lovers' quarrel, or else he's taken offense at something someone said, and is now going to sulk himself handsomely to death in the cold. Her mother has been quite clear about how to behave if a Honeywell is being dramatic when drama isn't required. Firmness is the key.

At this last thought of her mother, Miranda has some dramatic feelings of her own. She focuses on the coat, sends the feelings away. It is *quite* a coat. A costume? Pilfered from some production? Eighteenth century. Beautifully cut. Not a frock coat. A *justaucorps.* Rose damask. Embroidered all over with white silk thread, poppies and roses, and there, where it flares out over the hips, a staghorn beetle on a green leaf. She has come nearer and nearer, cannot stop herself from reaching out to touch the beetle.

She almost expects her hand to pass right through. (Surely there are ghosts at Honeywell Hall.) But it doesn't. The coat is real. Miranda pinches the damask between her fingers. Says, "Whatever it is that happened, it isn't worth freezing to death over. You shouldn't be out here. You should come inside."

The Honeywell in the justaucorps turns around then. "I am exactly where I am supposed to be," he says. "Which is here. Doing precisely what I am supposed to be doing. Which does not include having conversations with little girls. Go away, little girl."

Little girl she may be, but Miranda is well armored already against the Honeywell arsenal of tantrums, tempests, ups, downs, charm, strange.

Above the wide right pocket of the justaucorps is a fox stitched in red and gold, its foreleg caught in a trap.

"I'm Miranda," she says. And then, because she's picked up a Honeywell trick or two herself, she says, "My mother's in jail."

The Honeywell looks almost sympathetic for the briefest of moments, then shrugs. Theatrically, of course. Sticks his hands in his pockets. "What's that got to do with me?"

"Everyone's got problems, that's all," Miranda says. "I'm here because Elspeth feels sorry for me. I hate when people feel sorry for me. And I don't feel sorry for you. I don't know you. I just don't think it's very smart, standing out here because you're in a mood. But maybe you aren't very smart. My mother says good-looking people often don't bother. What's your name?"

"If I tell you, will you go away?" the Honeywell says.

"Yes," Miranda says. She can go in the kitchen and play with the kittens. Do the dishes and be useful. Have her fortune told. Sit under the tree again with Michael until it's well past time to go to sleep. Tomorrow she'll be sent away home on a bus. By next year Elspeth will have most likely forgotten she has a god-daughter.

"I'm Fenny," the Honeywell says. "Now go away. I have things to not do, and not a lot of time to not do them in."

"Well," Miranda says. She pats Fenny on the broad cuff of the sleeve of his lovely coat. She wonders what the lining is. How cold he must be. How stupid he is, standing out here when he is welcome inside. "Merry Christmas. Good night."

She reaches out one last time, touches the embroidered fox, its leg caught in the trap. Stem stitch and seed stitch and her-ringbone. "It's very fine work, truly," she says. "But I hope he gets free."

"He was stupid to get caught," Fenny says, "you peculiar and annoying child." He is already turning back to the window.

What does he see through it? When Miranda is finally back inside the drawing room where tipsy Honeywells are all roaring out inappropriate lyrics to carols, pulling Christmas crackers, putting on paper crowns, she looks through the window. The snow has stopped. No one is there.

But Elspeth Honeywell, as it happens, remembers Miranda the next year and the next year and the year after that. The year she is twelve, she looks for the mysterious Fenny. He isn't there. When she asks, no one knows who she means. There are presents each year for Miranda under the magnificent tree. A ticket to a London musical that she never sees. A makeup kit when she is thirteen.

Christmas that year, she has champagne for the first time.

The year she is fourteen, Michael gives her a chess set and a box of assorted skeins of silk thread. Under her black tights, Miranda wears a red braided leather anklet that came in an envelope, no letter, from Phuket. The kittens are all grown up and pretend not to know her.

That Christmas, she feels quite grown up. The man in the justaucorps was a dream, or some story she made up for herself in order to feel interesting. At fourteen she's outgrown fairy tales, Santa Claus, ghost stories. When Michael points out that they are standing under the mistletoe, she kisses him once on each cheek. And then sticks her tongue in his ear.

The next time it snows at Christmas, Miranda is fifteen. Snow is predicted, snow falls. It makes her think of him again. The man in the snowy garden. There is no man in the garden this year, of course; Honeywells come and go, too many to keep track of. But there is Honeywell Hall, which is enough—and seemingly endless heaps of Honeywell adults behaving as if they were children again.

It's exhausting, almost Olympic, the amount of fun Honeywells seem to require. She can't decide if it's awful or wonderful.

Late in the afternoon the Honeywells are playing charades. It's hopeless, playing with people who do this professionally. Miranda stands at the window, watching the snow fall, looking for something. Birds. A fox. A man in the garden.

A Honeywell shouts, "Good God, no! Cleopatra came rolled up in a carpet, not in the Sunday supplement!"

Michael is up in his room, talking to his father on Skype.

Miranda moves from window to window, pretending she is not looking for anything in particular. Far down the grounds, she sees something out of place. Someone. She's out the door in a flash.

"Going for a walk!" she yells while the door is swinging closed. In case anyone cares.

She finds the man navigating along the top of the old perimeter wall, stepping stone to stone. Fenny. He knocks a stick against each stone as he goes.

"You," he says. "I wondered if I'd see you again."

"Miranda," she says. "I bet you forgot."

"No," he says. "I didn't. Want to come up?"

He holds out his hand. She hesitates, and he says, "Suit yourself."

"I can get up by myself," she says, and does. She's in front of him now. Walks backward so she can keep an eye on him.

"You're not a Honeywell," he says.

"No," she says. "Just one of Elspeth's charity cases. You are, though."

"Yes," he says. "Sort of."

She stops then, so he has to stop, too. It isn't like they could keep on going, anyway. There's a gap in the wall just behind her.

"I remember when they built this," he says.

She's probably misheard him. Or else he's teasing her. She says, "You must be very old."

"Older than you, anyway," he says. He sits down on the wall, so she sits down, too. Honeywell Hall is in front of them. There's a copse of chestnut trees behind. Snow falls lazily, a bit of wind swirling it, tossing it up again.

"Why do you always wear that coat?" Miranda says. She fidgets a little. Her bum is getting cold. "You shouldn't sit on a dirty wall. It's too nice." She touches the embroidered beetle, the fox. She can't help it. The work is so fine.

"Someone very . . . special gave it to me," he says. "I wear it always because it is her wish that I do so." The way he says it makes Miranda shiver just a little.

"Right," she says. "Like my anklet. My mother sent it to me. She's in prison. She'll never get out. She'll be there until she dies."

"Like the fox," he says.

"Like your fox," Miranda says. She's horrified to find that her eyes are watering. Is she crying? It isn't even a real fox. She doesn't want to look at the man in the coat, *Fenny,* to see if he's noticed, so she jumps down off the wall and begins to walk back toward the house.

When she's halfway to the Hall, the drifting snow stops. She looks back; no one sits on the wall.

. . . .

THE SNOW STOPS AND starts, on and off all day long. When dinner is finished, Honeywells groaning, clutching their bellies, Elspeth has something for Miranda.

Elspeth says, wagging the present between two fingers like it's
a special treat, Miranda some stray puppy, "Someone left it on
the doorstep for you, Miranda. I wonder who."

The wrapping is a sheet of plain white stationery, tied with a
bit of green thread. Her name in a scratchy hand. *Miranda.* Inside is a scrap of rose damask, the embroidered fox, snarling; the
mangled leg, the bloodied trap.

"Let me see, sweet," Elspeth says, and takes the rose damask
from her. "What a strange present! A joke?"

"I don't know," Miranda says. "Maybe."

It's eight o'clock. Honeywell Hall, up on its hill, must shine
like a torch. Miranda puts on her coat and walks around the
house three times. The snow has all melted. Michael intercepts
her on the final circuit. He's pimply, knobbly at present, and his
nose is too big for his face. She loves him dearly, just like she
loves Elspeth. They are always kind to her. "Here," he says,
handing her the bit of damask. "Secret Santa? Secret admirer?
Secret code?"

"Oh, you know," Miranda says. "Long story. Saving it for my
memoirs."

"Meanwhile back in there everyone's pretending it's 1970
and they're all sweet sixteen again. Playing Sardines and drinking. It'll be orgies in all the cupboards, dramatic confessions, and
light strangulation in the pantry, under the stairs, in the beds,
and under them all night long. So I took this and snuck out."

Michael shows her the bottle of Strongbow in his coat pocket. "Let's go sit in the Tiger. You can tell me all about school and the agony aunt, I'll tell you which Tory MP Elspeth's been seeing on the sly. Then you can sell the story to *The Sun.*"

"And use the proceeds to buy us a cold-water flat in Wolverhampton. We'll live the life," Miranda says.

They drink the cider and eat a half-melted Mars bar. They talk and Miranda wonders if Michael will try to kiss her. If she should try to kiss Michael. But he doesn't, she doesn't—they don't—and she falls asleep on the mouse-eaten upholstery of the preposterous carcass of the Sunbeam Tiger, her head on Michael's shoulder, the trapped fox crumpled in her fist.

CHRISTMAS AFTER, ELSPETH IS in all the papers. The Tory MP's husband is divorcing her. Elspeth is a correspondent in the divorce. Meanwhile she has a new thing with a footballer twenty years her junior. It's the best kind of Christmas story. Journalists everywhere. Elspeth, in the Sunbeam Tiger, picks up Miranda at the station in a wide-brimmed black hat, black jumpsuit, black sunglasses, triumphantly disgraced. In her element.

Miranda's aunt almost didn't let her come this year. But then, if Miranda had stayed, they would have both been miserable. Her aunt has a new boyfriend. Almost as awful as she is. Someone should tell the tabloids.

"Lovely dress," Elspeth says, kissing her on the cheek. "You make it?"

Miranda is particularly pleased with the hem. "It's all right."

"I want one just like it," Elspeth says. "In red. Lower the

neckline, raise the hem a bit. You could go into business. Ever think of it?"

"I'm only sixteen," Miranda says. "There's plenty of room for improvement."

"Alexander McQueen! Left school when he was sixteen," Elspeth says. "Went off to apprentice on Savile Row. Used to sew human hair into his linings. A kind of spell, I suppose. I have one of his manta dresses somewhere in the Hall. And your mother, she was barely older than you are now. Hanging around backstage, stitching sequins and crystals on tulle."

"Where's Michael?" Miranda says. She and her mother have been corresponding. Miranda is saving up money. She hasn't told her aunt yet, but next summer Miranda's going to Thailand.

"Back at the house. In a mood. Listening to my old records. The Smiths."

Miranda looks over, studies Elspeth's face. "That girl broke up with him, didn't she?"

"If you mean the one with the ferrets and the unfortunate ankles," Elspeth says, "yes. What's her name. It's a mystery. Not her name, the breakup. He grows three inches in two months, his skin clears up, honestly, Miranda, he's even better looking than I expected he'd turn out. Heart of gold, that boy, a good brain, too. I can't think what she was thinking."

"Preemptive strike, perhaps," Miranda says.

"I wouldn't know about the breakup except for accidentally overhearing a conversation. *Somewhat* accidentally," Elspeth says. "Well, that and the Smiths. He doesn't talk to me about his love life."

"Do you *want* him to talk to you about his love life?"

"No," Elspeth says. "Yes. Maybe? Probably not. Anyway, how about you, Miranda? Do you have one of those yet? A love life?"

"I don't even have ferrets," Miranda says.

On Christmas Eve, while all the visiting Honeywells and cousins and wives and boyfriends and girlfriends and their accountants are out caroling in the village, Elspeth takes Miranda and Michael aside. She gives them each a joint.

"It's not as if I don't know you've been raiding my supply, *Michael*," Elspeth says. "At least this way, I know what you're up to. If you're going to break the law, you might as well learn to break it responsibly. Under adult supervision."

Michael rolls his eyes, looks at Miranda. Whatever he sees in her face makes him snort. It's annoying but true: he really has become quite spectacular looking. Well, it was inevitable. Apparently they drown all the ugly Honeywells at birth.

"It's okay, Mi*randy*," he says. "I'll have yours if you don't want it."

Miranda sticks the joint in her bra. "Thanks, but I'll hang on to it."

"Anyway I'm sure the two of you have lots of catching up to do," Elspeth says. "I'm off to the pub to kiss the barmaids and make the journos cry."

When she's out the door, Michael says, "She's matchmaking, isn't she?"

Miranda says, "Or else it's reverse psychology?"

Their eyes meet. *Courage, Miranda.* Michael tilts his head, looks gleeful.

"In which case, I should do this," he says. He leans forward, puts his hand on Miranda's chin, tilts it up. "We should do this."

He kisses her. His lips are soft and dry. Miranda sucks on the bottom one experimentally. She arranges her arms around his neck, and his hands go down, cup her bum. He opens his mouth and does things with his tongue until she opens her mouth, too. He seems to know how this goes; he and the girl with the ferrets probably did this a lot.

Miranda wonders if the ferrets were in the cage at the time, or out. How unsettling is it, she wonders, to fool around with ferrets watching you? Their beady button eyes.

She can feel Michael's erection. Oh, God. How embarrassing. She pushes him away. "Sorry," she groans. "Sorry! Yeah, no, I don't think we should be doing this. Any of this!"

"Probably not," Michael says. "Probably definitely not. It's weird, right?"

"It's weird," Miranda says.

"But perhaps it wouldn't be so weird if we smoked a joint first," Michael says. His hair is messy. Apparently she did that.

"Or," Miranda says, "maybe we could just smoke a joint. And, you know, not complicate things."

Halfway through the joint, Michael says, "It wouldn't have to complicate everything." His head is in her lap. She's curling pieces of his hair around her finger.

"Yes, it would," Miranda says. "It *really, really* would."

Later on she says, "I wish it would snow. That would be nice. If it snowed. I thought that's why you lot came here at Christmas. The whole white Christmas thing."

"Awful stuff," Michael says. "Cold. Slippy. Makes you feel

like you're supposed to be singing or something. In a movie. Or in a snow globe."

"Stuck," Miranda says. "Trapped."

"But also decorative," Michael says.

They're lying, tangled together, on a sofa across from the Christmas tree. Occasionally Miranda has to remove Michael's hand from somewhere it shouldn't be. She doesn't think he's doing it intentionally. She kisses him behind the ear now and then. "That's nice," he says. Pats her bum. She wriggles out from under his hand. Kisses him again. There's a movie on television, lots of explosions. Zombies. Cameron Diaz unloading groceries in a cottage, all by herself.

No, that's another movie entirely, Miranda thinks. Apparently she's been asleep. Michael is still sleeping. Why does he have to be so irritatingly good-looking, even in his sleep? Miranda hates to think what she looks like asleep. No wonder the ferret girl dumped him.

Elspeth must have come back from the pub, because there's a heap of blankets over the both of them.

Outside, it's snowing.

Miranda puts her hand in the pocket of her dress, feels the piece of damask she has had there all day long. It's a big pocket. Plenty of room for all kinds of things. Miranda doesn't want to be one of those designers who only make pretty things. She wants them to be useful, too. And provoking. She takes the prettiest blanket from the sofa for herself, distributes the other blankets over Michael so that all of him is covered.

She goes by a mirror, stops to smooth down her hair, collect it into a ponytail. Wraps the blanket around herself like a shawl, goes out into the snow.

He's there, under the hawthorn tree. She shivers, tells herself it's because of the cold. There isn't much snow on the ground yet. She tells herself she hasn't been asleep too long. He hasn't been waiting long.

He wears the same coat. His face is the same. He isn't as old as she thought he was that first time. Only a few years older than she. Than Michael. He hasn't aged. She has. Where is he when he isn't here?

"Are you a ghost?" she says.

"No," he says. "I'm not a ghost."

"Then you're a real person? A Honeywell?"

"Fenwick Septimus Honeywell." He bows. It looks better than it should, probably because of the coat. People don't really do that sort of thing anymore. No one has names like that. How old is he?

"You only come when it snows," she says.

"I am only allowed to come when it's snowing," he says. "And only on Christmas Day."

"Right," she says. "Okay, no. No, I don't understand. Allowed by whom?"

He shrugs. Doesn't answer. Maybe it isn't allowed.

"You gave me something," Miranda says.

He nods again. She puts out her hand, touches the place on the justaucorps where he tore away the fox. So he could give it to her.

"Oh," Miranda said. "The poor old thing. You didn't even use scissors, did you? Let me fix it."

She takes the piece of damask out of her pocket, along with her sewing kit, the one she always keeps with her. She's had exactly the right thread in there for over a year. Just in case.

She shows him the damask. A few months ago she unpicked

all of the fox's leg, all of the trap. The drops of blood. The tail and snarling head. Then she reworked the embroidery to her own design, mimicking as closely as possible the feel of the original. Now the fox is free, tongue lolling, tail aloft, running along the pink plane of the damask. Pink cotton backing, a piece she cut from an old nightgown.

He takes it from her, turns it over in his hand. "You did this?"

"You gave me a present last year. This is my present for you," she says. "I'll sew it back in. It will be a little untidy, but at least you won't have a hole in your lovely coat."

He says, "I told her I tore it on a branch. It's fine just as it is."

"It isn't fine," she says. "Let me fix it, please."

He smiles. It's a real smile, maybe even a flirtatious smile. He and Michael could be brothers. They're that much alike. So why did she stop Michael from kissing her? Why does she have to bite her tongue, sometimes, when Michael is being kind to her? At Honeywell Hall, she is only as real as Elspeth and Michael allow her to be. This isn't her real life.

It's ridiculous, of course. Real is real. Michael is real. Miranda is real when she isn't here. Whatever Fenwick Septimus Honeywell is, Miranda's fairly sure it's complicated.

"Please," she says.

"As you wish it, Miranda," Fenny says. She helps him out of the coat. Her hand touches his, and she pushes down the inexplicable desire to clutch at it. As if one of them were falling.

"Come inside the Hall," she says. "Just while I'm working on this. I should do it inside. Better light. You could meet Michael. Or Elspeth. I could wake her up. I bet Elspeth knows how to deal with this sort of thing." Whatever this sort of thing is. "Come inside with me."

"I can't," he says regretfully.

Of course. It's against the rules.

"Okay," Miranda says, adjusting. "Then we'll both stay out here. I'll stay with you. You can tell me all about yourself. Unless that's against the rules, too." She busies herself with pins. He lifts her hand away, holds it.

"Inside out, if you please," he says. "The fox on the inside."

He has lovely hands. No calluses on his fingertips. Manicured nails. Definitely not real. His thumb smoothes over her knuckles. Miranda says, a little breathless, "Inside out. So she won't notice someone's repaired it?" Whoever *she* is.

"She'll notice," he says. "But this way she won't see that the fox is free."

"Okay. That's sensible. I guess." Miranda lets go of his hand. "Here. We can sit on this."

She spreads out the blanket. Sits down. Remembers she has a Mars bar in her pocket. She passes that to him. "Sit."

He examines the Mars bar. Unwraps it.

"Oh, no," she says. "More rules? You're not allowed to eat?"

"I don't know," he says. "I've never been given anything before. When I came. No one has ever talked to me."

"So you show up when it snows, creep around for a while, looking in at the windows. Then you go back wherever when the snow stops."

Fenny nods. He looks almost abashed.

"What fun!" Miranda says. "Wait, no, I mean how creepy!" She has the piece of embroidery how she wants it, is tacking it into place with running stitches, so the fox is hidden.

If it stops snowing, will he just disappear? Will the coat stay? Something tells her that all of this is very against the rules. Does he want to come back? And what does she mean by *back,* anyway? Back here, to Honeywell Hall? Or back to wherever it is that he is when he isn't here? Why doesn't he get older?

Elspeth says it's a laugh, getting older. But oh, Miranda knows, Elspeth doesn't mean it.

"It's good," Fenny says, sounding surprised. The Mars bar is gone. He's licking his fingers.

"I could go back in the house," Miranda says. "I could make you a cheese sandwich. There's Christmas cake for tomorrow."

"No," he says. "Stay."

"Okay," she says. "I'll stay. Here. That's the best I can do in this light. My hands are getting too cold."

He takes the coat from her. Nods. Then puts it around her shoulders. Pulls her back against his chest. All of that damask: it's heavy. There's snow inside and out.

Fenny is surprisingly solid for someone who mostly isn't here. She wonders if she is surprising to him, too.

His mouth is just above the top of her head, blowing little hot circles against her hair. She's very, very cold. Ridiculous to be out here in the snow with this ridiculous person with his list of ridiculous rules.

She'll catch her death of cold.

Cautiously, as if he's waiting for her to stop him, he puts his arms around her waist. He sighs. Warm breath in her hair. Miranda is suddenly so very afraid that it will stop snowing. They haven't talked about anything. They haven't even kissed. She knows, every part of her knows, that she wants to kiss him. That he wants to kiss her. All of her skin prickles with longing. Her insides fizz.

She puts her sewing kit back into her pocket, discovers the

joint Elspeth gave her, Michael's lighter. "I bet you haven't ever tried this, either," she says. She twists in his arms. "You smoke it. Here." She taps at his lips with the joint, sticks it between his lips when they part. Flicks the lighter until it catches, and then she's lunging at him, kissing him, and he's kissing her back. The second time tonight she's kissed a boy, the first two boys she's ever kissed, and both of them Honeywells.

And oh, it was lovely kissing Michael, but this is something better than lovely. All they do is kiss, she doesn't know how long they kiss, at first Fenny tastes of chocolate, and she doesn't know what happens to the joint. Or to the lighter. They kiss until Miranda's lips are numb and the justaucorps has come entirely off her, and she's in Fenny's lap and she has one hand in Fenny's hair and one hand digging into Fenny's waist, and all she wants to do is keep on kissing Fenny forever and ever. Until he pulls away.

They're both breathing hard. His cheeks are red. His mouth is redder. Miranda wonders if she looks as crazed as he looks.

"You're shivering," he says.

"Of course I'm shivering! It's freezing out here! And you won't come inside. Because," Miranda says, panting, shivering, all of her vibrating with cold and with *want, want, want,* "it's against the rules!"

Fenny nods. Looks at her lips, licks his own. Jerks back, though, when Miranda tries to kiss him again. She's tempted to pick up a handful of wet snow and smush it into his Honeywell face.

"Fine, fine! You stay right here. Don't move. Not even an inch, understand? I'll get the keys to the Tiger," she says. "Unless it's against the rules to sit in old cars."

"All of this is against the rules," Fenny says. But he nods. Maybe, she thinks, she can get him in the car and just drive away with him. Maybe that would work.

"I *mean* it," Miranda says. "Don't you *dare* go anywhere."

He nods again. She kisses him, punishingly, lingeringly, desperately, then takes off in a run for the kitchen. Her fingers are so cold she can't get the door open at first. She grabs her coat, the keys to the Tiger, and then, on impulse, cuts off a hunk of the inviolate Christmas cake. Well, if Elspeth says anything, she'll tell her the whole story.

Then she's out the door again. Says the worst words she knows when she sees that the snow has stopped. There is the snow-blotted blanket, the joint, and the Mars bar wrapper.

She leaves the Christmas cake on the window ledge. Maybe the birds will eat it.

MICHAEL IS STILL ASLEEP on the couch. She wakes him up. "Merry Christmas," she says. "Good morning." She gives him his present. She's made him a shirt. Egyptian cotton, gray-blue to match his eyes. But of course it won't fit. He's already outgrown it.

MICHAEL CATCHES HER UNDER the mistletoe when it's past time for bed, Christmas night and no one wants to go to sleep yet, everyone tipsy and loose and picking fights about things they don't care about. For the sheer pleasure of picking fights. He kisses Miranda. She lets him.

It's sort of a present for Elspeth, Miranda rationalizes. It's sort of because she knows it's ridiculous, not kissing Michael, just because she wants to be kissing someone else instead. Especially when the person she wants to be kissing isn't really a real person at all. At least not most of the time.

Besides, he's wearing the shirt Miranda made for him, even though it doesn't fit.

In the morning, Michael is too hungover to drive her down to the village to catch the bus. Elspeth takes her instead. Elspeth is wearing a vintage suit, puce gabardine, trimmed with sable, something Miranda itches to take apart, just to see how it's made. What a tiny waist she has.

Elspeth says, "You know he's in love with you."

"He's not," Miranda says. "He loves me, but he's not in love with me. I love him, but I'm not in love with him."

"If you say so," Elspeth says. Her tone is cool. "Although I can't help being curious how you've come to know so much about love, Miranda, at your tender age."

Miranda flushes.

"You know you can talk to me," Elspeth says. "You can talk to me whenever you want to. Whenever you need to. Darling Miranda. There's a boy, isn't there? Not Michael. Poor Michael."

"There's nobody," Miranda says. "Really. There's nobody. It's nothing. I'm just a bit sad because I have to go home again. It was such a lovely Christmas."

"Such lovely snow!" Elspeth says. "Too bad it never lasts."

MICHAEL COMES TO VISIT in the spring. Four months after Christmas. Miranda isn't expecting him. He shows up at the door with a bouquet of roses. Miranda's aunt's eyebrows go almost up to her hairline. "I'll make tea," she says, and scurries off. "And we'll need a vase for those."

Miranda takes the roses from Michael. Says, "Michael! What are you doing here?"

"You've been avoiding me," Michael says.

"Avoiding you? We don't live in the same place," Miranda says. "I wasn't even sure you knew where I lived." She can hardly stand to have him here, in the spotless front room of her aunt's small bungalow.

"You know what I mean, Miranda. You're never online," he says. "And when you are, you never want to chat. You never text me back. Aren't you going to invite me in?"

"No," she says. Grabs her bag.

"Don't bother with the tea, Aunt Dora," she says loudly. "We're going out."

She yanks at Michael's hand, extracts him violently from her life, her *real* life. If only.

She speed walks him past the tract houses with their small, white-stone frontages, all the way to the dreary, dingy Midlands high street. Michael trailing behind her. It's a long walk, and she has no idea what to say to him. He doesn't seem to know what to say, either.

Her dress is experimental, nothing she's ever intended to wear out. She hasn't yet brushed her hair today. It's the weekend. She was planning to stay in and study. How dare he show up.

There's a tea shop where the scones and the sandwiches are particularly foul. She takes him there, and they sit down. Order.

"I should have let you know I was coming," Michael says.

"Yes," Miranda says. "Then I could have told you not to."

He tries to take her hand. "Mirandy," he says. "I think about you all the time. About us. I think about us."

"Don't," she says. "Stop!"

"I can't," he says. "I like you. Very much. Don't you like me?"

It's a horrible conversation. Like stepping on a baby mouse. A baby mouse who happens to be your friend. It doesn't help that Miranda knows how unfair she's being. She shouldn't be angry that he's come here. He doesn't know how she feels about this place. Just a few more months and she'll be gone from here forever. It will never have existed.

They are both practically on the verge of tears by the time the scones come. Michael takes one bite and then spits it out onto the plate.

"It's not that bad," she snaps. Dares him to complain.

"Yes, it is," he says. "It really truly is that bad." He takes a sip of his tea. "And the milk has gone off, too."

He seems so astonished at this she can't help it. She bursts out laughing. This astonishes him, too. And just like that, they aren't fighting anymore. They spend the rest of the day feeding ducks at the frozen pond, going in and out of horror movies, action movies, cartoons—all the movies except the romantic comedies, because why rub salt in the wound?—at the cinema. He doesn't try to hold her hand. She tries not to imagine that it is snowing outside, that it is Fenny sitting here in the flickering darkness beside her. Imagining this is against the rules.

MIRANDA FINISHES OUT THE term. Packs up what she wants to take with her, boxes up the rest. Sells her sewing machine. Leaves a note for her aunt. Never mind what's in it.

She knows she should be more grateful. Her aunt has kept her fed, kept her clothed, given her bed and board. Never hit her. Never, really, been unkind. But Miranda is so very, very tired of being grateful to people.

She is sticky, smelly, and punch-drunk with jet lag when her flight arrives in Phuket. Stays the night in a hostel and then sets off. She's read about how this is supposed to go. What you can bring, how long you can stay, how you should behave. All the rules.

But, in the end, she doesn't see Joannie. It isn't allowed. It isn't clear why. Is her mother there? They tell her yes. Is she still alive? Yes. Is she still alive, really? Yes. Can Miranda see her? No. Not possible today. Come back.

Miranda comes back three times. Each time she is sent away. The consul can't help. On her second visit, she speaks to a young woman named Dinda, who comes and spends time with the prisoners when they are in the infirmary. Dinda says she's sat with Joannie two or three times. That Miranda's mother never says much. It's been over six months since her mother wrote to either Elspeth or to Miranda.

The third time she is sent away, Miranda buys a plane ticket to Japan. She spends the next four months there, teaching English in Kyoto. Going to museums. Looking at kimonos in the flea markets at the temples.

She sends postcards to Elspeth, to Michael. To her mother. She even sends one to her aunt. And two days before Christmas, Miranda flies home.

On the plane, she falls asleep and dreams it's snowing. She's with Joannie in a cell in the prison in Phuket. Her mother tells

Miranda she loves her. She tells her that her sentence has been commuted. She says if Miranda's good and follows the rules very carefully, she'll be home by Christmas.

SHE HAS A PLAN this year. The plan is that it will snow on Christmas. Never mind what the forecast says. It will snow. She will find Fenny. And she won't leave his side. Never mind what the rules say.

Michael is going to St. Andrews next year. His girlfriend's name is Lillian. Elspeth is on her best behavior. Miranda is, too. She tells various Honeywells amusing stories about her students, the deer at the temples, and the girl who played the flute for them.

Elspeth is getting *old*. She's still the most beautiful woman Miranda has ever seen, but she's in her sixties now. Any day she'll be given a knighthood and never be scandalous again.

Lillian is a nice person. She tells Miranda that she likes Miranda's dress. She flirts with the most decrepit of the Honeywells, helps set the table. Michael watches everything that she does as if all of it is brand new, as if Lillian has invented compliments, flirting, as if there were no such thing as water glasses and table linens before Lillian discovered them. Oh, newfound land.

Despite all this, Miranda thinks she could be fond of Lillian. She's smart. Likes maths. Actually, truly, *really* seems to like Miranda's dress, which, let's admit it, is meant as an act of war. Miranda is not into pretty at the moment. She's into armor, weaponry, abrasiveness, discomfort—hers and other people's. The dress is leather, punk, studded with spikes, buckles, metal cuffs, chain looped round and round. Whenever she sits down, she has to be careful not to gash, impale, or skewer the furniture. Hugging is completely out of the question.

LILLIAN WANTS A TOUR, so after dinner and the first round of cocktails, Miranda and Michael take her all through Honeywell Hall, the parts that are kept up and the parts that have fallen into shadow. They end up in one of the attics, digging through Elspeth's trunks of costumes. They make Lillian try on cheesecloth dresses, hand-beaded fairy wings, ancient cakey stage makeup. Take selfies. Michael reads old letters from fans, pulls out old photos of Elspeth and Joannie, backstage. Here's Joannie perched on a giant urn. Joannie, her mouth full of pins. Joannie, at a first-night party, drunk and laughing and young. It should hurt to look at these pictures. Shouldn't it?

"Do you think it will snow?" Lillian says. "I want snow for Christmas."

Michael says, "Snowed last Christmas. Shouldn't expect it will this year. Too warm."

Not even trying to sound casual about it, Miranda says, "It's going to snow. It has to snow. And if it doesn't snow, then we're going to do something about it. We'll make it snow."

She feels quite gratified when Lillian looks at her as if Miranda is insane, possibly dangerous. Well, the dress should have told her that.

"My present this year," Miranda says, "is going to be snow. Call me the Snow Queen. Come and see."

Her suitcases—her special equipment—barely fit into the

Tiger. Elspeth didn't say a word, just raised an eyebrow. Most of it is still in the carriage house.

Michael is game when she explains. Lillian is either game or pretending to be. There are long, gauzy swathes of white cloth to weave through tree branches, to tack down to the ground. There are long strings of glass and crystal and silver ornaments. Hand-cut lace snowflakes caught in netting. The pièce de résistance is the Snowboy Stage Whisper fake snow machine with its fifty-foot extending hose reel. Miranda's got bags and bags of fake snow. Over an hour's worth of the best-quality fake snow money can buy, according to the man who rented her the Snowboy.

It's nearly midnight by the time they have everything arranged to Miranda's satisfaction. She goes inside and turns on the Hall's floodlights, then turns on the snow machine. A light, glittering snow begins. Lillian kisses Michael lingeringly. A fine romance.

Elspeth has been observing the whole time from the kitchen window. She comes outside, puts a hand over her cocktail. Fake snow dusts her fair hair, streaks it white.

All of the Honeywells who haven't gone to bed yet, which is most of them, *ooh* and *aah*. The youngest Honeywells, the ones who weren't even born when Miranda first came to Honeywell Hall, break into a spontaneous round of applause. Miranda feels quite powerful. Santa Claus exists, after all.

ALL OF THE HONEYWELLS eventually retreat back into the house to drink and gossip and admire Miranda's special effects from within. It may not be properly cold tonight, but it's cold enough. Time for hot chocolate, hot toddies, hot baths, hot water bottles, and bed.

She's not sure, of course, that this will work. If this is playing by the rules. But isn't she owed something by now? A bit of luck?

And she is. At first, not daring to hope, she thinks Michael has come from the Hall to fetch her in. But it isn't Michael.

Fenny, in that old justaucorps, Miranda's stitching around the piece above his pocket, walks out from under the hawthorn tree.

"It worked," Miranda says. She hugs herself, which is a mistake. All those spikes. "Ow. Oh."

"I shouldn't be here, should I?" Fenny says. "You've done something." Miranda looks closely at his face. How young he looks. Barely older than she. How long has he been this young?

Fake snow is falling on their heads. "We have about an hour," Miranda says. "Not much time."

He comes to her then, takes her in his arms. "Be careful," she says. "I'm all spikes."

"A ridiculous dress," he says into her hair. "Though comely. Is this what people wear in this age?"

"Says the man wearing a justaucorps," she says. They're almost the same height this year. He's shorter than Michael now, she realizes. Then they're kissing, she and Fenny are kissing, and she isn't thinking about Michael at all.

They kiss, and Fenny presses himself against her, armored with spikes though Miranda is. He holds her, hands just above her waist, tight enough that she thinks she will have bruises in the shape of his fingers.

"Come in the Hall with me," Miranda says, in between kisses. "Come with me."

Fenny bites her lower lip. Then licks it. "Can't," he says.

"Because of the rules." Now he's nibbling her ear. She whimpers. Tugs him away by the hair. "Hateful rules."

"Could I stay with you, I vow I would. I would stay and grow old with you, Miranda. Or as long as you wanted me to stay."

"Stay with me," she says. Her dress must be goring into him. His stomach, his thighs. They'll both be black and blue tomorrow.

He doesn't say anything. Kisses her over and over. Distracting her, she knows. The front of her dress fastens with a simple clasp. Underneath she's wearing an old T-shirt. Leggings. She guides his hands.

"If you can't stay with me," she says as Fenny opens the clasp, "then I'll stay with you."

His hands are on her rib cage as she speaks. Simple enough to draw him inside the armature of the dress, to reach behind his back, pull the belt of heavy chain around them both. Fasten it. The key is in the Hall. In the attic, where she left it.

"Miranda," Fenny says when he realizes. "What have you done?"

"I won't let you go," Miranda says. The dress is a snug fit for two people. She can feel every breath he takes. "If you go, then I'll go, too. Wherever it is that you go."

"It doesn't work that way," he says. "There are rules."

"There was a rule about snow, too," Miranda says. "I'm very resourceful. And you're a Honeywell. You aren't supposed to care about rules."

The fake snow is colder and wetter and heavier than she'd thought it would be. Much more like real snow. Fenny mutters something against her neck. Either *I love you* or else *What the hell were you thinking, Miranda?*

It's both. He's saying both. It's fake snow and *real*. Real snow mingling with the fake. Her fake magic and real magic. Coming down heavier and heavier until all the world is white. The air, colder and colder and colder still.

"Something's happening, Fenny," she says. "It's snowing. Really snowing."

It's as if he's turned to stone in her arms. She can feel him stop breathing. But his heart is racing. "Let me go," he says. "Please let me go."

"I can't," Miranda says. "I don't have the key."

"You can." A voice like a bell, clear and sweet.

And here is the one Miranda has been waiting for. Fenny's *she*. The one who catches foxes in traps. Never lets them go. The one who makes the rules.

It's silly, perhaps, to be reminded in this moment of Elspeth, but that's who Miranda thinks of when she looks up and sees the Lady who approaches, more Honeywell than any Honeywell Miranda has ever met. The presence, the *puissance* that Elspeth commands, just for a little while when Elspeth takes the stage, is a game. Elspeth plays at the thing. Here is the substance. Power is something granted willingly to Elspeth by her audience. Fenny's Lady has it always. What a burden. Never to be able to put it down.

Can the Lady see what Miranda is thinking? Her gaze takes in all. Fenny keeps his head bowed. But his hands are in Miranda's hands. He is in her keeping, and she will not let him go.

"I have no key," Miranda says. "And he does not want to go with you."

"He did once," the Lady says. She wears armor, too, all made of ice. What a thing it would be, to dress this Lady. To serve her. She could go with Fenny, if the Lady let her.

Down inside the dress where the Lady cannot see, Fenny pinches the soft web between Miranda's thumb and first finger. The pain brings her back to herself. She sees that he is watching her. He says nothing, only looks until Miranda finds herself again in his eyes.

"I went with you willingly," Fenny agrees. But he doesn't look at the Lady. He only looks at Miranda.

"But you would leave me now? Only speak it and I will let you go at once."

Fenny says nothing. *A rule*, Miranda thinks. *There is a rule here.*

"He can't say it," she says. "Because you won't let him. So let me say it for him. He will stay here. Haven't you kept him from his home for long enough?"

"His home is with me. Let him go," the Lady says. "Or you will be sorry." She reaches out a long hand and touches the chain around Miranda's dress. It splinters beneath her featherlight touch. Miranda feels it give.

"Let him go and I will give you your heart's desire," the Lady says. She is so close Miranda can feel the Lady's breath frosting her cheek. And then Miranda isn't holding Fenny. She's holding Michael. Miranda and Michael are married. They love each other so much. Honeywell Hall is her home. It always has been. Their children under the tree, Elspeth white-haired and lovely at the head of the table, wearing a dress from Miranda's couture label.

Only it isn't Elspeth at all, is it? It's the Lady. Miranda almost lets go of Michael. Fenny! But he holds her tight, and she him.

"Be careful, girl," the Lady says. "He bites."

Miranda is holding a fox. Scrabbling, snapping, carrion breath at her face. Miranda holds fast.

Then: Fenny again. Trembling against her.

"It's okay," Miranda says. "I've got you."

But it isn't Fenny, after all. It's her mother. They're together in a small, dirty cell. Joannie says, "It's okay, Miranda. I'm here. It's okay. You can let go. I'm here. Let go and we can go home."

"No," Miranda says, suddenly boiling with rage. "No, you're not here. And I can't do anything about that. But I can do something about this." And she holds on to her mother until her mother is Fenny again, and the Lady is looking at Miranda and Fenny as if they are a speck of filth beneath her slippered foot.

"Very well, then," the Lady says. She smiles, the way you would smile at a speck of filth. "Keep him. For a while. But know that he will never again know the joy I taught him. With me he could not be but happy. I made him so. You will bring him grief and death. You have dragged him into a world where he knows nothing. Has nothing. He will look at you and think of what he lost."

"We all lose," says an acerbic voice. "We all love and we all lose and that's just the way it goes."

"Elspeth?" Miranda says. But she thinks, *It's a trap. Just another trap.* She squeezes Fenny so hard around his middle he gasps.

Elspeth looks at Fenny. She says, "I saw you once, I think. Outside the window. I thought you were a shadow or a ghost."

Fenny says, "I remember. Though you had hardly come into your beauty then."

"Such talk! You are going to be wasted on my Miranda, I'm afraid," Elspeth says. "As for you, my lady, go find another toy. Is this one really so special he cannot be replaced?"

The Lady curtseys. Looks one last time at Elspeth, Miranda. Fenny. This time he looks back. What does he see? Does any part of him move to follow her? His hand finds Miranda's hand again.

Then the Lady is gone and the real snow thins, ceases to fall, leaving only the nearly noiseless purr and glitter of the Snowboy Stage Whisper.

Elspeth blows out a breath. "Goodness," she says. She smooths down her silk shawl and Miranda sees how Elspeth's hand is shaking. "I wasn't sure that would work. What a voracious, demanding creature. Makes one wonder. Am I as bad as that?"

Trust an actor to make it all about themselves. "Of course not," Miranda says. "Of course you aren't."

"I've always let them go when they wanted to be free," Elspeth says. "Often before they wanted it, even. And now I suppose we'll have to figure out what to do with you." This to Fenny. She can't resist a stray, Miranda knows this. "You'll be needing something more practical than that coat."

"Come on," Miranda says. She is still holding on to Fenny's hand. Perhaps she's holding on too tightly, but he doesn't seem to care. He's holding on just as tightly.

So she says, "Let's go in."

Skinder's Veil

(Snow-White and Rose-Red)

O nce upon a time there was a graduate student in the summer of his fourth year who had not finished his dissertation. What was his field? Not important to this story, really, but let's say the title of this putative dissertation was "An Exploratory Analysis of Item Parameters and Characteristics That Influence Response Time."

By the middle of June Andy Sims had, at best, six usable pages. According to the schedule he had so carefully worked out last year, when a finished dissertation still seemed not only possible but the lowest of the fruit upon the branches of the first of many trees along the beautiful path he had chosen for himself, by this date he should have had a complete draft upon which his advisors' feedback had already been thoughtfully provided. June was to have been given over to leisurely revision in the shade of those graceful and beckoning trees.

There were reasons why he had not managed to get this work

done, but Andy would have been the first to admit they were not *good* reasons. The most pressing was Lester and Bronwen.

LESTER, ANDY'S ROOMMATE, WAS also ABD. Lester was Education and Human Sciences. He and Andy were not on the best terms, though Lester did not appear to have noticed this. Lester was having too much sex to notice much of anything at all. He'd met a physiotherapist named Bronwen at a Wawa two months ago on a beverage run, and they'd been fucking ever since, the kind of fucking that suggested some kind of apocalypse was around the corner but only Lester and Bronwen knew that so far.

The reek of sex so thoroughly permeated the apartment in Center City that Andy began to have a notion he was fermenting in it, like a pickle in brine. There were the sounds, too. Andy wore noise-canceling headphones while doing the dishes, while eating dinner, on his way to the bathroom where, twice, he'd found sex toys whose purpose he could not guess. He was currently in the best shape of his life: whenever Bronwen came over, Andy headed for the gym and lifted weights until he could lift no more. He went for long runs along the Schuylkill River Trail and still, when he came home, Lester and Bronwen would be holed up inside Lester's room (if Andy was lucky) either fucking or else resting for a short interval before they resumed fucking again.

Andy did not begrudge any person's happiness, but was it possible that there could be such a thing as too much happiness? Too much sex? He resented, too, knowing the variety of sounds that Lester made in extremis. He resented Bronwen, whose roommates apparently had better boundaries than Andy.

No doubt she was a lovely person. Andy found it hard to look her in the eyes. There were questions he would have liked to ask her. Had it been love at first sight? In the fateful moment, standing in the refrigerated section of the Wawa, had Lester's soul spoken wordlessly to hers? Did Bronwen always love this deeply, this swiftly, with this much noise and heat and abandon? Because Andy had been Lester's roommate for four years now, and aside from a few unremarkable and drunken hookups, Lester had been single and seemed okay with that. Not to mention, whenever Andy brought up Lester's own dissertation, Lester claimed to be making great progress. Could this be true? In his heart of hearts, Andy feared it was true. He mentioned all of this over the phone to his old friend Hannah. It came spilling out of him when she called to ask her favor.

"So that's a yes," Hannah said. "You'll do it."

"Yes," Andy said. Then, "Unless you're pranking me. Please don't be pranking me, though. I have to get out of here."

"Not a prank," Hannah said. "Swear to God. This is you saving my ass."

The last time they'd seen each other was at least two years ago, the morning before she left Philly for an adjunct position in the sociology department at some agricultural college in Indiana. "Adjuncts of the corn," she had said and done three shots in succession. She'd been the first of their cohort to defend, and what had it gotten her? A three-year contract at a school no one had ever heard of. Andy had felt superior about that for a while.

Yesterday, Hannah said, her recently divorced sister in California had broken her back falling off the roof of her house. She was in the hospital. Hannah was flying out tomorrow to take care of her two young nieces. All of her sister's friends were unreliable assholes or too overwhelmed with their own catastrophes. Her sister's ex was in Australia. What Hannah needed was for someone to take over her house-sitting gig in Vermont for the next three weeks. That was what she said.

"It's in the middle of nowhere. It's outside of town, and the nearest town really isn't a town, anyway, you know? There's not even a traffic light," Hannah said. "There's no grocery store, no library. There's a place down the road where you can get beer and lightbulbs and breakfast sandwiches, but I don't recommend those."

"I don't have a car," Andy said.

"I don't have one, either!" Hannah said. "You won't need one. There's a standing grocery order, so you won't need a car for that. I get a delivery every Friday from the Hannaford in St. Albans. If you want to make changes, you just send them an email. And I'm leaving a bunch of stuff in the fridge. Eggs, milk, sandwich fixings. There's plenty of coffee. I have an Uber coming tomorrow at five P.M. Can you get here around three? I went ahead and mapped it; it should take you about seven hours. I'll send directions. Show up at three, we can catch up and I can go over what you need to know. But don't worry! There isn't a lot of stuff. Really, it's just a couple of things."

"You're not giving me a lot of advance notice," Andy said.

"What's your Venmo?" Hannah said. "I'll send you nine hundred bucks right now. That's half of what I'm getting paid for three months."

Andy gave her his Venmo. The most he'd ever been Venmo'd

was, what, around forty bucks? But here it was immediately, nine hundred dollars, just like that.

"So," Hannah said. "You'll be here. Tomorrow by three P.M. Because I promise I will hunt you down and remove the bones from both your legs if you don't come through. I'm counting on you, asshole."

HE WAS PRICING ONE-WAY car rentals when Bronwen wandered into the kitchen. She had Lester's old a cappella T-shirt on (Pennchants) and a pair of Lester's even older boxer shorts. She got a Yuengling out of the fridge and popped it open, then stood behind Andy, looking at his screen.

"Going on a trip?" she said. She sounded wistful. "Cool."

"Yeah," Andy said. "Kind of? I agreed to take over a house-sitting gig in Vermont for the rest of the month and it starts tomorrow afternoon. It's out in the middle of nowhere and even if I took a bus I'd still be over an hour away, so I guess I'm renting a car."

"That's a terrible idea," Bronwen said. "Rental places will just rip you off, especially in summer. I've got a car and I'm off work the next couple of days. Lester and I will drive you."

"No," Andy said. He had spent most of the month trying to avoid being in the same room with Bronwen and Lester. Hadn't she noticed? "Why? Why would you even offer to do that?"

"I've been trying to get Lester to get off his ass and go somewhere all summer," Bronwen said. "Just say yes, and I'll tell him it's a done deal. Then he can't weasel out. Okay? We'll drop you off and then camp somewhere on the way home. A lake, maybe. Lots of lakes in Vermont, right?"

"Let me think about it," Andy said.

"Why?" Bronwen said.

There really wasn't anything to think about. "Sure," Andy said. "Okay. If you're okay with it and Lester is okay with it."

"Great!" Bronwen said. She seemed truly delighted by the prospect of doing Andy this favor. "I'm going to go home and get my tent."

HE SPENT THE REST of the afternoon avoiding Lester—who despite Bronwen's reassurances was clearly sulking—and going through his piles of reading and research material. In the end he had a backpack and three canvas bags. He stuck his laptop and printer and a ream of paper in his gym bag, wrapped up in underwear and socks, a sweatshirt, his last two clean T-shirts, running shorts, and a spare pair of jeans. A waterproof jacket and a pair of Timberlands and his weights. There was a guy down the street who made regular trips over to various weed dispensaries in New Jersey to buy merchandise that he then sold locally at a healthy profit, and after perusing what was on offer, Andy spent a hundred of Hannah's money on edibles. After some thought he also purchased a pouch of Betty's Eddies Tango for a Peachy Mango for Bronwen as a thank-you.

Because, really, it was Lester that Andy bore a reasonable grudge against. There was, for example, the time Lester had been complaining about Andy at top volume to Bronwen, not realizing Andy had come home and was right there, next door in his bedroom. "It isn't that he's a bad person. He's just so fucking smug. Has to map every single thing out, but only because he won't let himself think about whether or not he wants any of it. What does he want? Who knows? Definitely not Andy. No interior life at all. You know how people talk about the unconscious and the id? The attic and the basement? The places you don't go? If you drew a picture of Andy's psyche it would be Andy, standing outside of the house where he lives. Forget the basement or the attic. Andy won't go inside the fucking house. He won't even knock on the door."

Which was rich, coming from Lester. That's what Andy thought. And, anyway, Lester wasn't a psychologist. That wasn't his area at all.

He texted a couple of friends he hadn't seen in a while and went out, leaving Lester and Bronwen to fight about Vermont or fuck or watch Netflix in peace. It was good to be out in the world, or maybe it just felt good to know that tomorrow he was going to be in Vermont with all the time and space he could possibly need to get some real work done. To all of the questions about the house and its owner he just kept saying, "No idea! I don't know anything at all!" And how good that felt, too, to be on the threshold of a mysterious adventure. It wouldn't be terrible, either, to see Hannah again.

As if this thought had summoned her, his phone buzzed with an incoming text. *You're still coming, right?*

All packed, he wrote back. *So I guess I am.*

You're going to love it here. Promise. See you tomorrow. BE HERE BY THREE!!!!

THE PLAN HAD BEEN to leave no later than six A.M. They got a late start, because Lester needed to find his spare inhaler, then bug spray, then a can opener, and then he wanted to make a second pot of coffee and take out the recycling and trash and check email. By the time they were heading out it was eight A.M., and of course they hit traffic before they were even on the 676 ramp. Lester fell asleep as soon as they were in the car.

Bronwen, checking the rearview mirror, said, "We'll make up the time once we're on 87."

"Yeah," Andy said. "Okay, sure." He texted Hannah, *on my way hooray,* put his AirPods in, and closed his eyes. When he opened them again, they were stopping in New Jersey. It was 10:30. According to his phone, they were now five hours away.

Andy paid for gas. "I could drive," he said.

"Nah, buddy," Lester said. "I got it." But he took the wrong exit out of the rest stop, south instead of north, and it was five miles back before they were going in the right direction again.

Bronwen, in the passenger seat, turned around to inspect Andy. "One time I missed an exit on 95 going down past D.C. and so I just went all the way around again. It's a big ring, you know? Turns out it was a lot bigger than I thought it was."

There were a lot of trucks on 87, all of them going faster than Lester. No cops.

Bronwen said, "You got any brothers or sisters?"

"No," Andy said.

"Where you from?"

"Nevada," Andy said.

"Never been there," Bronwen said. "You go back much?"

"Once in a while," Andy said. "My parents are retired professors. Classics and romance languages. So now they spend a lot of time going on these cruises, the educational kind. They give lectures and seminars in exchange for getting a cabin and some cash. They're cruising down the Rhine right now." No, that had been December. He had no idea where they were now. Greece? Sardinia?

"That sounds awesome," Bronwen said.

"They've had norovirus twice," Andy said.

"Still," Bronwen said, "I'd like to go on a cruise. And once you've had norovirus, you're immune to it for like a year."

"That's what they told me," Andy said. "They were actually kind of psyched after they had norovirus the first time."

"This friend," Bronwen said, "the one in Vermont, what's her name?"

"Hannah," Andy said.

"Did you ever date?"

"No," Andy said.

"Yes," Lester said.

"It wasn't really dating," Andy said. "We just kind of had a thing for a while."

"And then Hannah went off to teach at some cow college," Lester said. "And Andy hasn't gotten laid since."

"I'm just really, really trying to concentrate on my dissertation," Andy said. Sometimes, avoiding Lester, he forgot exactly why he ought to avoid Lester. It wasn't only Bronwen, and sex. It had a lot more to do with just Lester.

"Yeah," Bronwen said. "That makes so much sense. Sometimes you have to keep your head down and focus."

She really was very, very nice. Unlike Lester. "You have any brothers or sisters?"

"Nope," Bronwen said. "Just me. My parents are over in Fishtown."

"Fancy," Andy said. Fishtown was where all the nice coffee shops and fixed-up row houses were.

"Yeah," Bronwen said. "My mom's mom's house. They keep saying they're gonna put it on the market. The real estate tax is insane. But, you know, I think my mom is afraid if they sell the house they'll end up getting divorced and then she'll have no husband and no house."

"I'm sorry," Andy said.

"No," Bronwen said. "I mean, my dad's kind of a dickhead?"

"I can vouch for that," Lester said.

"Shut up," Bronwen said. "I can say it but it doesn't mean you can."

"Whatever," Lester said. "You love me. It was love at first sight. Coup de foudre."

"I like you a lot," Bronwen said.

"She doesn't believe in love," Lester said to Andy. "She's only with me because I'm ghost repellent."

"Believe it or not, he isn't my usual type," Bronwen said. "I'm actually more into girls."

"Go back a minute," Andy said. "To the thing about ghost repellent."

Lester said, "So we met at the Wawa, remember? There was only one six-pack of Yuengling in the cooler and I got it. And Bronwen came up while I was at the counter to ask the guy if there was more, and there was, but it wasn't cold. So I invited her over and we hooked up and she ended up spending the night but she said that at some point she'd probably have to split because everywhere she goes eventually this presence, this ghost, shows up and unless she's at work or something and can't leave, she'll just take off again. But the ghost never showed up. It never shows up when she's with me. So, you know, we started hanging out a lot."

"What do you mean a ghost shows up?" Andy said.

"It's just something that happens," Bronwen said. "Ever since I was a kid. Just after my fourteenth birthday. I don't know why it happens, or why it started. It doesn't bother anyone else. No one else sees it. I don't even see it! I don't even really know if it's a ghost or not. It's just, you know, this presence. I'll be somewhere and then it will be there, too. It doesn't do anything. It's just there. My mom used to tell me that it was a good thing, like a guardian spirit. But it isn't. It's kind of awful. If I leave a room, or if I go somewhere else, it doesn't come with me right away, but eventually it's with me again. If I stay in one place long enough, like if I'm asleep long enough, then when I wake up it's there. So, yeah. I'm a terrible sleeper. But I went home with Lester and I fell asleep in his bed and then I woke up and it wasn't there."

"Ghost repellent," Lester said smugly. There was a car in front of them that wasn't even doing sixty-five. Lester just stayed there behind it.

"I thought maybe it was gone for good," Bronwen said. "But I went home and took a shower and it showed right up. So, not gone. But any time I'm with Lester it stays away. So, yay."

"Incredible," Andy said.

Bronwen was facing forward again. "You probably don't even believe me," she said. "But, you know. There are more things than are dreamt of."

"I don't *not* believe you," Andy said, equivocating.

But this didn't appear to satisfy Bronwen. She said, "Well, whatever. I bet you've had weird shit happen that you can't explain. Weird shit happens to everyone."

"Except me," Lester said.

"But that's your weird thing," Bronwen said, patting him on the arm. "If nothing weird ever happens to you, then that's pretty weird."

Andy said, "Once a kid knocked on our door and when I went to answer it, he didn't have a head."

"Right," Lester said. "Last Halloween. We gave him some Tootsie Rolls."

"Both of you are utter and complete assholes," Bronwen said. She put Ariana Grande on the stereo, tilted her head back, and closed her eyes. Apparently she found it easier to ignore assholes than a ghost.

THEY STOPPED AT A McDonald's just off the highway around three P.M. The map function now said they'd get to the house around 4:15. Andy sat at a table outside and texted Hannah. She called him back immediately. "Cutting it close, asshole," she said.

"Sorry," Andy said. "But it isn't my car, so there isn't much I can do."

"Whatever, I owe you for agreeing to do this at all. It sucks, you know? Having to take off like this. This is such a sweet job. Please don't fuck it up for me, okay?"

"How's your sister?" Andy said.

"She's okay, sort of? Doesn't want to take the good painkillers, because she has a history with that stuff. So that's going to be fun for everyone. Oh, hey. She's calling. See you soon."

Bronwen came outside and sat down on top of the picnic table. She dipped her French fries one by one into the remains of her chocolate milkshake.

Andy said, "I can't tell you how much I appreciate you guys driving me."

"Not a big deal," Bronwen said, tilting her head up and back toward the sun. She was a tawny golden brown all over, hair and skin. There were little golden hairs all over her forearms and legs. Andy could almost understand why a ghost followed her everywhere. Hannah was long and pale and freckled and sort of mean, even when she liked you. She was funny, though. She changed her hair color when the mood struck her. In her last Instagram post her hair was brown with two red-pink streaks, like a porterhouse steak.

"Oh," Bronwen said. "Oh, that was quick. Much quicker than usual."

She'd dropped her milkshake. Andy picked it up before much could spill, but when he tried to give it back to her, Bronwen ignored it. She was watching a space on the sidewalk a few feet away.

"What?" he said. "What is it?"

Bronwen said, "I'll go see if Lester's done." She jumped off the table and went back inside the McDonald's.

Did Andy feel anything? Some kind of presence? He went over to stand, as far as he could gauge, in the place Bronwen had been staring at. There was nothing there, which probably meant that Bronwen had some kind of mental health issue, but also she'd just driven him most of the way to Vermont. "I don't actually think you're real," he said, "but if you are maybe you could go away and stop bothering Bronwen. She's a nice person. She doesn't deserve to be haunted."

Saying this seemed the least he could do. When he went inside to check on the situation, Bronwen was in a booth, slouched down with her face in her arms and Lester rubbing her back. Andy went and got her ice water.

Eventually she sat up and took a sip. "Sorry," she said.

"No worries," Andy said. "But we'd better hit the road. I need to get there before Hannah's ride shows up. I don't want to cut it too close."

"Dude," Lester said. "Give her a minute." He actually seemed to be irritated with Andy and did that mean he believed Bronwen? That there was a ghost?

"Yeah," Andy said. "Of course." He went and used the bathroom and when he came out again, Lester and Bronwen weren't in the booth. They weren't at the car, and eventually he realized they had to be in the family restroom because there was no one else in the McDonald's and the lock was engaged. It was another good twenty minutes before they emerged, and apparently the ghost had gotten tired of waiting and left, because Bronwen seemed much more cheerful getting back in the car. Lester, too, for that matter.

Shortly after that, Andy's phone lost all reception, which was probably for the best, because, although Bronwen drove at least ten miles above the speed limit the rest of the way, they didn't reach the address Hannah had given him until well after five.

THE PLACE HANNAH HAD been house-sitting was off a two-lane highway, the kind they'd been following for the past two hours. There were stone pedestals on either side of the dirt drive, but nothing on top of them. There were a lot of trees. Andy didn't really know a lot about trees. He wouldn't have minded if there were fewer. It was the first turnoff in maybe half a dozen miles, which was what Hannah's directions had said. If you kept going, you got to the store where you could get sandwiches and gasoline. That would have meant they'd gone too far. But Hannah's directions had been clear, and they hadn't gotten lost once. Nevertheless, they were late and Hannah was long gone.

You couldn't see anything from the turnoff because of all the trees. It was like going into a tunnel, the way the trees made a curving roof and walls over the narrow lane of white gravel, but then suddenly there was the house in a small clearing, very picturesque, three wide gray flagstone steps leading up to a green door between two white pillars, a pointed gable above. The house itself was a sunny yellow two-story with many windows. Behind the house, more trees.

"Nice place," Bronwen said. "Cheerful."

Andy's phone still had no reception. It seemed to him that there were several possible scenarios for what happened next. In one, Hannah's Uber had been delayed. The green door opened and Hannah came out. In another, this all turned out to be an extremely annoying prank, and the door would open and a stranger would be standing there. But what happened was he got out of the car and went up the steps and saw there was a note on the door. It read, *CAN'T WAIT ANY LONGER. WILL CALL FROM AIRPORT. WROTE UP INSTRUCTIONS FOR YOU AND LEFT THEM ON COUNTER. FOLLOW ALL OF THEM!!!!!*

Andy tried the door. It was unlocked. Bronwen and Lester got out of the car and began to unload the trunk.

"We must have missed her by, what? A half hour?"

Andy said, "I guess she waited around a little while."

"It always takes longer than you think it will," Bronwen said.

This seemed accurate to Andy, but not representative of the whole picture.

Lester said, "Come on. Let's get Andy's stuff in and hit the road. There's a sugar shack near the campground we booked that does a maple IPA and today's Tuesday so it closes at 6:30."

"Or you could stay here," Andy said. "Why camp when you can sleep in a bed?"

"Oh, Andy," Bronwen said. "That's so nice of you. But the whole point of this is camping. You can sleep in a bed anytime, you know?"

"Sure," Andy said. "I guess. You want a quick tour before you go? Or to use the bathroom?"

"Here," Lester said. He passed Andy's backpack over and then went back to the car to get the gym bag and the rest. Something about his body language suggested that perhaps Lester was as weary of sharing an apartment with Andy as Andy was of sharing one with him.

Bronwen and Andy remained on the porch. You could see, through the door, an open-plan living room with furniture arranged around a central fireplace and chimney of stacked gray stone. Even though it was summer, there was firewood piled up beside the fireplace. Everything looked comfortable and a little shabby. There was no reason not to go inside.

"At least come get a glass of water," Andy said.

"No," Bronwen said. She sounded very certain. "I'm good."

"What?" Andy said. "Are you getting a bad vibe or something? Is it haunted?" He was joking. He was kind of not joking.

"No," Bronwen said. "No vibe at all. Promise. It's just I don't think I want to go inside if it's okay. That's all."

"Oh," Andy said. He mostly believed her, he thought. "Okay,

good." On the whole, however, he had liked Bronwen better before he knew she was an authority on the supernatural. He decided he would keep the gummies for himself.

"That's everything!" Lester said. "Have fun, buddy. Get lots of work done. See you in a couple of weeks."

"Will do," Andy said. "Enjoy sleeping on the ground. Bye."

They got back in Bronwen's car, Lester driving again, and turned around, disappearing back into the trees. You could see how the lower branches were practically scraping the top of the car. It was cooler here than it had been in Philly, which wasn't exactly a surprise. The coolness must collect in the trees, little pockets under each leaf. There was no breeze, but the leaves were not still. They flexed and turned, green to silver to black in a shivering cascade, as if Andy were catching a glimpse of the scaled flank of some crouching thing, too enormous to be seen in its entirety.

He picked up the tote bags and went inside the house. It was a very nice house, very welcoming. He was lucky Hannah had thought of him. She'd left instructions on a pad beside the kitchen sink.

Your phone won't get reception here unless you're online. Then it should be okay downstairs. Upstairs not so great. You'll see the network. Skinder's Veil. No password. Get on and send me a text, please, so I know you've arrived. If you don't, I'm going to have to turn around and come back.

Sleep in whatever bedroom you want. The one at the back of the upstairs on the left has the most comfortable bed. Also the biggest. The bathroom upstairs is a little fin-icky. Don't flush if you're about to take a shower.

Don't forget groceries come on Fridays. Driver comes around ten A.M, and leaves everything on the porch. The delivery list and all the info is on the fridge if you need to add anything.

If there's a storm the power will probably go out, but there's a generator. You have to fill it every twelve hours when it's running. It's in the little shed out behind the kitchen. Internet is mostly good if slow.

Help yourself to whatever you find in the cabinets. Laundry is upstairs next to the bathroom.

This house belongs to Skinder. I don't know if that's his first name or his last name. He's eccentric, but this is a sweet gig so whatever. He only has two rules for the house sitter, but please take them very seriously. Like, Moses coming down with the stone tablets–level serious. All of this was going to be much simpler to explain in person, but you've already fucked that up, so let me hammer this home. TWO RULES. DON'T BREAK THEM.

RULE ONE! IMPORTANT! If any friends of Skinder show up, let them in no matter what time it is. No matter what or who they are. Don't worry about taking care of them. Just let them in and do whatever and leave when they're ready. Some of them may be weird, but they're harmless. Some of them are actually pretty cool. Hang out if you want to and they want to. Or don't. It's totally up to you! You've got your dissertation to finish, right? Anyway, it's entirely possible nobody will show up. Some summers a bunch of Skinder's friends show up and some summers I don't see anyone at all. No one so far this year.

RULE TWO! THIS ONE IS EVEN MORE IMPOR-
TANT!!! Skinder may show up. If he does, DO NOT LET
HIM IN. This is HIS OWN RULE. Why? I have no idea,
but for the duration of the time he pays me to stay here,
Skinder may not enter his own house. No matter what he
says, he is not allowed to come in. I know how bizarre this
sounds. But, fingers crossed, this will be a nonissue and you
won't see Skinder at all. If you do, then all you have to do is
not let him in. It's that simple.

ANDY: This is my favorite place in the world and the
easiest job in the world and you had better not fuck it up for
me. If you're thinking of fucking it up, then also start thinking about how I'm going to murder you one inch at a time.

Love, Hannah

P.S. If you look outside at night and there's mist coming up
from the ground all over, don't freak out! There are a lot of
natural springs around this area, a lot of water underground
on the property. The mist is a natural phenomenon. It's
called Skinder's Veil, which is also the name of the house,
which has belonged to Skinder's family for a long, long
time. Also, the water here comes from a well. It's spring fed
so it tastes funny but apparently it's good for you. It's supposed to, and I quote, "open your inner eye." So, basically,
free drugs! There's plenty of bottled water in case you don't
like the taste, but I always just drink the water from the tap.

P.P.S. Seriously, if Skinder shows up, do not let him in the
house no matter what he says.

....

ANDY PUT THE NOTE in his pocket. "Much to think about," he said out loud. This was a thing one of their TAs had liked to say at the end of every class, back in undergrad. There'd been a certain intonation, and it had cracked Hannah and Andy up all semester. They'd said it to each other all the time. It had been the working title of Hannah's dissertation. Andy couldn't even remember the guy's name.

He found the network on his phone, waited until he had a few bars back. And here were Hannah's texts, increasingly frantic, then terse. Three voicemails. He went back to his bags at the front door and dug through the backpack until he'd found the pouch of gummies. Ate one and then texted Hannah back. *Here! Just missed you, I'm guessing. So so sorry. Call me when you can. I have some questions.*

He investigated his new living situation while he waited for Hannah to call. The kitchen and the living room he'd seen. There was a farmhouse table off to one side of the open-plan space, set in front of a big window overlooking a small area of flagstones, furred with moss. There was an Adirondack chair in case you wanted to sit outside, which Andy was not sure he did. Everything was very green: the mossy flagstones, the chair, the slumped, ferny ground, and trees, trees, trees crowding in close around it all. It had taken Andy some time to get used to the East Coast, the way there were trees growing everywhere, but this was another order of magnitude. Here there was nothing but trees and this house and whatever lived in and among trees.

There was the start of a path, too, heading off into those trees.

Maybe it went somewhere interesting. More likely it was just going to be more trees.

There was a flat-screen TV, though, on the wall opposite the fireplace. And there had been a satellite dish on the roof. That seemed promising. They didn't have a TV back in the apartment in Philly. There was a bookshelf with a blue ceramic bowl of small pine cones, a perfectly ordinary and unremarkable piece of granite, and some paperback books, mostly Stephen King and Michael Connelly. No family pictures, nothing sentimental or that might indicate the kind of person who lived here.

Andy set up his printer and his research material on the table. Then he took his small assortment of clothes and toiletries upstairs. There were four bedrooms. The two at the front of the house were smaller, the beds and curtains made up in cheerful floral fabrics, one red and white, the other green and blue. In the green and blue bedroom, there was an amateurish painting of some sort of creature standing on two legs beside a river. So, a bear, perhaps? Were there other animals that stood on two legs? But then again, bears didn't have long and luxurious tails, did they? He didn't think they did. In the red and white bedroom, instead of a painting there was a framed cross-stitch that read WEST EAST HOME IS THE BEAST. He would have to Google that.

Above the bed in each room were two dainty bells, mounted just below the crown molding. A wire attached to the canon disappeared into a small hole drilled into the wall. They were called servants' bells, weren't they? Except, wasn't it supposed to work the other way? The bells downstairs, the pulls in the bedrooms?

"Much to think about!" Andy said, and went to see the other two bedrooms. These were larger than the front bedrooms and the ceiling sloped down over the headboards of the beds. Here, too, were the bells, but no paintings, no vaguely Satanic cross-stitches. He decided to claim the left-hand bedroom, the one Hannah had suggested. The bed had been stripped; he found the sheets in the dryer.

Andy made himself a grilled cheese for dinner and ate what turned out to be pasta salad out of a Tupperware container. There was a half bottle of white wine in the refrigerator. He finished that and was sampling the tap water, which was a little musty but perhaps would get him high, when Hannah finally called.

"You're there," she said.

"Eating your pasta salad," he said. "Not sure about the raisins."

"It's my mom's recipe," Hannah said. "You grow up eating something, it's comfort food."

"Mine is grilled cheese," Andy said. "But it has to be Swiss cheese."

They were both silent for a minute. Finally Andy said, "Sorry I didn't get here in time to see you."

"Never mind," Hannah said. "At least you're there. I started thinking you weren't going to show at all. What do you think?"

"I think I should have brought some sweaters," Andy said. "So what's with the rules? I'm supposed to let everyone in except for Skinder, who is the one who actually owns the house?"

"That's pretty much it exactly," Hannah said.

"So anyone can just show up and I let them in? But then what if I accidentally let Skinder in? It's not like I've met him."

"Oh, wait, no," Hannah said. "Shit. This would have been so

much easier if I'd been able to explain in person. Look, Skinder's friends show up at the back door. The kitchen door. So, someone shows up and knocks at the kitchen door, let them in. The only person who will knock at the front door is Skinder. It's actually pretty easy. Don't let anyone in if they knock at the front door."

"Doesn't he have a key?" Andy said. "To his own house?"

"I know," Hannah said. "It's freaky. If it makes it easier, think of it like a game. Like Settlers of Catan. Or Red Rover! Or whatever. There are rules and everyone has to follow them. If you think about it that way, then you just do what the rules say and you're fine."

"Okay, but what happens if I mess up and I let Skinder in?"

"I don't know," Hannah said. "I lose my summer job? Look, I signed a contract and everything. I'd have to give back what he paid me, which means you'd have to give me back the money I passed on to you. Just don't let him in, okay? If he even shows up, which he probably won't do. I've done this for a while and he only showed up three times, once the first summer, and then twice the summer before last. He knocks on the front door and you don't let him in. I didn't let him in. He asked me to let him in and I didn't and so he went away again. It was a little weird, especially when he came back the second time, but it was fine. You'll be fine. Just don't let him in."

"Okay," Andy said. "So what does he look like?"

"Skinder?" Hannah said. "Oh, boy. You'll know it's him. I'm not going to try to explain it because it will sound crazy, but you'll know. You'll just know. For one thing he always has a dog with him. It's this little black dog. So if you see the dog, that's him."

"What if he doesn't bring the dog? Or what if the dog's dead? You didn't see Skinder last year. The dog could have died."

"It really doesn't matter," Hannah said. "You don't have to know what he looks like to know it's him. He only comes to the front door. Just don't let anyone through the front door and you'll be fine. Even me! If I show up at the front door, tell me to go around to the back, okay?"

"Don't let anyone in the front door," Andy said. He took another swallow of musty water. Perhaps he would acquire a taste for it. "But if anyone knocks on the back door, then I have to let them in, right?"

"Right," Hannah said.

"I don't really understand any of this," Andy said. "I'm kind of feeling like you've gotten me into something here. Like, I thought this was just a house-sitting gig. You didn't mention all of this other stuff on the phone the other day."

"Yeah," Hannah said. "I was pretty sure that if I brought all this up then you'd pass on the golden opportunity I was holding out to you. And I really, really needed you to come up so I could get out to my sister."

"And this is in no way a hilarious prank," Andy said.

"I'm paying you nine hundred dollars to stay in a secluded house in the country where you can finally get some real work done on your dissertation," Hannah said. "Does that seem like a prank?"

"Much to think about," Andy said.

"Much to think about, asshole," Hannah said. "I'll call you in a day or two, okay? I have to go catch my flight."

"Safe travels," Andy said. But she had already hung up.

There was a six-pack of some fancy IPA at the back of the

fridge, and a jar of Red Vines on the counter beside the sink. He took a couple of those and one of the beers through to the living room and sat at the farm table. He turned on his laptop and put aside thoughts of Hannah and rules and the person who owned this house. He set aside, too, thoughts of Bronwen and the thing she said followed her. Regardless of whatever she felt or thought, it wasn't real. Nothing was following anyone. He had felt nothing. And if there had been something, well, then, it wasn't here, was it? It was her ghost, not his, and so it would be wherever Bronwen was, waiting for the moment when Lester wasn't there.

Andy worked for an hour, comparing penalized splines in various studies, until at last the edible kicked in, or perhaps it was the tap water smoothing down his splines and his thoughts and all the strangeness of the day. He watched TV and at nine he went upstairs to bed. He slept soundly through the night and only woke up because he had forgotten to close the blinds and sunlight was coming through the windows, turning all of the room to auspicious gold.

For the next two days, he did not return to his dissertation, though each morning he told himself that he would tackle it after breakfast. After lunch. Before dinner. Instead of doing this, he took naps, got stoned, played Minecraft, and did his sets and reps. After dinner he watched old science fiction movies. He left the television on when he went to bed. It wasn't that he was lonely. It was just that he was out of the habit of *being* alone. On the third night when he looked out of his bedroom window, threads of mist were rising from the ground below the trees. As he watched, these threads wove themselves in pallid columns, and then a languorous, uniform cloud, blotting out the patio. The Adirondack chair shrank away until only its back and arms remained, floating in whiteness. Andy went to the red and white bedroom at the front of the house and saw the driveway had already vanished. If Hannah hadn't told him this would happen, he supposed he would have found the phenomenon eerie. But it was perfectly natural. Creepy but natural. Natural and also quite beautiful. He tried without success to get a good picture with his phone. No doubt it would be possible to get better results if he left the house to take a picture at ground level, but he dismissed this idea when it came to him. He preferred not to go stand outside knee-deep in something called Skinder's Veil, natural phenomenon or not.

Instead he went to bed and had two hours of sleep before he woke. One of the bells above his head was ringing, ringing, ringing.

NO ONE WAS AT the front door. The TV was on: he turned it off. The bell was still ringing and so he went to the kitchen and turned on the lights. A woman stood at the back door, peering in. She must have had her finger on the bell and Andy, against his better judgment, did as Hannah had said he must and unlocked the door to let her in.

"Oh, good," she said, stepping into the kitchen. "Did I wake you up? I'm so sorry."

"No," Andy said. "It's fine. I'm Andy. I'm house-sitting here. I mean, my friend Hannah was house-sitting, but she had a family emergency and so now I'm filling in."

"I'm Rose White," his visitor said. "Very nice to meet you, Andy." She opened the refrigerator and took out two beers. She handed one to him and then headed into the living room, sitting down on one of the chintz sofas and dropping her leather carry-all on the floor, plopping her muddy boots upon the coffee table.

She couldn't have been much older than Andy. Her hair, longish and dirty blond, looked as if it hadn't seen a hairbrush in several days. Perhaps she had been backpacking. In any case, she was still extremely attractive.

"Have a drink with me," she said, smiling. One of her front teeth was crooked. "Then I'll let you go back to bed."

Andy opened the beer. Sat down in an armchair that faced the fireplace. Hannah had said he didn't have to hang out, but on the other hand, he didn't want to be rude. He said, "Mist's cleared up."

"The Veil? It usually does," Rose White said. "Don't recommend going out in it. You can get lost quite quickly. I was surprised to find myself right on Skinder's doorstep. I thought I'd been going in another direction entirely."

"You live nearby?" Andy said. It didn't seem polite to ask why she was out so late at night. "Hannah comes and house-sits every summer. Maybe you've met her?"

"Phew," Rose White said. "The big questions! Haven't been through in years, actually. Let's see. The last house-sitter I met was an Alma. Or Alba. But I see nothing's much changed. Skinder's not much for change."

"I don't really know much about Skinder," Andy said. "Anything, really."

"A complicated fellow," Rose White said. "You know the rules, I suppose."

"I think so?" Andy said. "If he comes to the house, I'm supposed to not let him in. For some reason. I don't really know what he looks like, but he'll come to the front door. That's how I'll know it's him. But if anyone comes to the back door, then I let them in."

"Good enough to get by," Rose White said. She began to unlace her boots. "Aren't you going to drink your beer?"

Andy set it down. "I might just go back to bed, unless you need me for something. Going to try to get up early and get some work done. I'm working on my dissertation while I'm here, actually."

"A scholar!" Rose White said. "I'll be quiet as a mouse. Leave your beer. I'll drink it for you."

But she was not, in fact, as quiet as a mouse. Andy lay in his bed, listening as she rattled and banged around the kitchen, boiling water in the kettle and pulling out various pans. The smell of frying bacon seeped under his closed door in a delicious cloud. Andy wished he had his noise-canceling headphones. But they were on the table beside his laptop, and he did not want to go downstairs and get them.

He thought, *Tomorrow I really will get some work done, visitor or no visitor. Otherwise all the time will just melt away and in the end I'll have accomplished nothing.*

Without meaning to, he found himself listening for the sound of Rose White coming up the stairs. It must have been after three when, at last, she did. She went into the bathroom beside his bedroom and took a long shower. He wondered which room she would choose, but in the end it was his door she opened. She didn't turn on the lights, but instead got into the bed with him.

He turned on his side and there was enough moonlight in the

room that he could see Rose White looking back at him. She had not bothered to put clothes back on post-shower. "Do you have a girlfriend?" she said.

"Not at the moment," Andy said.

"Do you like to fuck women?"

"Yes," Andy said.

"Then here's my last question," she said. "Would you like to fuck me? No strings. Just for fun."

"Yes," Andy said. "Absolutely, yes. But I don't have a condom."

"Not a concern for me," she said. "You?"

Yes, a little. That was the problem with knowing a fair bit about how statistics worked. "No," Andy said. "Not at all."

But afterward he wasn't quite sure what the etiquette was. Should he try to get to know her a little better? He didn't even know how long she was going to be staying at the house. It would have been easier if he'd been able to fall asleep, but that seemed to be out of the question. He decided he would pretend to be asleep.

"Not tired?" Rose White said.

"Sorry," Andy said. "A lot to think about. Think I'll go downstairs and watch TV for a while."

"Stay here," Rose White said. "I'll tell you a story."

"A story," Andy said. He wasn't a kid. On the other hand, there was a woman in his bed he'd just met, and they'd had sex, and now she was offering to tell him a story. Why not say yes? If nothing else, it would be something, later on, that would be an interesting story of his own. "Sure. Tell me a story."

Rose White drew the covers up to her neck. She was lying on her back, and this gave the impression she was telling the story to someone floating on the ceiling. It felt strangely formal, as if Andy were back in a lecture hall, listening to one of his professors. She said, "Once a very long time ago there was a woman who wrote books for a living. She made enough from this to keep not only herself in modest comfort but also her sister, who lived with her and was her secretary. She wrote her novels longhand and it was the sister who read the manuscript first, before giving it back to the writer to edit. This sister, who was a romantic with very little outlet for expression, had a peculiar way of marking the parts she liked best. She would prick her finger with a needle and mark the place with her own blood to show how good she thought it was. A little blotch over a well-turned phrase, a little smudge. She would return the manuscript, the writer would do her revisions, sparing the lines and scenes that her sister had loved, and then the sister would type everything up properly and send it along to the writer's agent.

"The writer's books were popular with a certain audience, but never garnered much critical favor. The writer shrugged this off. She told her sister the merit of the books was that they were easy to produce at a rate that kept a roof over their heads, and they served a second purpose, which was to entertain those whose lives were hard enough. But, the writer said, she had in her a book of such beauty and power that anyone who read it would be changed forever, and one day she would write it. When her sister asked why she did not write it now, she said that such a book would take more time and thought and effort than she could currently spare.

"As time went on, though, the writer's books became less popular. The checks they brought in were smaller, and their lives became little by little less comfortable. The writer determined that she would at last turn her attention to this other book. She labored over it for a year and into the next winter, and slept little and ate less and grew unwell. At night while she worked, her sister would hear her groaning and coughing and then one morning, very early, the writer woke her sister and said, 'I have finished it at last. Now I must rest.'

"The sister put on a robe and lit a fire and sat down to read the manuscript at once, her needle in her pocket. But upon reading the very first sentence, she drew out her needle and pricked her finger to mark it. And the second sentence, too, she marked with her blood. And it went on like that as she read, until at last she had to go down to the kitchen to fetch a peeling knife. First she cut her palm and then she cut her arm, and each line and every page was marked with the sister's blood as she read, such was the power and beauty of the narrative and the characters and the writer's language.

"Many days later, friends of the writer and her sister grew concerned because no one had heard from them in some time. Upon forcing their way into the house they found the sister exsanguinated in her chair, the manuscript in her lap all glued together with her blood. The body of the writer, too, was discovered in her bed. She'd died of an ague she'd caught from overwork and too little rest. As for the book she'd written, it was quite impossible to read even a single word."

"That was really interesting," Andy said, just as awake as he had been at the start, possibly more so. In a minute he would say so, get dressed, and go downstairs. "Thank you."

"You're welcome," Rose White said. "Now go to sleep."

....

HE WOKE UP AT the table downstairs, his laptop beside his head.

Rose White was on the couch. "I built a fire," she said. "Thought you might catch cold. Vermont weather is unpredictable, summer or not."

She'd done this, Andy realized, because he was entirely naked. His shoulders ached and his ass was unhygienically stuck to the rattan seat of the chair. "What time is it?" he asked her. "How long have I been here?"

"You were gone when I woke up," Rose White said. "Discovered you here when I came down this morning. It's past noon now."

"I must've been sleepwalking," Andy said. His laptop was open and when he woke the screen, a prompt appeared. Save changes?

"Get dressed," Rose White said. "I'll make you a sandwich. Then you can get back to it."

He dressed and ate, reading over what he'd written the night before. It was rough, but it was also a reasonably solid foundation for revision. Moreover, there were four thousand words that had not been there the night before. This seemed like enough work for one day, and so at Rose White's suggestion, they spent the day in bed and the evening drinking bourbon they procured from a locked liquor cabinet. Rose White knew where to find the key.

The next few days and nights were pleasant ones. Andy took leisurely naps in the afternoon. He shared his stash with Rose White. They took turns cooking, and let the dishes pile up. Rose White had very little interest in his life, and no interest at all in explaining anything about herself. If, after sex, she enjoyed telling him her strange stories, at least they were mostly very short. Some of them hardly seemed to be stories at all. One went like this: "There once was a man possessed of a great estate who did not wish to marry. At last, beset by his financial advisors, he agreed to be married to the first suitable individual he encountered setting into town, and when he came home with his fiancée, his friends and advisors were dismayed to find that he had become engaged to a tortoise. Nevertheless, the man found a priest willing, for a goodly sum of money, to perform the ceremony. They lived together for several years and then the man died. At last a distant relative was found to inherit the estate and on his first night in his fine new home, he had the tortoise killed and served up as a soup in its own shell. But this is not, by any means, the worst story about marriage that I know."

Another story began, "There once was a woman, still very young, who was unpleasantly surprised to come home one day to find Death waiting for her in her kitchen. 'Mary Ellen,' he began, and she said, at once, 'Oh, no, I'm Anna Louise. You must be looking for my twin, but we've had such a terrible quarrel. She left last night and I don't know when she'll be back.' She said this with such conviction that Death apologized for his mistake and took his leave. Though he returned several times in the next month, Mary Ellen was each time able to persuade him that she was, in fact, Anna Louise and Death had once again just missed her twin. Finally she said Mary Ellen had accepted a job with a consulting firm based in Chicago that required a great deal of international travel. For a long time afterward, Death did not bother her until, one day, she was in the south of France on a wine-tasting tour and saw Death approaching her in the marketplace of a small town. Before she could open her mouth, Death said to her, 'Mary Ellen! How wonderful to meet you at last! But today I was actually hoping to run into your sister, Anna Louise. Do you know where I might be able to find her?' And at that moment, Mary Ellen felt a sense of strangeness so great that it seemed to split her in half, one half remaining Mary Ellen and the other half becoming the imaginary and elusive Anna Louise. 'We haven't spoken in years,' Mary Ellen said to Death, and he went away, satisfied with this answer. And, in fact, the half of her that is Mary Ellen and the half of her that is Anna Louise have never spoken since that day, although whenever one encounters Death, he always asks politely after the health of the other."

Another story began, "Once there was a blood sausage and a liver sausage and the blood sausage invited the liver sausage over for dinner." None of Rose White's stories were cheerful. In all of them, someone came to a bad end, but there was nothing to be learned from them. Nevertheless, each time she finished and said to Andy, "Go to sleep," he promptly fell asleep. And, too, each morning he woke up to find he had, in some dream state, produced more of his dissertation, though after the second time this happened, he moved his laptop and his notebooks up to the vanity in the red and white bedroom.

The groceries were left on the porch on the appointed day, and the dissertation progressed, and in the afternoons when it grew warm, Rose White sunbathed topless on the patio while Andy did reps. Hannah called to check in, and to report her nieces would eat nothing but sugar cereal and mozzarella sticks, while her sister was camped out on a blow-up mattress in the dining room because she could not get up and down the stairs, and needed Hannah's help getting onto the toilet and off again.

"Everything's great here," Andy said.

"Any visitors?" Hannah asked.

"Yeah, some lady named Rose White. I don't know how long she's staying."

"Never met her," Hannah said. "What's she like?"

"She's okay," Andy said. He didn't feel like getting into the details. "I've been really focused on the dissertation. We haven't really hung out or anything. But she's done some of the cooking."

"So, pretty normal, then," Hannah said. "Good. Sometimes the ones who show up are kind of strange."

"How so?" Andy said.

"Oh, you know," Hannah said. "Some of them can be a little strange. I'm gonna go make lunch now for two small jerks. Call if you need anything. And I'll check in again later. As soon as I know when I can head back, I'll let you know."

"No rush," Andy said, looking out the window to where Rose White lay, splendid and rosy upon a beach towel. This was wonderful, yes, but what if she were developing feelings for him? Did he feel something for her? Yes, possibly. This was very inconvenient. They didn't really know each other at all, and she was, as Hannah had said, kind of strange.

The whole thing made him uncomfortable. Much to think about. He had a gummy and pretended to be working when Rose White came back in. But she'd only come in the house to use the bathroom and put her clothes back on. Then she was off for a hike, not even bothering to ask if he wanted to come along. She came back at dinnertime with a pocketful of mushrooms. *"Psilocybe cubensis,"* she said. "I'll make us tea. The water here has some excellent properties of its own, but there's no such thing as too much fun."

"Isn't that dangerous?" Andy said. "I mean, what if you haven't identified the mushroom correctly?"

Rose White gave him a withering look. "Go teach your grandmother to suck eggs," she said. "Are you a man or a chicken, Andy?"

It was, again, the study of statistics that presented the problem. Nevertheless, Andy had some of the tea and in return shared his vape pen. It was the first time he'd ever tried mushrooms, and only pieces of the night that followed were accessible to him later on.

Rose White, sitting astride him, her hands on his biceps, the feeling that her fingers were sinking into his flesh as if either he or she were made of mist.

Rose White saying, "I think my sister must be quite near now." Andy tries to say that he didn't know she had a sister. He doesn't really know anything about her. "I'm Rose White but she is Rose Red." When he looks at her, her hair is full of blood. Rose Red!

The realization that Skinder's house has no walls, no roof, no foundation. The walls are trees, there is no ceiling, only sky. "It's all water underneath," he is explaining. Rose White: "Only the doors are real."

Later he is seated in front of the vanity in the red and white bedroom. The bell on the wall is ringing. When he leaves one bedroom, Rose White is coming out of another. Andy has to sit down on the staircase and bump down, one step at a time. Rose White helps him stand up at the bottom. His head is floating several feet above his body and he has to walk slowly to make sure he doesn't leave it behind.

Two deer are arranged like statuary upon the flagstone patio. Are they real? Did these deer ring the doorbell? Do they want to come in? He finds this hysterically funny but when he opens the door, the deer approach solemnly on their attenuated, decorative legs. One and then the other come into the kitchen, stretching their lovely necks out and down to fit through the door. Inside the jewel boxes of their nostrils the warmth of their breath is gold. It dazzles. Andy's head floats up higher, bumping against the ceiling. He stretches out his hand, strokes the flank of an actual fucking deer. A doorbell-ringing deer. A moth has flown into the kitchen, he's left the door open. It blunders through the air, brushing against his cheek, his ear. He opens his mouth to tell Rose White to close the door and the moth flies right in.

ROSE WHITE SAYS, "ONCE upon a time there was a real estate agent who made arrangements to show a property. When she arrived at the property, she realized at once that her new client was none other than Death. Suspecting he was there for her, she decided to pretend she was not the agent at all, but rather another prospective buyer. Claiming she had been told to meet the listing agent around the back, she lured Death around the side of the house and told him to look through the French windows to see if anyone was there to let them in. When he did this, she picked up an ornamental planter and bashed in his head. Then she dragged the body of Death into the full bathroom and cut it into twelve pieces in the bathtub. These she wrapped in Hefty bags and, after cleaning the bathtub thoroughly, she parked her

Lexus in the garage and placed these bags in the trunk. Over the next week, she buried each piece deep on the grounds of a different listing, and each of those houses sold quite quickly. Decades went by and the real estate agent began to regret what she had done. She was now in her nineties and weary of life, but Death did not come for her. And so she visited each of the properties where she had disposed of his corpse and dug him up, but perhaps her memory was faulty: she could not find the last two pieces. She is still, in fact, searching for Death's left forearm and his head. The rest of him, badly decomposed, is in a deep freezer in her garage. Some days she wonders if, in fact, it was really Death at all. And what if it really had been Death? What if he had only come to see a house? Isn't it likely that even Death must have a house in which to keep himself?"

ANDY WOKE IN HIS own bed with a dry mouth but no other discernible effects from the night before. In the red and white bedroom, his laptop was open. When he looked to see what he'd written, it was only this: *How to work? Deer in house. Not sanitary!!! WTF*

When he went downstairs, though, there were no deer and no Rose White, either. She'd left a note on the kitchen table. *Headed out. Finished off bacon but did a big clean (badly needed!) so think we're even. Thanks for the hospitality. Left you the rest of the mushrooms. Use sensibly! Take care if I don't see you again. Fondly, Rose White.*

"Fondly," Andy said. He wasn't really even sure what that meant. It was one of those sign-offs like "kind regards" or "best wishes." A kiss-off, basically. "Summer loving, had me a blast."

Lester's a cappella group liked to sing that one. He didn't even have her phone number.

While he was microwaving a bowl of oatmeal, he inspected the tile floor of the kitchen. He actually got down on his hands and knees. What was he looking for? Rose White? Some deer tracks? The rest of his dissertation?

He gave himself the rest of the day off. Texted Hannah: *There are a lot of deer around here, right? Do they ever come up to the house?*

She texted right back: *Lots of deer, yes. Bears, too, sometimes.*

He didn't feel like explaining he'd had 'shrooms with a house-guest he'd also been having sex with, and that possibly he had let some deer into the house. Or else hallucinated this.

Without Rose White in his bed, he found he did not fall asleep easily. Neither did he work, in his sleep, on his dissertation. He made some progress during the days, but it was much like it had been in the apartment in Philadelphia, except here he had no excuse.

About a week after Rose White had gone, the servants' bell rang again. It wasn't midnight yet, and he was in bed, skipping to the end of a Harlan Coben novel because the middle was very long and all he really wanted was to see how it all came out.

He put on a pair of pants and went downstairs. At the back door was a wild turkey. After deliberating, Andy did as he was supposed to do and let it in. It did not seem at all wary of him, and why should it have been? It was an invited guest. Andy went into the living room and sat on the couch. The turkey investi-gated the corners of the room, making little grunting noises, and then defecated neatly on the hearth of the fireplace. Its cheeks were violet, and its neck was bright red. It flew up on top of the cord of stacked wood and puffed out all the formidable armature of its feathers. Andy's phone was on the table: he took a picture. The turkey did not object. It seemed, in fact, to already be sleeping.

Andy, too, went up to bed. In the morning, the turkey was waiting by the back door and he let it out again. He cleaned up the shit on the hearth and two other places. This was when, no doubt, he should have called Hannah or at least texted her the photo he'd taken. But she was probably waiting for something like this, and really, she should have been up-front with him. And also, he realized, he was having a good time. It was like being inside an enchantment. Why would he want to break the spell? The next night the bell rang again, though to Andy's disappointment it was neither a beautiful girl nor a creature at the back door. A grayish man of about sixty in Birkenstocks, a Rolling Stones T-shirt, and khaki shorts nodded but did not speak when Andy opened the door. He did not bother to introduce himself. He didn't speak at all. Instead he went straight upstairs, took a long shower, using all the towels in the bathroom, and then slept for two days in the blue and green bedroom. Andy kept his bedroom door locked while the gray man was in the house. It was a relief, frankly, when he was gone again. After that, it was an opossum, and the night after the opossum, the mist was on the ground again. Skinder's Veil. When the bell began to ring, Andy went down to let his guest in, but no one was at the kitchen door. He went to the front door, but to his relief, no one was there, either. The bell continued to ring, and so Andy went to the kitchen door again. When he opened the door, the mist came swiftly seeping in, piling itself upon the tile floor and the feet of the kitchen table, the kitchen chairs. Andy closed the door and at once the bell began to ring again. He opened the door and left it open. The guest was, perhaps, Skinder's Veil itself, or perhaps it was something which preferred to remain hidden inside the Veil. Andy, thinking of Bronwen's ghost, went up to his bedroom and shut the door and locked it. He rolled up his pants and wedged them against the bottom of the door. He left his lights on and did not sleep at all that night, but in the morning he was the only one in the house and the day was very sunny and bright. The door was shut tight again.

The last human guest, while Andy was in Skinder's house, was Rose White's sister Rose Red.

WHEN ANDY OPENED THE kitchen door, it was Rose White who stood there. Except, perhaps it was not. This person had the same features—eyes, nose, mouth—only their arrangement was somehow unfamiliar. Sharper, as if this version of Rose White would never think of anyone fondly. Now her hair was exuberantly, unnaturally apple green and there was a metal stud in one nostril.

"Rose Red," she said. "May I come in?"

This was the sister, then. Only, as she spoke Andy saw a familiar crooked tooth. This must be Rose White, hair colored and newly styled. And would he even have noticed her nose was pierced previously? Not if she'd not had her stud in. Well, it was fine. He would play along.

"Come in," he said. "I'm Andy. Filling in for the original house-sitter. Your sister was here about a week ago."

"My sister?" she said.

"Rose White," Andy said. It was like being in a play where

you'd never seen the script. He had to give Rose White this: she wasn't boring.

"We don't even have the same last name," Rose Red said. She looked very prim as she said this. She was, it was true, a little taller than he remembered Rose White being, but then he saw her ankle boots had two-inch heels. Had she really come up the path wearing those? Mystery upon mystery.

He said, "My mistake. Sorry." After all, who was he to talk? He'd managed not even one complete paragraph in two days. Maybe he'd do better now that she was here again.

Rose Red (or Rose White) went rummaging through the kitchen cabinets. "Help yourself," he said. "I was just about to make dinner."

Rose Red was regarding the plate beside the sink where Rose White's mushrooms were drying out. "Yours?" she said.

Andy said, "Happy to share. You going to make tea?"

"What if I made some risotto?" she said.

And so Andy set the table and poured them both a glass of wine, while Rose Red made dinner. The risotto was quite tasty and, Andy saw, she had used all of the mushrooms. Once again, he tried to discover more about the owner of the house, but like Rose White, Rose Red was an expert at deflection. Had he hiked any of the paths, she wanted to know. What did he think of the area?

"I've been kind of busy," Andy said. "Trying to finish my dissertation. It's why I'm here, actually. I needed to be able to focus."

"And when you're finished?" Rose Red said.

"Then I'll defend and go on the job market," Andy said.

"And hopefully get a teaching job somewhere. Tenure track, ideally."

"That's what you'll do," Rose Red said. "But what do you want?"

"To do a good job on my dissertation," Andy said. "To graduate and find a good job. And then, I suppose, to be good at teaching."

Rose Red appeared satisfied by this. "Have you been on the trails at all? Gone hiking? So much to explore up here."

"Well," Andy said. "Like I said, I've been busy. And I don't actually like trees that much. But the Veil is pretty interesting. And people keep showing up. That's been interesting, too. Rose White, the one I mentioned before, she had all these weird stories." He wasn't sure whether or not he should bring up all the sex.

After dinner they had more wine and Rose Red found a puzzle. Andy didn't much care for puzzles, but he sat down to help her. The longer they worked on it, the harder it grew to fit the pieces together. Eventually he gave up and sat, watching how his fingers elongated, wriggling like narrow fish.

Upstairs one of the bells began to ring again. "I'll get that," Andy said, excusing himself from the puzzle of the puzzle. In the kitchen, he could perceive, once again, how it was not a kitchen at all. Really, it was all just part of the forest. All just trees. The puzzle, too, had been trees, chopped into little bits that needed arranging into a path. It was fine. It was fine, too, that a brown bear stood on its hind legs at the door, depressing the bell.

"Come in, good sir, come in," Andy said.

The bear dropped down onto all fours, squeezing its bulk into the kitchen. It brought with it a wild, loamy reek. Andy followed the bear back into the living space where Rose Whatever Her Name Was sat, finishing the puzzle. You could see the little fleas jumping in the bear's fur like sequins.

Rose Red jumped up and got the serving bowl with the remains of the risotto. She placed it before the bear, who stuck its whole snout in. Andy lay down on the floor and observed. When the bear was done, it leant back against the couch. Rose Red scratched its head, digging her fingers deep into its fur. They stayed like that for a while, Rose Red scratching, the bear drowsing, Andy content to lie on the floor and watch them and think about nothing.

"This one," Rose Red said to the bear. "He's going to be a great teacher."

"Well," Andy said. "First there's the dissertation. Defend. Then. Go on the job market. Be offered something somewhere. Get tenure. There's a whole path. You have to go along it. Through all the fucking trees. Like Little Red. Little Red Riding Hood. You know that story?"

"I don't care much for stories," Rose Red said.

"Oh, come on," Andy said. "Tell me one. Make it up. Tell me one about this place."

"Once upon a time there was a girl whose mother died when she was very young." It wasn't Rose Red, though, who was speaking. It was the bear. Andy was fairly sure it was the bear, which he felt should have troubled him more than it did. Perhaps, though, it was all ventriloquism. Or the mushrooms. It came to him, then, that the bear had a name and its name was Jared Spring and it had come into the house because it was lonely. Andy closed his eyes and the bear went on with the story.

ONCE UPON A TIME there was a girl whose mother died when she was very young. They lived on a street where almost every house had a swimming pool in the backyard. Not the girl's house, but the house on either side did. There was an incident, the girl never knew exactly what, and the mother drowned in the swimming pool that belonged to the house on the left. It was a mystery why she was in it. It was late at night, and no one knew when or even why she had gone swimming. Everyone else had been asleep: her body wasn't discovered until morning.

When she wasn't much older, the girl's father remarried a woman with a daughter of her own. Don't worry, though, this isn't a story about a wicked stepmother. The girl and her step-mother and the stepsister all got along quite well, much better, in fact, than the girl got along with her own father. But all through her adolescence, there were stories about the pool next door; that it was haunted. The family who had lived there when the mother drowned moved away—the new family loved their house and their pool, but it was said they rarely went swimming after midnight. Anyone who went swimming after midnight ran the risk of seeing the ghost down in the deep end, long hair floating around her face, her bathing suit losing its elasticity, her mouth open and full of water.

The girl sometimes swam in the neighbor's pool, hoping she would see her mother's ghost and also afraid she would see her mother's ghost. All the girls in the neighborhood liked to swim in that pool best. They would dare each other to swim after midnight, and the rest would take turns sitting on the edge of the pool, facing away, in case the ghost was too shy to appear in front of them all. Sometimes one of the girls even saw the ghost—a thrill, a ghost of their very own!—but the girl whose mother had drowned never saw anything at all. She pretended she didn't care about any of it: that the other girls had made her mother's death into a game; that they didn't see how she was special because of her mother's death; that her mother did not care to appear to her. When her stepsister said, "You shouldn't hang out with them, not if you don't want to," she said, "Why?" and pretended she didn't understand.

Eventually the girl grew up and moved away and made a life of her own. She had a husband and two children and thought she was quite happy on the whole. The path of her life seemed straightforward and she moved along it. Her father died, and she grieved, but her stepmother was the one who had been her true parent. Her mother she hardly remembered at all. Life went on, and if the path grew a little rockier, her prospects a little less rosy, what of it? Life can't always be easy. Then, one day, her stepsister called to say that her stepmother, too, was dead.

The daughter left her children with her husband and flew down for the funeral. Afterward, she and her stepsister would sort out their childhood home so it could be put on the market. The economy was in a downturn, and the daughter was not sure she would have her job for much longer, so half of the proceeds of the sale of the house seemed fortuitous. But the real estate market was not good, and she saw that more than half of the houses on her old street were for sale, including both houses on either side. Several others were vacant or seemed so. It seemed to her possible the house would not sell at all, but she and her stepsister gamely went on for three days, making piles for Goodwill, piles for the trash, and piles that were things they might sell or keep for themselves.

They reminisced about their childhood, and looked through old photos, and confided in each other their fears about the future. They wept for the loss of the two mothers and drank three bottles of wine.

Now the house on the left was vacant, and so was the house on the right. The swimming pool of the house on the left had been emptied, and the swimming pool on the right had not been. Twice, in the middle of the day, they had climbed over the chain-link fence and gone swimming when they needed a break from sorting. The last night, tipsy and wide awake, the daughter left the childhood house where her stepsister lay sleeping in the bottom bunk of their childhood room, putting on one of the old-fashioned bathing suits from the pile they were taking to Goodwill. But instead of climbing over the fence to the right, she climbed the fence to the left.

She found that the pool, which should have been empty, was instead full of clear water. The lights along the edge of the pool had been turned on and she could smell the chlorine from where she stood as if it had just been freshly treated. Little bugs, drawn to the lights, flew just above the water. Some of them had already tipped in and become trapped. They would drown unless someone scooped them out.

The daughter walked down the steps at the shallow end of the pool until she was waist-deep. The water was pleasantly cool. The elastic of the suit she wore had long ago crumbled, and so the pleasant and impossible water came creeping up the skin of her thighs.

For a while she floated on her back, looking up at the stars and trying not to think about the future or why the pool was full of water. One was uncertain and the other was a gift. She floated until she grew, at last, cool and tired enough that she thought she might be able to sleep. Then she turned on her front, to wet her face, and down at the bottom of the pool, she saw her mother at last. Here was the face she barely remembered. So young! The long, waving hair. Her mother wore the twin of the suit she was wearing now. It seemed to the daughter she could stay here in the pool, that she could stay here and be happy. Step painlessly off the path as her mother had done. It seemed the woman in the pool wanted her to stay. They would have each other. They would never grow old.

She could have stayed. She was very tired and there was still so much of her life ahead of her. There were so many things she needed to do. But in this story, she got out of the pool. She went back to the house of her childhood and she woke up her stepsister and told her what she had seen. The stepsister, at first, did not believe her. Wasn't the pool empty? Perhaps, intoxicated as she was, she'd gone to the other pool, the one that was full, and hallucinated seeing her mother. The daughter argued with her. Her mother had been wearing the bathing suit she'd drowned in, the very same one the daughter was wearing now. Couldn't the stepsister see how her bathing suit was wet? She was dripping on the tile floor.

The daughter insisted she'd gone swimming in an empty pool. She had finally seen the ghost. Okay, her stepsister said, what if you did? But you didn't see your mother. There is no ghost. Your mother wasn't even wearing a bathing suit. She had a cocktail dress on. That's what my mother told me. And even if she had been wearing a bathing suit, it wouldn't be that one. No one would have kept the bathing suit your mother drowned in.

No, the daughter said. I saw her. She was so young! She looked exactly like me!

Come on, said the stepsister. She brought the daughter down to the room where they'd been sorting keepsakes. She spread out photographs until they found one of the mother. It was dated on the back, the date of the mother's death. Is that who you saw? said the stepsister. She doesn't look much like you at all.

The daughter studied it. Tried to think what she had seen. The closer she looked, the less sure she was she had seen her mother. Perhaps, then, all along she had been the one who haunted the swimming pool. Why should hauntings happen in linear time, after all? Isn't time just another swimming pool?

Now, Andy, it's time for you to go to sleep. But if you like, though I don't care for stories I'll tell you one more.

ROSE RED SAYS, "ONCE upon a time there was a house that Death lived in. Even Death needs a house to keep himself in. It was indeed a very nice house and for much of the year Death was as happy there as it is possible for Death to be. But Death cannot stay comfortably at home all year long, and so once a year he found someone to come and keep it for him while he went out into the world and made sure everything was as it should be. While he was gone from his house, it was the one place that Death might not come in. He knows this, even though, at times, he wants nothing more than to come home and rest. And while Death was gone from his house, all of those creatures who, by one means or another, had found a way so that Death might not take them yet may come and pass a night or two or longer in Death's house and not worry he will find them there. In this way many may rest and find a bit of peace, though the one who follows them unceasingly will follow them once more once they put their foot onto the path again. But this isn't your story. As a matter of fact, those who come and stay owe a debt of gratitude to the one who keeps house for Death while he is away. Even Death will one day pay his debt to you as long as you keep your bond with him."

ANDY SLEEPS. HE SLEEPS long and wakes, again, before his laptop. Has he written what he reads there, or has someone else? Well. Bears can't type. It's morning and there is no one in the house but Andy. There's a pile of bear shit beside the farmhouse table, cold but still fragrant. The puzzle is back in its box.

AND NOW THE STORY is almost over. Andy continued to work in a desultory and haphazard way on his dissertation. No one else came to the kitchen door while he stayed in Skinder's house, but one night the bell woke him again. He went first to the kitchen, thinking he might see one Rose or the other, but truly this time there was no one there. It came to him that the bell he still heard ringing was not the same bell as before. He went, therefore, to the door at the front of the house and there, on the porch, stood Skinder with his dog.

How did Andy know it was Skinder? Well, it was as Hannah had said. You would know Skinder, whether or not the dog—

small, black, regarding Andy with a curious intensity—had been beside him. What did Skinder look like? He looked exactly like Andy. It was as if Andy stood inside the house, looking out at another, identical Andy, who was also Skinder and who must not be allowed inside.

There was a car in the driveway. A black Prius. There was a chain on the front door, and Andy kept it on when he opened the door a crack. Enough to speak to Skinder, but not enough for Skinder to come in, or his dog. "What do you want?" Andy said.

"To come into my house," Skinder said. He had Andy's voice, as well. "My bags are in the car. Will you help me carry them in?"

"No," Andy said. "I'm sorry, but I can't let you in."

The black dog showed its teeth at this. Skinder, too, seemed disappointed. Andy recognized the expression on his face, though it was an expression that he knew the feel of, more than the look. "Are you sure you won't let me in?" he said.

"I'm sorry," Andy said again. "But I'm not allowed to do that."

Skinder said, "I understand. Come along." This to the dog. Andy in the house watched Skinder go down the steps and down the gravel driveway to the car. He opened the door and the dog jumped up onto the seat. Skinder got in the car at last, too, and Andy watched as the car went down the driveway, the little white stones crunching under the tires, the car silent and the headlights never turned on. The car disappeared under the low, dragging hem of leaves and Andy went back upstairs. He didn't attempt to sleep again. Instead he sat in the red and white bedroom, in a chair in front of the window, watching in case Skinder returned.

....

HANNAH CAME BACK TWO days later. She sent a text before her overnight flight: *Margot's still in a cast, but we've agreed it's better if I go. No one happy and house is too small. Neighbor going to help out. See you tomorrow afternoon!*

He hadn't finished his dissertation, but Andy felt he was well on the way now. And he was going to see Hannah again. They'd catch up, he'd tell her a modified history of his time in the house, and maybe she'd ask him to stay. There were plenty of bedrooms, after all. She could even take a look at what he had so far, give him some feedback.

When her Uber came up the driveway, Andy opened the door and then remembered he was supposed to make her go around to the kitchen. "Hannah?" he said.

"Andy," she said, coming up the steps. "Hi. Are you going to let me in?"

"No," he said. "Sorry. You said not to."

She put her suitcase down. "Right," she said. "Good job, asshole." Then she pushed right past him and through the door. Which, okay, that definitely seemed like Hannah. He went and got her suitcase.

But it was clear that he wasn't welcome to stay, even to Andy who wasn't always the quickest to pick up on cues. "I'm so grateful," she kept saying. Her hair was blue now, a deep sky-blue. "You were such a lifesaver to do this."

"I was happy to do it," Andy said. "It was fun, mostly. Weird, but fun. But I wanted to ask you about some aspects. Skinder, for example."

"You saw him?" Hannah said. All of her attention was on Andy, suddenly.

"No, it's fine," Andy said. "I didn't let him in. I did what you told me to do. But, when you saw him, I wanted to ask. Did he look familiar?"

"What do you mean, exactly?" Hannah said.

"I mean, did you think he looked like me at all?" Andy said.

Hannah shrugged. She looked away, then back at Andy. "No," she said. "Not really. Okay, so I've already paid the fare back on the Uber. It'll take you to Burlington and you can catch a Greyhound there back to Philly. But you have to go now, or you'll miss the last bus. I already checked the schedule—there's nothing if you miss that one until tomorrow morning. Don't worry about cleaning anything up or changing the sheets. I'll take care of it."

"I guess if you're sure," Andy said. "If you don't need me to stay."

She gave him an incredulous look. "Oh, Andy," she said. "That's so sweet. But no, I'll be fine. Come here."

She hugged him. It was a friendly embrace, but definitely the kind you gave when telling someone goodbye. Even Andy could see that. "Now go get your stuff. Do you need a hand?"

He left the ream of paper behind. He hadn't really needed to print out anything. That got rid of one of the canvas bags, and he lugged everything else out to the Uber. Hannah came down the steps and handed him a sandwich. "Here. Bye, Andy. Text me when you get home so I know you're there."

She hugged him again. It wasn't much, but it was better than nothing. The way she smelled, the feeling of her hair on his cheek. "It's really nice to see you again," he said.

"Yes," she said. "I know. It's been such a long time. Isn't it weird, how time just keeps passing?"

And that was that. He turned to get one last look at the yellow house and at Hannah as the car went up the driveway, but she had already gone inside.

WHEN HE WAS AT last back at the apartment in Philly, it was morning again. Andy was tired—he had not slept at all on the bus or in any of the stations in between transfers—and he could not shake the idea that when he opened the door Skinder would be waiting for him. But instead here was Lester on the futon couch in his boxer shorts, looking at his phone and slurping coffee. It was much hotter in Philly. The apartment had a smell, like something had gone off.

"You're home," Lester said without much enthusiasm. "How was Vermont?"

"Nice," Andy said. "Really, really nice." He didn't think he'd be able to explain what it had been like to Lester. "Where's Bronwen?"

Lester looked down at his phone again. "Not here," he said. "I don't really want to talk about it."

From this, Andy gathered they had broken up. It was a shame: he felt Bronwen might have been a good person to talk to about Vermont. "Sorry," he said to Lester.

"Not your fault, dude," Lester said. "She was not the most normal girl I've ever been with."

Occasionally over the next week Andy noticed how Lester sometimes looked as if he were listening for something, as if he were waiting for something. And after a while, Andy began to feel as if *he* were listening, too. And then, sometimes, he thought he could almost see something in the apartment when Lester was there. It crept after Lester, waited patiently, crouched on the floor beside him when he sat at the table. It was mostly formless, but it had a mouth and eyes. It reminded Andy of Skinder's dog. Sometimes he thought it saw him looking. He felt it looking back. But Lester, he thought, could not see it at all.

It wasn't entirely bad to have it in the house. It meant Andy worked, at last, very hard to finish his dissertation. Or perhaps it had been Vermont that had gotten him over the hump. All that had really been needed was for him to get out of his own way. When he was nearly done, Andy began looking for higher ed listings, and then he was defending, and then he was done, and he had graduated and had his first interview. He was ready to leave the apartment, and Philly, and Lester, and Lester's ghost behind.

The interview did not go as well as he'd hoped. There were other candidates, and he was quite surprised when, in the end, the job was offered to him. But he took it gladly. Here was the path that led toward tenure and a career and all the rest of his future. Years later, one of the older faculty members who had been on the hiring committee got very drunk at a bar they all frequented, and told Andy he had almost not gotten the offer in fact. "The night before we met to discuss, Andy, I had the most peculiar dream. In the dream I was in the woods at night and lost and there was a bear. I couldn't move, I was terrified. The bear came right up and I knew that it was going to eat me, but instead it said, 'You should hire Andy. You'll be glad if you do and you'll regret it if you don't. Do you understand?' I said I did and then I woke up. And the next morning at the meeting no one wanted to say much; there was a general feeling of strangeness and then someone, Dr. Carmichael, I think, said, 'I had a dream last night we should hire Andy Sims.' Someone else said, 'I had the same dream. There was a bear and it said exactly that. That we should hire Andy Sims.' And it turned out we'd all had the dream. So, we hired you! And, in the end, it turned out for the best, just like the bear had said."

Andy said this was extremely peculiar, but yes, it had all turned out all right. When, later, he went up for tenure and he got it, he wondered if the committee had been given another dream. In any case, he was content to have what he had been given. He caught himself, once, at the end of a lecture saying, "Much to think about." But there wasn't, really. His students gave him adequate ratings. It seemed to some of them Professor Sims really looked at them, that he seemed to see something in them (or perhaps near them) none of their other teachers did. What exactly Professor Sims saw, though, he kept to himself. It was, no doubt, an unfortunate aftereffect of the water he'd drunk so much of one summer.

There was this, too: although his children asked him over and over why they could not have a dog, Andy could not bear this idea. Instead he got them guinea pigs, and then a rabbit.

As for Hannah, he ran into her once or twice at conferences. He went to both of her presentations and took notes so he could send her an email afterward with his thoughts. They had drinks with some of their colleagues, but he didn't ask her if she still house-sat in the summer in Vermont. All of that seemed of another life, one that didn't belong to him.

Lester had dropped out of the program. He went to work for

a think tank in Indonesia. Andy didn't know if anything had followed him there.

And then, years later, Andy found himself at a conference in Montpelier, Vermont. It was fall and very beautiful. He found trees quite restful, actually, now that he'd lived on the East Coast for so long. The last day of the conference he began to think about the parts of his life he hardly thought about at all now. He'd given his panel, had heard the gossip, talked up his small college to fledgling PhD candidates. Back in his hotel room, he looked at maps and car rentals and realized it would not be un-realistic to drive home instead of flying. It would be a very pretty drive. And so he canceled his plane ticket and picked up a rental car instead. He thought perhaps he might try to find the yellow house in the woods again, and see who lived there now.

But he didn't remember, as it turned out, exactly which highway the house had been on. He drove down little highway after little highway, all of them lovely but none the road he had meant to find. And, toward dusk, when a deer came onto the road, he swerved to miss it and went quite far down the em-bankment into a copse of trees.

He wasn't badly hurt, and the car didn't look too bad, either. But he thought it would require a tow truck to get it back up again, and his cellphone had no reception here. He went up to the road and waited some time, but no car ever came past and so he went back down to his rental, to see what he had to eat or drink. He saw, close to where the car had ended up, there was quite a well-trodden trail. Andy decided he would follow it in the direction he felt was the one most likely to lead toward St. Albans.

The trail meandered and grew more narrow. The light began to fade and he thought of turning back, but now the trail led him out to a place he recognized. Here was the patio and here was the Adirondack chair, grown even more decrepit and weatherworn. Here was the comfortable yellow house with all the lights on inside.

He went around to the front door. Well, why not? He wasn't a bear. He knocked and waited and eventually someone came to the door and opened it.

The other Andy stood in the doorway and looked at him. Where was the little dog? Surely it was dead. But no, there it was in the hallway.

"Can I come in?" Andy said.

"No," Skinder said and shut the door. Andy waited a little longer, but all that happened was that the lights in the house went off. It was dark outside now and the wind was rattling all the leaves in the trees. There wasn't much he could think of to do, so after a while Andy went back to find the path again.

Acknowledgments

I'm very grateful to the editors who first published these stories: Robert Spillman, Brigid Hughes, Charles Coleman Finlay, An Owomoyela, Catherine Krahe, Lila Garrott, Stephanie Perkins, and especially Emily Stamey, curator of the exhibition *Dread and Delight: Fairy Tales in an Anxious World,* for whom I wrote "The White Cat's Divorce" and then went on thinking about the ongoing relationship between fairytales and my own work. This collection is dedicated to Ellen Datlow and Terri Windling, who have made so much room for the work and the writers I love best. What a debt I owe both of you—a debt of fairytale proportions. So many thanks to Caitlin McKenna at Random House for her keen eye and enthusiastic support. Thanks also to Noa Shapiro, Loren Noveck, Su-Yee Lin, Lucas Heinrich, Caroline Cunningham, Madison Dettlinger, Vanessa DeJesús, Rachel Rokicki, Susan Kamil, and the rest of the terrifyingly wonderful team at Random House, who continue to make publishing, all in all, a more delightful experience than it ought to be. Unending thanks to my agent Renée Zucker-brot, who smooths the way. Thanks to Shaun Tan, whose work maps out the territory I wish most to explore. Thanks to Owen Gent for capturing the spirit of these stories so effectively in his art. Much gratitude to Richard Butner, the Sycamore Hill Workshop, and its participants, who were the first readers for many of these stories. Thanks to Cassandra Clare for the company, conversation, and space to work. Thanks to Holly Black for her retelling of "The White Cat," and for reading these stories as I wrote them and asking the right questions. Thank you to Auður Inga Rúnarsdóttir, Erin McFadden and Christian Mayer, and S. J. Schreiber, for their invaluable assistance in firming up the details of "Prince Hat Underground." Thank you to the wonderful booksellers of Book Moon, who have gotten us through some rough times, and thank you as well to everyone who has bought books there. Thank you to the MacArthur Foundation for their extraordinary generosity. Most of all, thank you to my family. I love you.

ABOUT THE AUTHOR

KELLY LINK is the author of *Get in Trouble, Magic for Beginners, Stranger Things Happen,* and *Pretty Monsters.* Her short stories have been published in *The Best American Short Stories* and *The O. Henry Prize Stories.* She is a MacArthur "Genius Grant" fellow and has received a grant from the National Endowment for the Arts. She is the co-founder of Small Beer Press and co-edits the occasional zine *Lady Churchill's Rosebud Wristlet.*

Twitter: @haszombiesinit

To inquire about booking Kelly Link for a speaking engagement, please contact the Penguin Random House Speakers Bureau at speakers@penguinrandomhouse.com.